David Sylvian

The Last Romantic

David Sylvian
The Last Romantic

Martin Power

OMNIBUS PRESS
LONDON · NEW YORK · PARIS · SYDNEY

Cover designed by Mike Bell Design
Picture research by Nikki Lloyd

ISBN: 0.7119.8391.7
Order No: OP48193

Exclusive Distributors:
Book Sales Limited,
8/9 Frith Street,
London W1V 5TZ, UK.

Music Sales Corporation,
257 Park Avenue South,
New York, NY 10010, USA.

The Five Mile Press,
22 Summit Road,
Noble Park,
Victoria 3174, Australia.

To the Music Trade only:
Music Sales Limited,
8/9 Frith Street,
London W1V 5TZ, UK.

Typeset by Galleon Typesetting, Ipswich.
Printed and bound in Great Britainby MPG Books (Hartnolls) Ltd.

A catalogue record for this book is available from the British Library.

www.omnibuspress.com

Contents

Introduction

November 4, 1995
Royal Festival Hall, London

It's a touching moment for both artist and audience. Humorous, strange, but above all, touching. Following a two hour "retrospective" show that saw him reclaim his musical past and drop a hint or two about his musical future, David Sylvian shuffles awkwardly to the front of the stage to take a final bow. The applause is enthusiastic, but in that terribly British way. In other words, no one drops their programme while clapping. Sylvian smiles, waves and then seems ready to make his exit. However, just before he can cut and run, a tall and imposing figure emerges from somewhere in the front stalls and walks towards him. Sylvian appears unsure for a moment. There is a definite pause in the hall.

Beaming a mighty smile, the man from the front stalls extends a hand in Sylvian's direction. Sylvian grasps it with his own. The Royal Festival Hall promptly comes alive. In a matter of seconds, the singer is besieged with admirers, men and women shyly offering their arms towards the stage. Caught unawares, Sylvian does his best to shake each hand and return each smile. In truth, he looks more than a little confused. After a minute or so, confusion leads to embarrassment and Sylvian saunters off. The applause continues.

June 1998

Some sixteen years after he walked away from pop stardom, David Sylvian still commands a fearsome level of admiration from his followers. And still has difficulty dealing with it. Though he hasn't had a 'hit' since 1984, he continues to sell records, fill out auditoriums, and just as importantly, gain the grace and favour of his artistic contemporaries. Sylvian's sometime musical partner, Robert Fripp, sums him up thus: "He's a lovely man and I like him supremely. Gorgeous voice, enigmatic lyrics, fabulous synthesiser sounds." Tears For Fears frontman Roland Orzabal describes Sylvian as a songwriter who "turns pop music into art", with a "poetic and painterly" gift for melody. One of his closest friends and most enduring collaborators, the redoubtable Holger Czukay, says that "David is such a sensible person, such a spiritual person". And Great Britain's most respected classical composer, John Tavener, finds Sylvian's music more than agreeable: "I like his slow-moving harmonic lines, (they) put me in mind of Randy Newman, one of the very few pop artists I really like."

At the start of David Sylvian's career, such high praise would have been inconceivable. As part of the South London based group Japan, he came in for some of the most vitriolic criticism of the late Seventies: "New York Dolls rip-offs", "catarrhal dronings" and "a grotesque stench of musical decay" were a few of the more choice descriptions of the band's original look and sound. When Japan re-invented themselves as a youthful Roxy Music in 1980, the response accorded them wasn't much better: "Japan's pastel pleasantries seem like so much wrapping paper inside which is concealed a cheap plastic gift." Yet, by 1982, the self same band were being lauded as the future of British pop, their music described as "gorgeously erotic" and "perfectly evanescent". In short, they were the cream of the 'new romantic' crop. Nonetheless, following a stream of hit singles and sold-out concerts they promptly imploded, collapsing under the weight of romantic entanglements and their own internal contradictions.

For Sylvian, Japan's dissolution marked the beginning of his real work, with the songwriter pursuing an increasingly eclectic course that allowed him to enter the realms of the avant-garde, as well as forge alliances with the world of art and literature. He also chose to abandon the heavily stylised image that had brought him success in the first place in favour of a nondescript appearance and positively spectral public profile. However, his music became arguably better, taking on a depth and texture only hinted at in his younger days. His lyrics, too, grew stronger and more complex, with notions of spirituality and self-doubt jostling alongside dry satire and, on occasion, sly wit.

At times, following his progress has been difficult. The philosophical contradictions, sporadic negativity and continuing scorn he has shown towards his own musical output have all made it hard to get a handle on where Sylvian is coming from, or indeed, going to. Simon Napier-Bell, who managed Japan at the height of their fame, glimpsed "a profound disquiet" within the singer, an emotional turbulence of sorts, that found Sylvian constantly backing away from stardom when it presented itself. Yet, for him, it remained part of the charm. As it surely does for his fans.

A working class South London boy who has subsequently become one of the UK's more arcane melodic exports, Sylvian's life and career has seen him through pop stardom, experimental photography, continuing spiritual exploration and some inspired collaborative efforts with the likes of Ryuichi Sakamoto, Holger Czukay and Robert Fripp. There has also been marriage, children, musical reconciliations and bitter fall-outs along the way. Yet each stage of the process, each subtle reinvention has been clearly marked in the development of his voice – from dry rasp to worn groove. That voice alone makes for a truly fascinating story.

Acknowledgements

This book would not have been possible without the kindness of four friends who not only provided a wealth of David Sylvian/Japan related material, but more importantly, offered sage advice, honest opinion and when required, several drinks. All thanks then to Stephen Joseph, David Kelly, Andrew Robinson and Colin Stewart.

Additionally, my grateful thanks and appreciation go to the following people who willingly gave up their thoughts and time for this project: Dave Ball, Harry Beckett, B J Cole, Holger Czukay, Mark Isham, Ian Maidman, Simon Napier-Bell, Ann O'Dell, Roland Orzabal, Anton Sanko, John Tavener, John Taylor, Danny Thompson, Suzanne Vega.

Again, for help, assistance and the opening of some firmly shut doors, my enduring thanks go to Kirsty Allen at Real World, The American Federation Of Musicians, Applehead Sound, Ron Fierstein, Tanya at Firstars, Future Sound Of London, Karen Harding, Kate Hanson, Brian Howell, John Hughes at L B of Lewisham, April at Isham, Andy Linehan, Steve Malins at The Numan Group, everyone at the Musicians Union, Mark at Mute Records, Alice at Native Management, Steve at New Note, Opium (Arts) Ltd, Siobhan Paine, Johnny Rogan, Harish Shah, Sharon Kelly and Carol Lawrie at Sony, Andy Stephens, those helpful chaps at Uncut, Mark Vernon, John Viner, Virgin Records and Gaby Wilson at Pet Shop Boys Partnership (perhaps I'll have better luck next time). Also Phil Lewis and Gerry Laffy for the title of my first chapter.

For providing additional source material for this book, I would also like to express my gratitude and appreciation towards the following individuals: Jason Ankeny, Linden Barber, A J Barratt, Jack Barron, Max Bell, Ian Birch, John Bungey, Chris Carr, Nick Coleman, Huw Colingbourne, Richard Cook, Paul Davies, Adrian Deevoy, Kerry Doole, Paul Du Noyer, Mark Ellen, Dede Fedele, Kathleen Galgano, Steve Gett, John Gill, Tim Goodyer, Louise Gray, Ray Gun, Lynn Hanna, Steve Holtje, Patrick Humphries, Richard Jackson, Andrea Jones, Andrew Jones, Peter Kane, Gibson Keddie, Jamie Kemsey, Biba Kopf, Nile Larsen, Carole Linfield, Nick Logan, Sam Molineaux, Paul Morley, Jimmy Nicol, Craig Peacock, Ian Penman, Kelly Pike, Arthur A. Pitt, Elissa Van Poznak, Mark Prendergast, Anthony Quinn, Ronnie Randall, Simon Reynolds, Dave Rimmer, Chris Roberts, David Lee Roth, Anton Rush, Robert Sandall, Richard Scott, Jim Shelley, Tony Stewart, Jane Suck, Steve Sutherland, David Toop, Don Watson, Josef Woodard, Rob Young. I must also express particular gratitude to Paul Rymer and also to Jonas Warstad and Lech Linkiel, who together run the Japan web-site, Assemblage. Thanks to their diligent research, I became aware of several Japan related magazine articles of which I had no prior knowledge.

I consulted the following magazines and newspapers during the course of my research, and in some cases extracted interview material: *Bassist, Creem, Details, Electronic & Music Maker, The Face, The Independent, Melody Maker, Mojo, Music Life, Music Technology, New Musical Express, Q, Record Collector, The Sunday Times, Time Out, the Vintage Magazine Company* and *The Wire*. The same applies to the following magazines which have ceased publication: *Blitz, Flexipop, Juke, Keyboard Review, New Sounds New Styles, No 1, Record Mirror, Sounds, Vox* and *Zig Zag*.

Several honourable mentions: firstly, hats off to Andrew King for aiding, abetting, providing and linking. My shout, I believe. As ever, I also remain indebted to Chris Charlesworth, who besides showing patience and understanding, continues to separate the wheat from the chaff on my behalf – not the easiest of tasks, I suspect. Another king big thanks goes to Helen Donlon for retrieving some tasty morsels from the most obscure places, and opening up shop at all hours of the day and night. Also, for her generosity and help on this, and indeed several other projects, my thanks and appreciation go to Lucy Hawes. For providing valuable research material (and the opportunity to have a chuckle at those Eighties haircuts), I thank Kevin Grant. And for her efforts in trying to track down the elusive Mr Costello, I remain obliged to Nikki Russell. As always, my heartfelt thanks to Hilary and, of course, David Sylvian himself.

Additional Acknowledgements: John Kelly, Stuart Maconie, Sylvie Simmons, Phil Sutcliffe, John L Walters, Rob Young, Jayesh (the noblest of wine merchants), the *Independent*, the *Irish Times*, *Wire.*

A special thanks to Colin Wilson, whose books *The Outsider* and *The Misfits* remain the definitive portrayal of "the man who sees too much, too deep". Both publications provided much needed inspiration whilst researching this project.

1

Dreaming Of Japan, High Places And Guitar Solos

David Sylvian was born on February 23, 1958 in Stone Park, Beckenham, Kent. His given name was David Alan Batt, a present from a resolutely working class South London family. By the time he was eighteen, Sylvian had given the present back.

His father Bernard, a plasterer by trade, and mother Sheila (née Stone) lived in Venner Road, Sydenham, in the London Borough of Lewisham. Their home was a stone's throw from Penge East railway station, and only a few minutes walk from Crystal Palace Park. On December 1, 1959, David's younger brother Stephen was born in a Sydenham Maternity Hospital. With the clan now numbering five (Sylvian has a sister three years his senior), matters became difficult for the family both financially and emotionally. "My father had a fantastic struggle dealing with the fact that he had to work really hard to bring up kids,' Sylvian later said. "He was really unhappy with his life and this would show itself in aggression, sometimes towards his family. It was the only way he could let out his frustration."

A quiet child, Sylvian's primary school days were largely unremarkable but for the fact that he exhibited more interest in painting and music than English and maths. He attributed the latter to his sister's guiding influence. "My sister brought music into the house for the very first time," he told *Vox*'s Jamie Kemsey. "She was listening to Motown and a lot of soul." By his own admission "a pretty neurotic kid", music would provide the young Sylvian with a critical support system, as well as act as a comforter of sorts. "It was an escape as well as an emotional release," he said.

Though candid in the extreme about much of his public life, Sylvian has been less than forthcoming on his early childhood days, preferring to avoid the subject whenever possible. On the odd occasion that he has offered a snippet or two of information, a protective veil still remains. "I never enjoyed my childhood," he once remarked. "In fact, I've managed to block most of it out . . . I can't cope with it. I don't know why. It was nothing to do with my parents. I guess I was just over-sensitive. I responded very badly to my environment."

The environment to which Sylvian was referring was mid-Sixties Lewisham, an area that was desperately trying to stabilise itself both in terms of its ever-changing cultural values and reduced financial prosperity. As with many London suburbs at the time, Lewisham and Catford were dealing with a high influx of immigrants, their arrival bringing about problems of social integration and class resentment. While these concerns would eventually steady themselves, a lack of government/local authority development funds meant that the area continued to decay in a civic sense, with both schools and public amenities suffering badly. Though everyone who lived in Lewisham in the late Sixties will talk fondly of the "sparkling newness" of Ladywell Public Swimming Baths or the superb fruit and veg market, the area was equally well known for a huge amount of second-hand car dealerships and regular fights outside MacDonalds restaurant (coincidentally the first MacDonalds to open in the UK). In short, Sylvian was a sensitive child growing up in a tough neighbourhood.

Things became progressively tougher when at the age of eleven, he found himself a student at Catford Boys School, then located on the junction of Stainton Road and Brownhill Road, just seconds away from the busy South Circular route. According to one local resident, Catford Boys was "little more than a training ground for thugs", though in truth, it was no worse than any other comprehensive school in the surrounding area. It subsequently closed in 1991, the majority of its records lost in the move from original site to local authority offices. A petrol station marks its memory.

Consolidating the role he played at primary school, Sylvian seemed content to sit at the back of the class, feigning interest whenever his teachers demanded it. However, he was slowly making friends, with one fellow student, Anthony Michaelides, standing out from the crowd. Born July 24, 1958, Michaelides (soon to be rechristened Mick Karn) was already something of a musician when he met Sylvian. After tentative experiments with both the violin and mouth-organ, Karn was guided by his teachers in the direction of the bassoon, in which he soon proved proficient. In fact, Catford Boys were so sure of his talent that they put the youngster forward for an audition with the London Schools Symphony Orchestra. To his horror, Mick passed with flying colours. As his success at the trial had depended on cheating the examiners (Karn had learned his set piece by ear, as he was wholly incapable of sight-reading the sheet music in front of him), the next six months were spent desperately trying to keep up with his fellow pupils, an experience he later described as both "traumatic" and "devastating". However, he was soon relieved of his teenage burden.

"On the way home to Catford after my first LSSO concert," Karn later revealed to *The Wire*'s Louise Gray, "my bassoon was stolen by a group of skinheads. They asked me what was in the case. I told them. They showed me a broken bottle. I gave them the case. Very simple. The school wouldn't buy me another bassoon, so in retaliation, I bought a bass for £5 from a kid at school and got together with David who was already playing acoustic guitar."

The guitar David was playing had been a Christmas gift from his father, who bought his younger brother Steve a set of drums at the same time. Though he only knew a few chords, Sylvian soon began to experiment with linking stray melodies together. "I started writing songs when I was thirteen," he later confirmed. "They were just rubbish." Steve was equally dismissive of his first efforts with a set of sticks. "I didn't spend years listening to big-name drummers when I got my first kit," he said. "What happened was that on one particular day, I knew I was going to get my first kit, so I sat down and listened to the drumming on one particular record. It could have been a complete flop."

Sylvian's decision to try and form a group came soon after purchasing his first single, a mint copy of 'Telegram Sam' by Marc Bolan's T-Rex. In stark contrast to the sweet but inoffensive Motown grooves that activated his initial interest in music, Bolan's greasy combination of low-slung guitars and high-octane glamour seemed to offer Sylvian passage to an alternative world. It didn't take long to connect the notion of temporary transportation to one of more permanent release. "Being in a band was the *only* escape from an environment that was a pretty insensitive place," he later said. In truth, it was an idea and philosophy he shared with just about every working-class kid who picked up a musical instrument.

Once the fledgling trio became more confident in their appointed roles, a definite 'glam-rock' influence began to rear its head, with the latest singles by David Bowie, The Sweet and Roxy Music all purchased, duly dissected and musically attempted – albeit badly. "I could only play a little bit of rhythm guitar," Sylvian recalled, "and Steve could only play a few percussion instruments . . ." Karn, however, was beginning to make definite progress. "I'd been pressing [on the bassoon] so hard for so long," he said, "my fingers were already hard, so it was easier to play good bass." In deference to his talent, David and Steve appointed Mick lead singer, a role he grudgingly accepted.

As the group's aspirations began to gather speed, the decision was made to align themselves more fully with their dandified heroes. Hence, at the grand old age of fifteen, the trio arrived at Catford Boys replete with dyed hair and carefully applied make-up. Sylvian's naïveté to the predicament in which he was placing himself still seems touching to this day. "We thought the kids would rebel and follow us," he later told the *Melody Maker*. "They didn't." In fact, what his classmates did was beat the living daylights out of him. His reaction was to return to school the next day in even more distinctive apparel. "It made me more determined," he told *Flexipop*'s Huw Collingbourne. "I've always been extremely stubborn, and that helped me along at the time." While David was content to receive his daily beating, his parents were beginning to worry. "It was a cause for concern for them . . . they often used to try and persuade me to change my appearance, mainly for the sake of a peaceful life." Despite their repeated attempts to get him to change course, Sylvian persisted.

One of the few kids not to run a mile every time David and Mick turned a corner was Richard Barbieri. A model student at the time, Barbieri shared many of the same classes as Sylvian and Karn. However, his prowess at sports meant he had little to fear from associating with Lewisham's most effeminate-looking duo. "Catford Boys was dead rough," Richard later said, "and David and Mick always used to get beaten up for wearing earrings and dyeing their hair. I never had any trouble though, because I was the captain of the school football team!"

Born on November 30, 1957, Barbieri shared some similarities with both Karn and Sylvian. Like Mick, his parents were of Mediterranean origin, though Richard's lineage was Italian as opposed to Greek-Cypriot. He was also extremely interested in music, with hard rock bands like Led Zeppelin and progressive groups such as Emerson, Lake and Palmer forming the backbone of his record collection. Nonetheless, though Barbieri had toyed with the idea of playing keyboards, he wasn't particularly interested in joining a band. Therefore, he was able to keep a strategic distance from the increasingly rebellious duo.

After months of playground scuffles and warnings from teachers regarding his appearance, Sylvian was eventually asked to leave Catford Boys School. With no trade or profession in sight, the onus was now on him to turn an obsession into a career. "Being in a band was a means of getting away . . ." he later told *Record Collector*'s Mark Prendergast, ". . . of making money and sticking together as friends."

The group got their first opportunity to play live at Mick Karn's brother's wedding. Yet, when the time came to actually face his family, the bassist refused to go on. Legend has it (though it's never been fully substantiated) that David agreed backstage to take on vocal duties to ease his friend's nerves. Whatever the truth of the story, when the curtain went up, Sylvian was at the microphone. A hundred or so guests subsequently witnessed Japan's début performance. One suspects they left unimpressed.

It is also difficult to establish the exact truth concerning the origins of the band's name, apparently decided upon shortly after this inaugural gig. Some accounts suggest that Sylvian pulled the name Japan out of a hat only hours before the group were due to perform their first professional concert in South London in 1974. Others suggest the trio decided on Japan after attending a central London party packed with Oriental businessmen. It has even been suggested that the name was inspired by a discarded travel brochure they found on a bus. Whatever the truth about the name's origins, Sylvian has always loathed it. "It came out of the air when we were desperate. I hated it then. I still do."

By late 1975, Japan were ready to expand their line-up. After several semi-successful gigs playing cover material in and around the Catford and Lewisham area, the group came to the conclusion that the only way to capture the full-blooded rock/glam sound they so desperately sought was to add a lead guitarist to their ranks. An advertisement was duly placed in the 'Musicians Wanted' column of weekly music paper *Melody Maker*. The original specification read "Japan seek lead guitarist aged between 17–18". The man who got the job was 22 and married with two children. His name was Rob Dean.

Four years older than his colleagues (he was born on

April 23, 1955), Dean hailed from Clapton, East London, a part of the capital almost entirely alien to Mick, Steve and David. An extremely down-to-earth character, whose guitar style fell somewhere between the no-nonsense flash of Bowie sideman Mick Ronson and the more blues-orientated bluster of Led Zeppelin's Jimmy Page, Rob had impressed the trio not only with his musicianship, but also his keen sense of humour. In fact, within months of joining Japan, he had gained two distinct nicknames: 'Boblett' and 'Mr Ordinary', the latter as much a jibe at his reluctance to wear make-up or outrageous clothes as it was to do with his status as a settled family man.

A chance meeting with an old schoolmate provided Japan with their fifth and final member. Since leaving Catford Boys with a brace of 'O' Levels, Richard Barbieri had been busy forging a path for himself in the world of finance, specifically as a trainee clerk in Barclays Bank. Nonetheless, when Sylvian heard that Barbieri had recently purchased an organ, an invitation was cordially extended to join the band. As Richard only knew three or four chords at best, it was a brave decision on David's part.

The newly expanded Japan spent much of the winter of 1975 rehearsing. Whereas previously the group had relied on covers of standard glam rock tunes and old Tamla Motown hits for their live set, Sylvian now began to draft in many of his own compositions, with original songs like 'Stateline' sitting back to back with radical reworkings of The Rolling Stones 'Heartbreaker' and Eric Clapton's take on Bob Marley's 'I Shot The Sheriff'. Since neither Karn nor Dean seemed particularly interested in contributing song ideas, it was left to the singer to exert definite control over the direction the band was taking. Setting a precedent for the future, Sylvian duly rose to the challenge.

On February 14, 1976, Japan emerged from their rehearsal rooms to provide support for emerging London power-pop act The Fabulous Poodles. Both their style and sound was markedly more professional, with the previously stage-shy

Sylvian beginning to accept his role of front-man. All leopard-skin jackets, pink and blond peroxide hair and mock street-punk attitude, Japan were a sum of their visual influences: Patti Smith, Iggy Pop, Richard Hell on the one hand, glam, Motown and soul on the other. Nonetheless, the all pervading influence that hung over the group like a vulture was undoubtedly The New York Dolls, the searing, hedonistic American proto-punk act who were in their death throes at the time. One only had to look at the cover of the Dolls' seminal 1973 album *Too Much, Too Soon* and Japan's latest physical incarnation to realise that the similarities simply crushed the differences. In truth, the resemblance was to be the bane of their young lives.

To speed up their ascent to stardom, the group made a decision to place another advertisement in the *Melody Maker*, this time for a manager. The man that took the bait was Danny Morgan, a talent scout who was serving an apprenticeship of sorts to one of rock music's more colourful managerial figures, the mercurial Simon Napier-Bell. A larger-than-life character with an instinctive understanding of how the music business worked, Napier-Bell had risen to prominence in the late Sixties due to his involvement with the semi-legendary London group The Yardbirds and velvet-voiced pop chanteuse Dusty Springfield. By the early Seventies, he added the discovery of Marc Bolan and T-Rex to his distinguished CV. After handling Bolan's affairs, Napier-Bell decided to go into semi-retirement, though he was only in his mid-thirties at the time. However, life in Paris soon lost its lustre ("It was quite boring doing nothing"), and he found himself back in London looking for a band. Japan more than filled the criteria.

"Japan were found by Danny Morgan after they put an advertisement in the *Melody Maker*," recalled Napier-Bell. "He was a great guy, Danny, a pain in the arse, but a persistent pain in the arse. He kept calling me saying, 'I've found this amazing group. You've got to see them.' So, in the end, I did."

Though Napier-Bell was used to meeting many a band, his

reaction on encountering Japan was one of profound shock. "David was just extraordinary – a cross between Mick Jagger and Brigitte Bardot. His voice was a cross between everyone I'd ever heard. And then you met Mick, who was his twin, both with long orange hair down to their waists. And even when you'd met David's twin, you then met his brother. The whole thing was just unbelievable. Anyone in the music business would just have to say, 'these guys are going to be huge mega-stars . . .', so I signed them up."

Napier-Bell's original idea was to oversee Japan, rather than act as a "hands-on" manager. Nevertheless, the plan drastically changed when "man-in-charge" Danny Morgan started to exhibit signs of over-spending. "When I met Japan," he recalled, "I agreed to sign them up to my company for publishing and recording, and give them a small advance. But Danny Morgan was to actually manage them. So I gave him some money, but he was just a mess. I gave him *£10,000,* and he came back two weeks later with the money all gone. He'd bought them a van and equipment, drove it somewhere and got it stolen. Of course, he hadn't insured it . . ."

Japan found themselves rapidly plunged into a promotional whirlpool of activity. After seeing out a quite awful two-week residency at the Big End Club in Munich, Germany (an engagement to which the band had committed themselves before signing with Napier-Bell), they were bought onto two nationwide tours with acts at opposite ends of the musical spectrum – newly active punks The Damned and seminal hippie/ex-Traffic drummer Jim Capaldi. In a way, it was perfect casting. Japan were neither new nor old, sitting somewhere uncomfortably in the middle. Unfortunately, due to a five-year break from the music business, their manager was under the impression that his charges represented the cutting edge of British pop. "I'd been away for ages," said Napier-Bell. "I didn't realise they based their whole look on The New York Dolls. They were so bright and sharp . . . fun. They thought they knew what they were doing. Of course, they didn't."

The situation was confirmed when Japan's early demo tapes were hawked around to British record companies. In short, they couldn't get arrested. "CBS Records sent me a letter saying, 'Japan have great potential'," said their manager, " 'but we're not in the potential business.' Another response came back from RCA referring to 'the appalling bass playing of Mick Karn'. They said we had to get another bass player, or teach him how to put his fingers on the frets . . .' "

Sylvian remained philosophical about the rejections. "The image of the band doesn't portray our music at all," he told journalist Arthur A. Pitt. "A lot of people get the wrong idea about us, which is a shame. It would be the easiest thing in the world for me to stop wearing make-up, but I can't as it would be too much of a compromise. Personally I feel confident wearing it." As David would later admit, the make-up, clothes and ambi-sexual posturing fulfilled a dual purpose. First, it was a disguise with which to face his audience. Secondly, it was a persona that allowed him not to face himself. Both masks would become redundant in time.

Simon Napier-Bell finally found Japan a record deal with Hansa/Ariola, a German based company best known for foisting Boney M on the world. Eager to break the British market, Hansa had recently bought offices in London and began advertising their arrival with remarkable gusto. "All over London, there were huge billboards for Hansa," Napier-Bell remembered, "appalling things. They looked like advertisements for Marks & Spencer!" In order to both promote themselves and secure a brace of new acts, the company announced a talent contest of sorts, with the prize being a record deal. "It wasn't a talent contest in the way that there were judges sitting there," said Napier-Bell. "About three hundred groups went along, and one by one Hansa filtered through them until they got the ones they wanted. Japan got the deal mainly through image. When you see an image that brilliant, your immediate thought is 'That's enough in itself'. Adequate music will do. But, I mean Hansa hadn't got a clue at that point. They'd come from Germany. They didn't know what was going on, or the fact that punk was going to explode . . ."

Shortly after signing with the label, Sylvian nearly got Japan thrown off again by announcing the fact that some of the group were changing their names. He was to become David Sylvian. His brother Stephen was to be Steve Jansen. And Anthony Michaelides was reborn as Mick Karn. At no point during the discussions was it suggested that the chosen surnames were remarkably similar to those of David Johansen and Sylvain Sylvain, The New York Dolls' lead vocalist and rhythm guitarist. "David announced the band's new names and Hansa were bloody horrified. They wanted to renege on the contracts," said Simon Napier-Bell. After several heated arguments, Sylvian got his wish and the group retained their contract.

While Japan were now a "going concern", there was still one major behind-the-scenes problem to contend with, Richard Barbieri's inability to extract a tune from a piano. Salvation came via electronics. "In many ways," laughed Simon Napier-Bell, "Richard was to be the musical success story in Japan. I mean, they only put him in the band because he had a Woolworth's organ! He was always in danger of being thrown out in the early days, so he used to come round to my flat in Wigmore Street and I used to teach him to play the piano. And he struggled and he struggled until we got a synth. Then *everything* changed. He just instinctively understood synthesisers and electronics. No more problems."

Following a spate of gigs within the London area, including dates at the Rock Garden and Islington's Hope And Anchor, Japan embarked on their first studio sessions for their new record company . . . Following several gigs within the London area, Japan embarked on their first studio sessions for their new record company. These were overseen by Hansa's staff producer, Steve Roland, principally known for his involvement with fresh faced Sixties popsters, Dave Dee, Dozy, Beaky, Mick

& Tich. Eager to give Japan's thick rock sound a more commercial air, Roland decided to bring in two female backing vocalists to augment Sylvian's voice. The experiment went badly. "Steve's high point in the studio," recalled Simon Napier-Bell, "was when he got two black girls in to do the backing vocals. After they started singing, Roland said to them, 'Sorry, sorry, that's a bit flat.' The girls shouted, 'Flat?', and Steve said, 'No, No, I mean sharp . . .' They screamed 'Sharp?' Steve then said, 'Oh, well, er . . . somewhere in between . . .' That was the end of his production duties with the band." The two tracks Japan cut with Steve Roland are still 'missing in action'.

The man who took Roland's place was Ray Singer, an industry veteran who had previously worked with the likes of The Easybeats and The Sarstedt Brothers, as well as a number of reggae artists. "Ray was somebody who loved to work with a live band," said Napier-Bell, "and actually, he was very good for Japan." Though both group and producer would subsequently fall out in later years, Japan seemed to click with Singer almost immediately on meeting him. Sessions were booked at London's Audio International Studios, where within three weeks the band had laid down all the songs that would constitute their first album. To ensure quality control, Ray Singer spent a further four weeks mixing the tracks. At the time, Mick Karn was enthusiastic about the results. "It's the best thing since sliced bread!" he exclaimed to journalist Chris Carr. Nonetheless, their manager knew there were several hurdles yet to overcome. "You always know when you're meeting a star," explained Napier-Bell. "What you don't know is when that person will become a star . . ."

It was to be a long wait.

2

Howls And Shrieks

In March, 1978, Japan released their first single on Hansa Records, a cover of Barbra Streisand's 'Don't Rain On My Parade'. The original melody, written for the musical/film Funny Girl was pure Broadway from start to finish: witty, infectious and immaculately performed. Sadly, Japan's version was none of these things. More 'gruesome mutilation' than 'inspired homage', the band seemed to view the song as little more than a convenient way of quickly establishing punk/new wave credibility. Hence the listener was treated to a cacophonous racket of screeching guitars, clattering percussion and hideously overwrought vocals. In truth, 'Don't Rain On My Parade' brought out the very worst in David Sylvian, his out of tune drawl rendering the track almost unbearable at times. Though such rampant pillaging of an established classic was undoubtedly meant to make Japan appear dangerous and controversial, no-one (least of all the record buying public) took any notice. The single sunk without trace.

One month later the band's débu album, *Adolescent Sex*, was shipped to stores. In short, it was a profound disappointment. Largely bereft of any decent tunes, the LP saw Japan ping-ponging between stodgy funk-rock ('Performance', 'The Unconventional') and poorly realised heavy metal ('Adolescent Sex' itself). There were a few moments of light relief. The closing track 'Television' was likeable enough, with Sylvian growling lines like "You've got blasphemy with a smile," and "Insomnia sleeps with you nights" over a suitably acerbic musical background. 'Communist China' too, was a creditable stab at hard rock dynamics. Though the song had little to do with Communism (or China for that matter), the clever chord changes, stop-start rhythms and overall lyrical bile ("Here's penetration for you") hinted at some future promise. But taken as a whole, *Adolescent Sex* represented no real threat to the more innovative bands trawling the UK club circuit at the time. When one compared Japan to the likes of Siouxsie And The Banshees, The Only Ones or The Skids, they sounded terribly dated, a bitter after-taste of the glam rock years.

The critics remained divided over the LP's worth: "Wow, maaan, what's this?" wrote *Sounds* scribe Jane Suck. "It's really, ah, good! . . . Japan make the bomb that detonated. Filthy rock'n'roll utilising everything . . ." *Record Mirror*'s Kelly Pike was equally giving: "Japan – a new five piece band, who look like The New York Dolls, and sound a million miles apart." Nonetheless, *New Musical Express* (in the critical ascendant at the time due to their solidarity with punk culture) didn't like Japan at all. "I've got the first birth of a band called Japan here," wrote journalist Tony Stewart, "and it's still-born. There's such a grotesque stench of musical decay that my stylus refuses to go near it again."

Such a vituperative attack was surely a reaction to the way the group were being marketed as much as the music itself. While then current new-wave acts like Magazine and XTC were content to play down their musical talent behind slow waves of low-key advertising, Japan were being plugged as if they were the second coming. Full page adverts of the quintet blazed from the pages of the rock press, with one poster conveying a particularly seedy image of David Sylvian brandishing a Japanese ceremonial sword, presumably there to reinforce the group's name. Another (now infamous) campaign tried to trade on the band's ambivalent sexual allure, showing a stray hand entering a zipper on a pair of jeans. 'Get Into Japan!' screamed the accompanying copy. In the wake of

The Sex Pistols and The Clash, the use of such hedonistic imagery only served to alienate the group from their more protest friendly peers.

Sylvian, however, was keen enough to point out that his lyrics on *Adolescent Sex* dealt with current issues: " 'Performance' is about minority groups in politics," he revealed to journalist Chris Carr, "and 'Lovers On Main Street' is about prostitutes . . . Someone came in the other day who thought 'Wish You Were Black' was a love song. It's not. It's a protest song about the National Front. Because of the way I write people think it's a love song and that surprises me." In all honesty, it shouldn't have. With lines such as "I know, I wish you were black, but it ain't no use singing gospel, she ain't never coming back," it was almost impossible to discern what David was actually referring to. The same could be said of many of the songs on *Adolescent Sex*. Though some of his lyrical observations were undoubtedly clever, giving an impression of knowing sexuality and casual cynicism, one instinctively felt Sylvian drew more on his imagination than actual experience. Still, it is easy to forget, in lieu of later achievements, that he was only twenty years old when *Adolescent Sex* was released.

To ensure further promotion of the LP, Japan undertook their first nation-wide tour of the UK, providing support for American heavy metal/art rock combo Blue Oyster Cult. Even on paper, the pairing was patently ridiculous. While Japan were guitar-driven, their peroxide image and camera-friendly pouts were a far cry from the blood, thunder and Viking beards of Blue Oyster Cult. Selling the band into the hearts of the British rock audience was one thing, but Seventies heavy metal fans were notorious for giving short shrift to any form of posing, preferring their heroes to be as hirsute and unscrubbed as possible. The classic 'Christians to the lions' scenario beckoned.

On April 27, 1978 at Bristol's Colston Hall, Japan got their first real taste of negative criticism. Shortly after they took to the stage the boos began in earnest, with insults and bottles following soon after. To their credit, the band roughed it out, playing a repertoire drawn mainly from *Adolescent Sex*, but the howls and shrieks of derision that accompanied their set made for a chilling baptism of fire. The response accorded them at Manchester's Apollo Theatre the next night was even worse. Something had to be done. Japan's manager Simon Napier-Bell offered Sylvian a possible solution. "I said, 'David, I've got to teach you something. You've got to go to the front of that stage and take charge of that audience. Just walk to the front, stand there and look at them. Then they'll barrack you. And the more they barrack you, the more you stand there and look at them. And (soon enough), they'll get bored making noise and you've won. All you've got to do is stand there with enough confidence until they back down.' "

The test came on the third night of the tour in front of a particularly bloodthirsty Glaswegian audience. "In the middle of an enormous barracking at the Glasgow Apollo, David actually did it," recalled Napier-Bell. "He stopped the song, and just looked round. And all of a sudden this enormous smile came on his face. He realised there was nothing to be scared of. After a while, the audience shut up and he finished the song. Absolutely extraordinary . . ." Though crowd reaction to the band remained hostile throughout the tour (with some real frights occurring at Liverpool's Empire Theatre and Newcastle's City Hall), Japan arrived back in London for a two night stop-off at Hammersmith Odeon on June 4/5 with all limbs intact. Sylvian had learned a priceless lesson: "It was an invaluable experience for us," he later told the *Melody Maker*'s Steve Gett, "because if you cope with an audience like that, you can cope with anything . . ."

The hostility the group faced on the Blue Oyster Cult tour was borne out by the poor sales of *Adolescent Sex* in the UK. Far too lightweight to appeal to serious rock aficionados, and carrying too many 'old-guard' sensibilities to interest fans of the new-wave, Japan found themselves uncomfortably placed in a musical no-man's land. Sylvian attributed their dilemma to the eclectic nature of both band and album. "It's people that listen to [*Adolescent Sex*] once and gauge it on first impressions who don't like it," he told Chris Carr. "It's one of those albums that you've got to listen to, get into and try and understand what we're doing, because we are not going to come along with what's been done already. We're trying to do something completely different."

In August, 1978, Hansa Records again tested the commercial waters with the release of Japan's second single, 'The Unconventional'. One of the least interesting tracks from *Adolescent Sex,* the song only saw the light of day because its title drew attention to the group's eccentric visual appearance. Unfortunately, 'The Unconventional' was up against stiff competition, with Siouxsie And The Banshees' marvellous début 'Hong Kong Garden' and The Stranglers' 'Walk On By' released around the same time. While Siouxsie clambered to No 7, and The Stranglers No 21, Japan failed to chart. Blue Oyster Cult, in the meantime, rubbed salt into the wounds by scoring their biggest UK success yet, with the band's Byrds-inflected ode to death '(Don't Fear) The Reaper' reaching No 16 on the Top 30.

Smarting from the commercial body-blow dealt them by British audiences, Japan ventured across the Atlantic in September, 1978 for their first (and last) US dates. Four shows where performed in all, (two on the East Coast, two on the West), but the reception accorded the band by American crowds was little better than the one they'd left behind. "It was at a time when punk was at its height," Mick Karn later recalled, "and we weren't accepted at all. [Consequently], David built up a phobia about ever going there again, so we never made it back." Japan's manager, Simon Napier-Bell, summed up the ill-fated visit: "Critically quite successful, but nobody turned up . . ."

As was standard industry practice in the late Seventies, Japan were given precious little time to contemplate their mistakes. Consequently their second album, *Obscure Alternatives,* was in the shops by October 1978. A much stronger and more rounded effort than *Adolescent Sex*, the LP (again produced by Ray Singer) made great use of the darker side of the group's sound. There was still the odd throw-away, with the Mott The Hoople-like raunch of 'Automatic Gun' and 'Sometimes I Feel So Low' adding precious little to already established themes, but elsewhere some progression was apparent.

On 'Love Is Infectious' for instance, the band were experimenting with quirky time changes and almost atonal guitar interplay. 'Deviation' consolidated the approach, marrying a frenetic tempo to the first stirrings of Mick Karn's rubbery bass style. The song also marked Karn's recorded début as a saxophonist, his positively subterranean brass stabs adding flavour where required. 'Rhodesia' caught Japan in a reggae mood, though they were only partially successful in capturing the inherent sense of space so crucial to the true Kingston sound.

However, three tracks stood out in earnest. With 'Suburban Berlin', Sylvian had written his first truly interesting pop song, the composition ably contrasting moody, spiteful verses against a laconic, yet eminently memorable chorus. If his lyrics were still a little too clever for their own good – "Domestic training, a woman's intuition . . . a love is churning out on factory lines" – they had at least found a home in a halfway decent tune. " 'Suburban Berlin'," said David, "is like comparing pre-war Germany with the Nazi thing [now] around in England." The German city of Hamburg was also prominently featured in the words to 'Deviation', the song itself a wry commentary on a brief affair Sylvian indulged himself in while on tour earlier in the year. "It was five days of constant pressure," the singer recalled, "and you can tell by the [words] what [I] think of Hamburg."

The title track, 'Obscure Alternatives', also provided fine musical drama, with agitated guitars, burping basses and under-fed percussion creating a suitably opaque atmosphere for Sylvian's nascent drawl: "Zero down to zero," he complained.

"Come catch me as best you can." Yet it was the album's final moment, 'The Tenant', that held the key to Japan's possible future. Best described as a subtle fusion of *Low*-period Bowie and the gentler work of 19th century French romantic composer Erik Satie, the instrumental's elegant piano flourishes, sweet-toned guitar and plaintive sax all hinted that Sylvian might be onto something of real worth: " 'The Tenant' was the first time I'd sat down at a piano," he later recalled. "I started writing on the keyboard after that. It made a dramatic change in the music . . . it became more melodic . . . and I began to understand more about chord structures."

Although guitarist Rob Dean described Japan's collective endeavours on *Obscure Alternatives* as "A sequence of musical passages combined into one entity," the cover of the record revealed that one of the "entities" was starting to stand out a little more than the others. Whereas *Adolescent Sex*'s artwork had presented Japan wholly as a group, photographer Fin Costello's cover shot for their latest album pulled David out of the ranks and placed him firmly in the spotlight. It was the first real sign that Sylvian was becoming more comfortable in his role as front-man. And, more tellingly, a disquieting omen of things to come.

To accompany the release of *Obscure Alternatives*, Japan took to the road, performing selected dates at Manchester's Mayflower Club on November 18, 1978 and London's Lyceum on November 26. Nonetheless, despite recent evidence to suggest that the group were starting to find some musical form, the press remained scathing towards them. " 'Rhodesia' favours a metallic, clinical dub rhythm, a funk bass pattern and an ill-fitting space synthesiser and heavy rock guitar," wrote *NME*'s Mark Ellen. "Vocalist David Sylvian's disregard for rhythm ensures that his catarrhal dronings reduce the whole thing to a mincing electric death." He continued: " 'Love Is Infectious' – where layers of unconnected jarring sounds are stacked up under more glutinous vocal drooling – is just a mass of chaotic noise." Ellen's review of Japan's appearance at the Music Machine in early December was actually one of the kinder ones published.

Like *Adolescent Sex, Obscure Alternatives* failed to chart in the UK, though the album did stir up some commercial interest in Canada. In fact, the only success Japan had managed to muster thus far was a brief appearance in the Dutch Top 30, where 'Adolescent Sex' had been released as a single. Suffice to say, the band found themselves struggling. "Japan obviously had no relevance to current music in the UK," said Simon Napier-Bell. "They were completely out of touch with what was going on. In fact, they had no interest in what was going on. The image was a complete rip-off of The New York Dolls . . . it was just a complete disaster. But," he conceded, "they were charming."

Within months of releasing *Obscure Alternatives,* Japan would completely abandon both the image and music that saw them vilified by critics and ignored by the public. Yet, the seam of ill-fitting, dandified rock the group so diligently mined in the late Seventies did prove inspirational to some. London-based hard rock outfit Girl gained some notoriety by utilising a similar look and sound on their 1980 début LP *Sheer Greed.* And early Eighties Finnish quintet Hanoi Rocks bore more than a passing resemblance to Japan circa 1978, with their peroxide-blond singer/sax-player Mike Monroe a veritable doppelganger for David Sylvian before he made the acquaintance of a good hairdresser. Sadly, neither band could really push their music past the prejudices of the rock world they were so desperate to enter. As was the case with Japan, audiences weren't quite ready to embrace another round of effeminate looking young men playing loud guitars.

Ultimately, Sylvian would later refer to *Adolescent Sex* and *Obscure Alternatives* only as "mistakes", taking the view that, "We got the first album wrong, so we did another and that was wrong as well." He also blamed youth and circumstance. "If you make mistakes," David told *NME*'s Paul Morley in 1982. "It's difficult . . . to escape. I know the first album (was) rubbish, that all the hype that went with it was wrong, but we were just five boys being naïve and trying to get something together. (Yet) all that stubbornness, ignorance and naïveté we paraded then was a strength in a way – a blindness that enables you to get through those bad periods. We were pushed towards the outrageous and it was past the age of outrage. We struggled against it and it came out a caricature."

3

A Change Of Emphasis

By the winter of 1978, Japan were in serious trouble, both artistically and financially. Their manager, Simon Napier-Bell, had plunged himself into real debt trying to break the band, but LP sales remained perilously low. Even the record company were beginning to ask questions about their future. Nevertheless, the crisis Japan found themselves facing seemed only to strengthen their resolve, with the group drawing on the 'all for one, one for all' mentality so redolent throughout their years at Catford Boys School. "The five of us will sit in a room," said David Sylvian, "and we won't say a thing, and if someone comes into the room, they'll feel very uncomfortable. We're that close. We can sit for hours . . . not say a thing in a room of silence." Such youthful solidarity was undoubtedly touching, but it did little to solve their current dilemma.

Temporary salvation was on the way with the belated release of the band's first album, *Adolescent Sex*, in Japan. Though the LP actually hit the shelves in the UK some months before, the group's management/publicists realised that, if handled right, much could be made of Japan's name and image in the Far East. After all, in terms of sales, the Japanese record-buying market was the third biggest in the world, with only the USA and Great Britain purchasing more units per capita. The strategy hatched to break the band was nothing if inspired. "We made a plan for Japan [the country]," recalled Napier-Bell, "where three to four months before the album came out there would be intensive press and pictures . . . but no music – obviously because the music wasn't right. I mean, the kids who followed music in Japan were eleven to fourteen years old . . . and into Cheap Trick and Kiss. They weren't ready for [Japan's] complicated sound."

He continued: "But [in the end], it worked brilliantly. We managed to get a 30,000 fan club before the record came out . . . based on press and pictures. Then the LP came out and it sold 30,000 copies. [Unfortunately], there were then 30,000 disappointed kids! But they were already in love with the look of the group, so they had to listen to the album and get to like it. In a way, we'd educated these kids into [listening to] something intelligent. That way, as they got older, they stayed with the band."

Japan had to postpone their first visit to the Far East for a month or so because of illness – Sylvian came down with a throat problem, perhaps due to the way he was manipulating his vocal chords at the time – but by March, 1979, they found themselves in Tokyo, in the midst of thousands of adoring pre-pubescents. There was also a keen level of interest shown in the group by some markedly older female fans. "Massive groupie situation," Richard Barbieri later recalled to *Q*, "[but] we tended to ignore it for quite a few years. Thought we were above all that. [Later] we decided that we wanted to have a good time."

Japan guitarist Rob Dean was equally dismissive of the attention foisted upon them: "We're not really into having a dozen girls on each arm everywhere we go," he told *Record Mirror*'s Kelly Pike in 1978. "In fact, a dressing room full of simpering females from the moment you come offstage is a nuisance we can do without . . . I suppose we're just not interested enough." Long live rock'n'roll.

In stark contrast to their low profile appearances in the UK, the group's first concert in Japan was held at the imposing Budokan Theatre. "The first gig they did in Japan was the Budokan," recalled Napier-Bell. "Before that, the biggest solo gig they'd done was The Red Lion in Hammersmith to 140 people. Then they go straight through to the Budokan – 11,000 seat capacity sold out three days in a row."

Though the dichotomy must have been irritating at the time, Japan's continued success in the Asian territories would provide them with a much-needed financial life-line for some time to come. "For years, they went to Japan for two weeks," says Napier-Bell, "played huge gigs, came back to England and then did nothing."

Napier-Bell's remarks were borne out by the group's less than triumphant homecoming gig at North London's Rainbow Theatre in April, 1979. While they were in fine musical form, playing a selection of material culled from both *Adolescent Sex* and *Obscure Alternatives* – 'The Unconventional', 'Automatic Gun' and the drab 'Suburban Love' were all duly covered, though the band had mercifully dropped 'Heartbreaker' and 'Don't Rain On My Parade' from their set by this time – the theatre itself was less than half-full, a clear (and disturbing) sign that British audiences continued to view the group with suspicion, or worse, contempt.

As chief songwriter/band leader, the pressure was now on David Sylvian to turn their fortunes around. His first decision (approved by his colleagues) was to dispense with the services of producer Ray Singer. "On *Obscure Alternatives*," David later told the *Melody Maker*'s Steve Gett, "our relationship with [Ray] wasn't too hot in the end. I don't really think he understood what we were doing, and I'd like to take half the songs on the album back into the studio and re-mix them."

Sylvian's next move, on the face of it, was extremely surprising, but ultimately quite inspired. Rather than approach an established rock producer with the home demos he'd recently recorded for Japan's third album, he chose instead to fly to Los Angeles and meet with Giorgio Moroder, a producer/songwriter best known at the time for penning Donna Summer's No 1 hit 'I Feel Love'. Although Moroder had worked with rock and pop acts in the past (he and partner Pete Bellotte were the men responsible for Chicory Tip's 'Son Of My Father'), he was predominantly associated with disco groups like Silver Convention and Summer. Nonetheless, Sylvian's recent compositions veered more towards keyboards than they did guitars. Therefore he was eager to utilise Moroder's proven ability with swirling synthesisers and up-tempo beats. "After playing him the songs," David recalled, "he said if he was going to produce us he would like to co-write one [with me]." Cornered, but pleasantly so, Sylvian agreed to the alliance.

The result of the Sylvian/Moroder collaboration, 'Life In Tokyo', was Japan's strongest single yet. It also marked a formidable and lasting change in the way the group administrated their overall sound. Dispensing completely with the rock guitar ballast of previous endeavours, Richard Barbieri's clean, synthetic lines were pushed well to the fore, freeing up critical space for the rhythm section to perform the task of making the music come alive. Karn and Jansen rose to the challenge admirably, providing both punctuation, and a real sense of swing. Sylvian's voice too, was markedly changed. Without an arsenal of over-driven guitars to compete with, his trademark rasp had cooled to an almost soul-like croon. Aside from the largely irritating female backing vocals (presumably tacked on to the track to give it further commercial allure), 'Life In Tokyo' represented Japan's best chance yet of cracking the UK Top 30. Unfortunately, when the single was released in May 1979, it sank without trace.

Though Japan had initially entertained the idea of recording another single ('European Son') with Moroder, the commercial failure of 'Life In Tokyo' marked the end of their association with the producer. Sensing disaster, Hansa Records' accountants began to circle like vultures. "Peter Meisel [head of Hansa Records] called me and said, 'When is David going to write a hit?' " recalled Simon Napier-Bell. "I said, 'I don't know . . . he's trying.' Meisel then said, 'It's because we give them £20 a week – that's the problem. Cut off the money, then he'll write a hit!' "

Japan's response to their ever-growing problems was to cut and run. Subsequently, they relocated their base of operations to New York, where fledgling song ideas and arrangements were worked upon. Having lost their US record deal due to poor sales, the move also gave the group a much needed opportunity to peddle their wares to any interested parties, among them Epic in the US. In the meantime, the search for a suitable producer continued, with Sylvian interviewing several potential candidates for the job. The singer originally had his eye on John Punter, a mercurial talent perhaps best known for work with Roxy Music's Bryan Ferry (1973's *These Foolish Things* and 1974's *Another Time, Another Place*), but the producer was already engaged on another project at the time. Fortunately for Japan's future prosperity, Sylvian spent so much time writing new material that by the time he'd finished, Punter had become available. Returning to the UK, Japan and their new producer entered London's Air Studios in the autumn of 1979 to begin work on the group's third LP. By February 9, 1980, it was in the shops.

Entitled *Quiet Life,* the record consolidated the approach evinced on 'Life In Tokyo', but with a crucial note of harmonic sophistication added to the band's sound. In fact, the greatest surprise was just how far Japan had progressed as musicians. Keyboard player Richard Barbieri, by his own admission a slow starter, was now central to the realisation of Sylvian's songs, his fine grasp of chordal textures generating an almost orchestral dimension to tunes such as 'In Vogue' and the title track itself. Drummer Steve Jansen had also shed many of his more rockist tendencies, pursuing instead an altogether more elegant and eclectic groove (his stick-work on 'Alien' and 'The Other Side Of Life' are highlights particularly worthy of mention). By simply turning down the volume, Rob Dean established himself as a guitarist of note, supplying the band with a clipped and percussive edge. However, the award for most frightening advance in technical facility surely belonged to Mick Karn, whose combination of off-kilter, almost deranged bass-lines and stabbing saxophone breaks on *Quiet Life* announced his arrival as a world-class musician.

And so to the tunes themselves. Thankfully, David Sylvian seemed to have learned much from his experiences with Giorgio Moroder. Instead of continuing to indulge his infatuation with American musical forms, *Quiet Life* saw the songwriter move into distinctly European territories, with tracks such as 'Halloween' and 'Fall In Love With Me' both light years away from the thick rockist soup of *Adolescent Sex*. In essence, the only concession made on the LP to the USA was a subtle cover version of 'All Tomorrow's Parties', the rather doleful social lament from The Velvet Underground's enormously influential 1967 début album.

The album emphasised David's development as a lyricist and balladeer, and seeping into both 'Despair' and 'The Other Side Of Life' were the first signs of the gentle melancholia and desire for emotional or physical escape that would prove so important to Japan's final years. A proud first cousin to Erik Satie's 1880 masterpiece *Trois Gymnopédies*, 'Despair's gently plucked piano, sorrowful saxophone and spare drum machine offered further evidence that *Obscure Alternatives*' 'The Tenant' had opened a door through which Sylvian would find even more fertile areas of composition.

Perhaps the only criticism one could make was that by choosing to sing the song in French, he was laying himself open to charges of pretension. Yet, *Quiet Life*'s closing moment, 'The Other Side Of Life', was largely immune from censure. A captivating ballad that utilised all of Japan's newfound musical strength, the song at last found Sylvian rejecting clever word-play in favour of more bitter-sweet lyrical imagery: "These single occasions we seem to share stumble and fall . . . she comes and goes . . . the other side of life."

The woman responsible for the stirring string arrangements on 'The Other Side Of Life' and 'In Vogue' (another of *Quiet Life*'s high points) was Ann O'Dell, a long-time friend of both Japan's manager Simon Napier-Bell and producer John

Punter. However, when she was first approached about writing orchestral parts for the album, O'Dell was less than enthusiastic. "To be honest," Ann recalled, "I wasn't keen because I was a [committed] musician and I wasn't impressed with the people who'd formed bands via art school rather than music school. I didn't like Roxy Music for the same reason." Her mood lightened when she heard Sylvian's songs. "David was very charismatic, and his material was strong. As an arranger, it's always nice when you find something that you can contribute to . . . that challenges you. There was more to David's songs than Bryan Ferry's songs."

O'Dell was more than qualified to make such an assessment. Aside from arranging strings on the platinum selling album *Hooked On Classics*, she had spent much of the Seventies actually working with Bryan Ferry, contributing orchestral parts to 'Smoke Gets In Your Eyes', 'Tokyo Joe' and the 1977 album *The Bride Stripped Bare.* O'Dell had even played keyboards on Ferry's world tour of the same year.

And therein lay the potential problem. When one investigated *Quiet Life* more thoroughly, uncomfortable parallels began to surface between Japan's new sound and Roxy Music's "clinical sheen". The Andy McKay inspired saxophone lines on 'Alien', Phil Manzenera-like sustained guitars on 'All Tomorrow's Parties', and Sylvian's subtle conversion from a rasping vocal style to a more mild-mannered croon all pointed towards a certain degree of homage. It was an angle duly picked up on by the music press. "Although [Japan] may seem full-steam ahead, seamlessly 'European' to you," wrote *NME*'s Ian Penman, "it all sounds slyly studied Roxy *Stranded* to us ancients, Ferry's smoky closures accentuated and crowded into one watery fiction."

The facts spoke for themselves. *Quiet Life* was produced by John Punter, who had worked as an engineer for Roxy Music and also produced Bryan Ferry's first two solo LPs. Ann O'Dell's presence consolidated the connection. Even Japan's manager readily acknowledged the link. "David changed from

Marc Bolan/David Bowie to Bryan Ferry overnight," recalled Simon Napier-Bell. "Hansa Records went completely berserk."

Despite the charges of plagiarism that accompanied the release of *Quiet Life,* even the most hardened cynic had to concede that Japan's new musical direction was far superior to the one they had left behind. This was born out when the band started to pick up their first real support from the music press, with *Melody Maker*'s Steve Gett and *Sounds* editor Geoff Barton both aligning themselves to Japan's cause. If overall critical acceptance was still some way off, Sylvian was at least beginning to sound like a man who knew his time was at hand. "I'm only interested in being successful on my own terms," he told Steve Gett. "I'm not going to do things I don't enjoy. It's far more important to me to have an album that I'm happy with and that gives something rather than one that sells millions."

Ironically, *Quiet Life* became Japan's best selling LP to date, entering the UK charts at No 53 in the second week of February, 1980. Attendance levels at the band's concerts also improved, with two shows at London's Venue selling out in late January. For their audience, these dates represented the first real chance to view the group's new image. And quite striking it was too, with fashionable leather box jackets and well-cut pegs replacing Leopard-skin coats and torn jeans. The lions' manes that once constituted hairstyles for the band had been consigned to the scrapheap with the emphasis now on cleverly styled wedges and carefully teased fringes. Taken as a whole, Japan's new sound and style seemed to bode well for the future. Nonetheless, there were several problems to overcome first, most of them involving money.

4

Doodle And Croon

Throughout the summer of 1979, Japan had been on the brink of splitting up. Though youthful arrogance carried the group through the first wave of critical scorn, a combination of poor record sales and continued financial hardship had begun to seriously weaken their determination to succeed. Even the notoriety they had found in Japan seemed a hollow victory, with critics more than eager to point out that it was looks rather than musical ability that won over their Asian audience. However, faith in their own talent was largely restored during the recording of *Quiet Life.* "I really enjoyed making *Quiet Life,*" Richard Barbieri later told *Keyboard Review,* "because it was a happy time and a real consolidated group effort." For David Sylvian, the album represented a watershed of sorts. "We started *Quiet Life* with a concept of 'sound' whereas we'd previously just thrown songs together. I just grew up very quickly in the six months between the second and third album. I saw where I was."

Despite the fact that *Quiet Life* had lifted Japan into the UK charts for the first time, they were still a financial drain on both their record company and management. "There was a point when I thought I just had to stop," recalled Simon Napier-Bell. "By then I was £150,000 in debt and it was going nowhere. [So] I called the band up and said, 'I [want] to have a really important meeting.' I was going to tell them I was really sorry but I had to give up. I was really worried, because they were friends and always so enthusiastic. I didn't sleep well the night before. Anyway, the meeting came and they turned up one after the other, all beautifully dressed . . . almost shining. And they said, 'What's the meeting about, Simon?' And I said . . . 'We've really got to decide how we're going to crack this!' I just couldn't do it . . ."

The decision was made to record a cover of Smokey Robinson's 'I Second That Emotion' for single release. If a hit, the song might promote just enough interest in *Quiet Life* to see the album into the Top 30, thereby solving everyone's financial problems. Suffice to say, like every Japan single before it, 'I Second That Emotion' failed to chart. As a consequence, Hansa Records refused to finance a fourth album for the band. For Napier-Bell, it was breaking point. "I got Peter Meisel alone, and he agreed to let Japan go."

After meetings with several companies, including CBS and RCA, both band and management felt Richard Branson's Virgin Records was offering the best all-round deal. "We went to Virgin," Sylvian said at the time, "because they have a natural enthusiasm which you just don't find in record companies very often. And the people there are very young."

Yet shortly after Japan signed contracts, all hell broke loose. "As soon as Meisel's wife [also a Hansa director] heard what had happened, she said, 'We haven't let them go at all,' " explained Napier-Bell. "She screamed and yelled, and had a huge fight with Peter. And Peter, who was always scared of his wife, refused to admit to her that he'd told me they could go. (It ended up) as a big court case that cost a lot of money."

The situation was eventually settled out of court by the band's lawyers. "It was resolved by council finding precedents for a verbal release which had been gone back on, because of course, there was nothing on paper," recalled Napier-Bell. "We eventually found two from 1916, where artists' contracts had been verbally terminated, and then someone had gone back on the agreement."

While Japan were now free to pursue their new contract with Virgin, Hansa Records were still due a termination fee from the band. "We knew that unless we settled out of court," Sylvian later recounted, "the name we'd built up would be lost and there'd be no point in coming back. So we had to settle and give them a lot of money, which got rid of the advance from Virgin."

The only obstacle now remaining in Japan's path was the money they owed their manager. Obviously in a generous (or positively psychic) mood, Napier-Bell decided a write-off was the best way forward. "The point was this," he said, ". . . when we started at Virgin, the band owed me – on paper – well, I can't honestly remember the exact figure, but roughly £150,000 to £200,000. A ridiculous amount of money. And even if you're starting afresh, if you say to the band, 'You owe me £200,000,' they're just going to break up. They aren't going to look at it logically. So I figured 'write it off', and if they do well, I'll get 20% [of their income]." Overall, it proved to be a wise decision.

In October, 1980, Japan's first single/EP for Virgin Records was released. Entitled 'Gentlemen Take Polaroids', the song established a clever musical bridge between the refined groove of *Quiet Life* and the band's forthcoming LP. Utilising crystal-cut guitars, snap-shot percussion and a swaying, gently infectious melody, 'Gentlemen Take Polaroids' allowed Sylvian to further indulge his new-found penchant for romance: "There's a girl downtown I'd like to know, I'd like to slip away with you, and if you said you loved me . . . how could I mind?" Backed up with three instrumental tracks, 'The Experience Of Swimming', 'The Width Of A Room' (written by Rob Dean and Richard Barbieri respectively) and the extremely Enoesque 'Burning Bridges', '. . . Polaroids' nestled into the UK charts at No 60, the highest position the group had yet achieved with a single.

A month later, Japan's fourth LP was released. Its title, *Gentlemen Take Polaroids,* was no great surprise to anyone who had bought the recent single. In essence, the album represented a consolidation of the musical themes explored on

Quiet Life, but with more emphasis placed on arrangements, harmony and space. Though the approach added a polite, almost dignified element to Sylvian's songs, it also neutered much of their emotional content, with the listener having to work hard to find a connection with the music.

Still, there was much to admire about the record. Both 'My New Career' (featuring an exquisite violin solo from session ace Simon House) and 'Methods Of Dance' were exceedingly elegant compositions, and the group's cover of 'Ain't That Peculiar' (yet another Smokey Robinson song) allowed Karn, Jansen and Barbieri a golden opportunity to flex their instrumental muscles. On 'Swing', Japan actually achieved the distinction of out-Roxying Roxy Music on a track that somehow managed to advance many of the ideas Bryan Ferry toyed with on the albums *Stranded* and *Manifesto*. In fact, John Punter, the producer of *Gentlemen Take Polaroids*, to this day sees 'Swing' as the zenith of Japan's recorded career.

Lyrically, David Sylvian was busy unifying many of the topics he'd raised on *Quiet Life*, with travel and escape to foreign climes still much on his mind. "Tell me when the work is done, tell me when the day is through," he sang on 'Swing'. "And I'll drive safely in my car, taking islands in Africa." The weather, too, occupied his thoughts, with sun, wind, rain and storm all comprehensively name-checked throughout the album. By presenting these images of almost colonial existence, where climate dictated mood and pace of life, Sylvian came across as a bored, if occasionally ardent tourist within his own compositional territories.

As was usual with Japan, the album's final tracks managed to drop a few broad hints as to the next stage in the band's musical development. Therefore, listeners were treated to the gentle stirrings of 'Nightporter', a direct descendant of *Obscure Alternatives*' 'The Tenant' and *Quiet Life*'s 'Despair', and Sylvian's most direct homage yet to the work of Erik Satie. However, where 'Nightporter' differed from David's previous work was in the seemingly introspective nature of its lyrics:

'Could I ever explain this feeling of love, it just lingers on, the fear in my heart that keeps telling me which way to turn . . .' While *Quiet Life*'s 'In Vogue' and 'The Other Side Of Life' had both flirted with the concept of self-reflection, 'Nightporter' marked the first real example of Sylvian using first person narrative to convey a sense of longing and regret to his audience. Sadly, much of the song's emotional impact was lost in a syrupy sea of cellos, oboes and Satie-inflected piano. In short, passion had been replaced by pastiche. It was a deficiency Sylvian would correct in coming years.

Gentlemen Take Polariods' concluding tune, 'Taking Islands In Africa' also represented a precursor of things to come, marking as it did the first recorded collaboration between Sylvian and Yellow Magic Orchestra keyboard player Ryuichi Sakamoto. In many ways, the two had been gravitating toward each other ever since Japan achieved stardom in Sakamoto's homeland in early 1979. While Yellow Magic Orchestra meant little in international terms, their capable blend of traditional Oriental music and up-to-the-minute electro-pop had ensured them an almost hallowed status in their native Japan. As a consequence, Ryuichi and main musical partner Yukihiro Takahashi were treated as the country's first genuine rock stars, with foreign invaders Japan the only real threat to them in sales terms.

Yet, rather than pursue a path of mutual enmity, Sylvian and Sakamoto had actually become firm friends. When YMO played at London's Venue club in October, 1979, David was part of the audience. Ryuichi duly returned the compliment in July, 1980, by interviewing the singer for *Music Life,* Japan's biggest selling rock magazine. With Sylvian becoming ever more interested in Oriental culture and sound, it was only fitting that his association with Sakamoto would lead the way to Japan's first instrumental foray into World music.

The alliance took place during the summer of 1980, when Sakamoto found himself working at Central London's Air Studios on his second solo LP *B-2 Unit.* As chance would have it, Japan were across the corridor completing overdubs on *Polaroids.* Suffice to say, chords were swapped and a song was born. The result of their collaboration (on which Sakamoto picked up a co-writing credit) was a clever yet subtle fusion of standard Japan sheen and distinctly Oriental sounding keyboards to which David added an atypically optimistic lyric. As was now standard practice with Sylvian, he appropriated the song's title from a lyric he had already written for the track 'Swing'.

Backed by a heavy promotional campaign, which saw one major record chain use the ill-advised slogan 'For Japan, Nippon Down To Our Price', *Gentlemen Take Polaroids* finally broke the band into the Top 50, with the album making a semi-creditable appearance at No 45 in late November, 1980. The music press remained unimpressed. "The emphasis is on an immaculately precise blend of doodle and croon," wrote *NME*'s Paul Du Noyer. "If only Japan's music was as eloquent as it's elegant . . . they lavish tender loving care on the surface sound – a beautifully polished, empty shell of a sound. [It's] such exquisitely shaped music – even if it often seems shamelessly derivative and early Roxy, most notably in Sylvian's morose warble – [it] is in itself an achievement of sorts."

Melody Maker's Patrick Humphries was equally parsimonious with his praise. "There is something infinitely unsatisfying about this album, from the false image of the band to the hollow songs they perform. If Roxy Music were not alive and well, it would be necessary to invent them, and Japan might fill that vacuum. But Roxy are still with us . . . which negates the reason for the existence of a band like Japan – unless Sylvian can tear himself away from his hall of mirrors. Japan," Humphries concluded, "take all the constituent parts of the Roxy manifesto, and conspicuously fail to add anything at all."

If the rock press were trying to halt Japan's progress by giving them bad reviews, the strategy wasn't working. A scheduled date at London's Lyceum on November 27 sold out within hours. "The turning point was the Lyceum," Simon

Napier-Bell confirmed, "but the day before the band were to appear, David refused to do it. I knew enough about artists to know he was being insecure, but this was different. I didn't know what to do. I just wanted to grab him by the hair . . . so I ended up frightening him. He had to do that gig."

For Japan's manager, it was another in a long line of attempts on Sylvian's part to sabotage his chance at pop stardom – a trait that more usually manifested itself in the studio. "If anyone said, 'That's a good song', or 'That's commercial' or 'That'll be a hit', he threw it out. Every bloody time. He even went beyond that. He'd actually make the record, finish it, overdub it, and it would only take someone to come in the studio and say, 'That's brilliant', and bang!, it was out the window. He was terrified of being condemned for being commercial. He could live with being condemned as esoteric or peculiar, but he couldn't live with [being called] commercial. The only thing he could hold onto was that his music was weird, or beyond understanding." Perhaps for Sylvian, the struggle was worth more than the prize. "If we wanted to be pop stars, why would we put ourselves in for hard times?" he once asked. "Why would we go through the chores of making this type of music?"

Ultimately, the minute David Sylvian set foot on stage at London's Lyceum, his fate was sealed. Instead of being greeted with the usual round of cat-calls, insults and flying bottles, he found himself gazing at an audience that looked just like him. The age of the new romantic had arrived.

5

The Smell Of Greasepaint, The Avoidance Of Crowds

While Japan were ensconced in Central London's Air Studios creating the anodyne pleasures of *Gentlemen Take Polaroids*, a musical sea change was taking place outside in the UK pop scene. After four years of unrivalled dominance, the punk/new wave explosion that had promised so much to so many was finally beginning to show signs of fizzling out, with commerce and capital superseding desire and anger. The Sex Pistols' Johnny Rotten was now John Lydon, a man in search of a suitable Public Image. The Clash had long since torn up their contractual agreement to provide urban terrorism for the masses, preferring instead to whittle away their time performing in American casinos. And Generation X's Billy Idol was just about to destroy any credibility punk might have left by launching an extremely vulgar, but still occasionally entertaining, solo career under the guidance of financial whiz-kid/Kiss manager Bill Aucoin. It had all gone terribly wrong – or right – depending on your point of view.

The first visible sign of a musical changing of the guard had actually come as early as June 1979, when Gary Numan's Tubeway Army stormed to the top of the charts with the synthesised drones of 'Are Friends Electric?'. Unlike punk, which depended on a combination of energy and vitriol to make its point, Numan's music was all robotic rhythms, jerky keyboards and dispassionate lyricism. It was also a hugely refreshing alternative to what had come before. Nonetheless,

Gary Numan was to remain a singularity on the British music scene for some time to come.

That situation changed dramatically in July, 1980, when long-time pop contenders Ultravox got to No 3 in the UK charts with the single 'Vienna'. All flighty synthesisers, anaemic percussion values and soaring, melodramatic vocals, 'Vienna's commercial success confirmed what the staff at many a fashionable London night spot had already known for months. In short, the 'new romantics' had arrived.

As a cultural movement, new romanticism was little different from any other scene that had come before it, from Mod to Glam. Essentially, it depended on three things – fashion, music and a base of operations from which to formulate its strategy. The fashion element was easy enough to encapsulate. In direct opposition to punk, where the general idea was to make oneself as unattractive as possible, new romantics revelled in glamour, with carefully but generously applied make-up, gravity defying hairstyles and immaculately cut clothes all essential items on the agenda. The overall look was distinctly European, almost a direct homage to the sense of decadence and style found in 1920's German cabaret.

The music embraced new technology. Therefore, pure-toned synthesisers and mechanical sounding drum machines provided an able replacement for scrawny guitars and aggressively bashed cymbals. Taking its cue from David Bowie's Berlin period (*Heroes*, *Low*) and the minimalism of Kraftwerk, the sound of new romanticism was one of anaesthetised passion, where form was as important as content. In short, it was a music of emotional displacement.

The movement took root in several of London's hipper night clubs, with Blitz, Club For Heroes and, to a lesser extent, Le Kilt providing a perfect gestation ground for new romantics to hone their look, philosophy and studied indifference. For would-be New Romantics who lived north of Watford, all was not lost. Birmingham's Barbarellas club also indulged the sect, as did many niteries throughout Leeds, Manchester and even Newcastle.

As with all movements, new romanticism couldn't stay underground for long. After Ultravox scored a bull's-eye with 'Vienna', noted cultural/musical magpie David Bowie quickly aligned himself with the cult he had, in part, created. Hence, many 'faces' from the new romantic scene were drafted in to provide "visual ambience" for the promotional video to his single 'Ashes To Ashes'. As The Thin White Duke intoned the sorry conclusion to Major Tom's tale directly into camera (dressed in a Pierrot's outfit, no less), a veritable legion of London's latest fashion moths paraded behind him. The novelty value of the video alone assured Bowie the No 1 spot in the UK charts in August 1980.

By September, a subsidiary branch of new romanticism, labelled 'Futurism', was also starting to make its presence strongly felt in the North of England. In truth, the futurists actually pre-dated the "Blitz kids", but due to geographical location, it had taken time for the London-based music press to sit up and take notice of the trend. However, when over 5,000 fans showed up to watch the West Yorkshire based duo Soft Cell perform at the 'Futurama 2 Science Fiction Music Festival' in Leeds, journalists were duly dispatched to find out what all the fuss was about. Within months, they would find themselves venturing still further north to Sheffield, where Phil Oakey's Human League were beginning to plan their assault on the UK charts.

Ultimately, it mattered little whether one addressed the movement as 'New Romanticism' or 'Futurism'. The centralised core of both schools depended on the same values: a return to glamour, the use of synthesisers to create pristine, clean-cut melodies and an overall air of emotional distance. Of course, David Sylvian and Japan had been trading on such values for nearly two years, which rather handily placed them at the forefront of the next big thing in British pop music.

The crowd that attended the band's show at London's

Lyceum on November 27, 1980, were well aware that Japan were being tipped as pop's brightest hopes. After all, a number of carefully placed signs had alerted them to the fact: a wholesome, crisply produced single called 'Gentlemen Take Polaroids', a clever, yet alluring publicity campaign that promoted the group's new album as a fashionable alternative to the music of The Police and The Jam and, above all, the news that David Sylvian was recently voted 'The World's Most Beautiful Man' – an honour, incidentally, that caused the singer to approach his manager and publicity agent with murder in mind. "It was brilliant PR by our publicist, Connie Filippello," recalled Simon Napier-Bell. "David had changed his hairstyle, and she thought up this brilliant idea of saying he had just been voted 'The World's Most Beautiful Man' in Japan. Of course, David went completely bonkers about it. He came into the office and said I had to fire Connie. He didn't want to be built up on that basis . . . but it was done."

The result of all this was that the Lyceum was *the* place to be for the hipper elements of London's club crowd. Thankfully, Japan rose to the occasion, handing in a show of considerable musical worth and more than a little style. The set list itself was a mixture of old and new, with *Obscure Alternatives* 'Rhodesia' placed alongside 'My New Career' and 'Methods Of Dance'. 'Alien' and 'Quiet Life' also made an appearance, as did the as yet unreleased 'European Son'. All songs were duly dispensed in the clean, vaguely analytical style that Japan seemed to have made their own.

The musicians, too, were well settled into their appointed stage roles. Richard Barbieri was a studious presence, seemingly more concerned with synthesiser settings than the audience in front of him. Drummer Steve Jansen promoted a bookish air, one eye permanently fixed on the middle distance, the other carefully concealed behind a well-placed fringe. Mick Karn remained the natural entertainer of the band, hobbling backwards and forwards on the stage while letting loose some positively eerie sounds from his bass guitar. And Rob Dean hid his growing dissatisfaction with Japan's increasingly keyboard-driven sound behind a series of sways, smiles and edgy guitar fills.

David Sylvian had by now found his feet as master of ceremonies. The scowls and screams of Japan's early years well behind him, he now conveyed a calm, almost sedate stage presence, with the lower register vocal style débuted on 'Life In Tokyo' availing him the opportunity to sustain notes rather than strangle them. And if his range and delivery still recalled the dulcet tones of Bryan Ferry it was, in the end, a matter for critics to chew upon. After all, the teenagers that packed the Lyceum seemed more concerned with emulating Sylvian's hairstyle than debating whether his voice was his own.

In truth, Japan's appearance at the Lyceum marked a major breakthrough for the band, not only confirming their worth as a creditable live act but, more importantly, aligning them with a cultural movement that was about to break wide open in the UK. But there were still a few dissenting voices in the crowd. "Japan," wrote the *Melody Maker*'s Steve Sutherland, "who continue to pollute our public auditoriums with paint, powder and poofy hairdos . . . a conveyor belt of sound without climax or depth, beginning to end." The *NME* took the more traditional route. "Japan's current sound is one long, diffuse out-take from Roxy Music's *Flesh and Blood.*"

The critical drubbings the group received did little to stunt their growth. By May of 1981, they were appearing to packed houses across the UK, with dates at Norwich University (May 8), Leeds' Tiffanys club (10) and Edinburgh Odeon (12). The tour ended with two well-received performances at Hammersmith Odeon (16/17), the concerts notable for the fact that Japan had effectively doubled their pulling power in the capital within the space of five months.

The band's appeal in the country of Japan had also risen markedly, with fans doing almost anything to take home a piece of their heroes. "It was quite upsetting at the time of *Gentlemen Take Polaroids,*" Mick Karn told *Smash Hits*' Elissa Van Poznak. "We had to have our own floor at hotels with guards at the lifts. The girls look so gentle, and you think, 'Oh, they can't harm me'. But one day we made the mistake of going through the lobby and *they had chains, all types of weapons*. They actually tried to coil the chain round your feet and pull you to the ground. We all managed to make the lift except Richard." Mercifully, Barbieri survived the ordeal.

Japan's spiralling success remained a double-edged sword for David Sylvian. Though he was very nearly a 'star', the demands placed upon him as the face of the band were beginning to take their toll. At the top of his hate list were live engagements. "There are certain traditions within the rock business that you tend to get sucked into," he told *Juke*'s Andrea Jones. "You don't realise you're doing it until after a year or two . . . and then you realise the things you're doing don't make you happy. You don't enjoy it and wonder why you're doing it. For myself, it's touring. That's the first thing you get sucked into, because when you're young and you form a band, the first thing you try and do is play live . . . we've been putting a lot into our live performances and I still don't enjoy it." Mick Karn later confirmed Sylvian's remarks. "I was probably the only one who enjoyed (touring)," he told *Bassist* magazine. "David hated it. Absolutely hated it."

Another irritation for Sylvian was the growing level of homage accorded him by fledgling new romantic groups, with one Birmingham-based act particularly besotted with both his style and look. "Duran Duran came along and stole David's image," said Simon Napier-Bell. "They came day after day and begged him to produce them." When Sylvian made it clear he wasn't interested, the band allegedly found another solution. "Every one of them copied David's looks, so you had five David look-alikes," Napier-bell laughed. "Then they very sensibly went off, and instead of making esoteric Japan music, they recorded good, old-fashioned four to the floor disco music. So, in the end, they got the hits with the Japan look."

From a financial perspective, it made perfect sense for Japan to align themselves with new romanticism. After all, by the summer of 1981, the trend was in full swing, with Spandau Ballet, Visage, Depeche Mode and The Human League all scoring hits in the UK Top 20. Should Sylvian have wished it, one well aimed publicity campaign could easily have established him as one of the founding fathers of the movement. However, his response was to distance Japan from any form of association with the cult. "It's fancy dress," he stated coldly. "Dressing up to be something, to play a part, just for one night. That's something we've *never* done." The remark only helped reinforce the belief that Sylvian continued to perceive both himself and his band as 'outsiders' with no allegiance to any stylistic flag or passing musical fad. Ultimately, it was both an inclination and philosophy that would serve him well in years to come.

For the time being, though, he had to be content with playing the role of emergent pop celebrity. In May of 1981, Japan had come perilously close to cracking the UK Top 30 with the release of a new single, 'The Art Of Parties' – the first taster from their forthcoming album. Backed by a tour and heavy press coverage, '. . . Parties' skittering funk groove and jittery lyrical drive – "Once I was young, once I was smart, now I'm living on the edge of my nerves . . ." – took the band to No 45 in the charts, the highest position they had yet achieved. Nevertheless, real success finally came when Japan's old record company, Hansa, decided to capitalise on their back catalogue. In September, 1981, a compilation of material culled from *Adolescent Sex, Obscure Alternatives* and various aborted singles and B-sides was released under the rather suitable title *Assemblage.* Though some of the songs actually dated back as far as the winter of 1977 ('Stateline'), *Assemblage* still managed to push Japan into the UK Top 30 for the first time, with the album reaching No 26. To further assist sales, Hansa released a re-mixed version of 'Quiet Life' as a single. It subsequently became the group's first Top 20 hit, reaching No 19 on the charts in October. After nearly four years in the commercial wilderness, they had finally arrived.

Sadly, guitarist Rob Dean wasn't around to witness the

festivities, having left the band after their recent UK tour. Increasingly disenchanted with the musical direction Japan were taking (he had only contributed to four tracks on *Gentlemen Take Polaroids*), and eager to find a more suitable home for his talents, Dean moved to Los Angeles in the summer of 1981. "We were really holding him back," Sylvian said at the time. "He'd have ideas but I wouldn't allow them, wouldn't give him enough room to grow, so it was only natural for him to go." After a brief tenure with pop punks Vivabeat, Dean subsequently joined Gary Numan's touring band in 1982, where ironically, he found himself performing 'She's Got Claws', a song Numan had co-written with Mick Karn. Released as a single in September 1981, 'She's Got Claws' had reached No 6 in the UK. By 1986, Rob found himself collaborating with an up and coming Irish vocalist/songwriter called Sinéad O'Connor.

With or without Dean, Japan were still on the cusp of international stardom. Their latest LP was scheduled for release at the end of November, 1981 and all signs pointed towards gold or platinum sales. They had the respect and admiration of their musical contemporaries, and according to one journalist, the "coolest image in rock'n'roll". In short, it was all theirs for the taking. Suffice to say, everything went horribly, horribly wrong.

6

Vindication

On November 28, 1981, Japan's fifth studio album, *Tin Drum*, was released. Flying in the face of current British pop, the LP saw the group abandon all vestiges of their former life in favour of a radically new direction that investigated both Far Eastern culture and traditional music. The most striking aspect of the record was the fact that Japan used synthesisers and electronic percussion to emulate the native sounds of that region. By fusing new technology with ancient values, they also made their best record to date.

The distinctly Oriental theme of *Tin Drum* was driven home with striking force by songs such as 'Sons Of Pioneers', 'Still Life In Mobile Homes', the swaying instrumental 'Canton' and the second single drawn from the album 'Visions Of China', which reached No 32 on the UK charts. To accompany the foreign tonalities created by Richard Barbieri, Mick Karn and Steve Jansen, Sylvian presented a lyrical world where adherence to the principles of hard work, communal living and respect for one's elders all combined to create a utopian world. Yet, if one scratched just below the surface, a strong satirical undercurrent was also in evidence. "We walk backwards, say nothing . . . we're living our visions of China." The gift for satire returned on 'Cantonese Boy'. "We're singing, marching through the fields," sang a wry sounding Sylvian. "We're changing the lives we've led for years . . . Red Army calls you . . . the call of the crowd."

"My fascination with the East has always been because it's a totally different culture," Sylvian later explained to *NME*'s Ian Penman. "I've never actually been to China. My fascination for it is purely in terms of imagery. I'm not really dealing with Chinese problems or the society as such. A lot of the ideas come from totally different places." He continued: "I think the Japanese way of life is a much better way of working in terms of society . . . the way they live their lives is based on old ideals and traditions, as well as modern technology. That's why it works, they've kept their morals and values."

Elsewhere on *Tin Drum*, lyrical notions of romance, melancholia, travel and escape each raised their head, with the song 'Talking Drum' providing a suitable home for all of them at once. "I take the car, I travel round . . . but now I'm scared, now I'm lost in love . . . your burning bridge, my talking drum . . ." But it was 'Ghosts' that provided Sylvian with the breakthrough he had sought for so long. A strange, seductive ballad in which its writer expressed notions of ambiguity, regret and hope in equal measure, 'Ghosts' was David Sylvian's first direct step towards revealing a glimpse of what was going on inside him. "Once I was so sure, now the doubt inside my mind comes and goes, but leads nowhere . . ." The "simple life", it seemed, was no longer there. "At the time I wrote the lyrics," he recalled, "I wasn't happy with them, I wasn't 100% sure . . . there's a lot of me in there. But I'm not a depressive . . . I enjoy my depressions. I actually find 'Ghosts' optimistic, not pessimistic. In fact, I think on the whole album there's a feeling of hope all the way through."

That hope was realised by the musicians that gave life to Sylvian's songs. In fact, Jansen, Karn and Barbieri had excelled themselves throughout *Tin Drum*, creating a sound that could almost be classified as the musical equivalent of science fiction. Incapable now of playing a standard four bar progression even if their lives depended upon it, the trio chose instead to pursue an uncanny blend of off-the-wall rhythmic shunts, jaw-dropping bass fills and truly alien-sounding keyboard textures. "Me and David spent days in the studio programming synthesisers," Richard Barbieri later told *Keyboard Review.* "It was a very laborious process, but creatively satisfying . . . it was the first album where we actually produced something . . . completely original."

Though Steve Jansen's contribution to *Tin Drum* was of equal worth, natural modesty prevented him from basking in too much glory. "I know very little about the technical side of drumming, and I'm going to stay that way," he said at the time. "I don't like talking about drums. The subject bores me. I just like hearing them." Renowned jazz trumpeter/soundtrack composer Mark Isham, who would soon make the acquaintance of both Jansen and Barbieri was more than eager to sing their musical praises. "Steve's an excellent drummer," said Isham. "His style comes from a concept. He's very melodic . . . very compositional, every beat has a specific construction to it. Richard's a sound designer. He's got a tremendous sense of orchestration with electronics and keyboards. They're both remarkable musicians."

Another man who could take pride from his work on *Tin Drum* was Steve Nye. A founding member of the avant-garde instrumental group, The Penguin Cafe Orchestra, Nye had replaced John Punter as Japan's producer for their latest album. Though a quieter, more reflective presence than the affable Punter, Nye had in fact played a crucial part in 'de-Roxyfying' the band's sound, availing them an opportunity to find their own musical path rather than follow in the footsteps of Bryan Ferry et al. In short, if John Punter's brief had been to free Japan from their rockist tendencies, then Steve Nye's principal task was to allow them to sound like *themselves.* So impressed was Sylvian with Nye's overall approach that he continues to work with the producer to this day.

A fine album, full of unclouded melodies, excellent musicianship and more than a little thought, *Tin Drum* succeeded in getting Japan some of the best reviews of their career. "The music (un)moves with caressing precision," proclaimed *NME*'s

Paul Morley. "Gorgeously erotic, perfectly evanescent. It accepts transitoriness, yet delights in sensation." Morley heaped praise on Sylvian too. "The LP is also a triumph for David Sylvian, the sensitive individual, the deep feeling loner, his voice stricken on the tensions between confidence and gloom, whose lyrics are a questing expression of love and loss, doubt and despondency. His old clumsiness at describing his position, at probing his passion has been replaced with a sublime simplicity."

However, it wasn't all wine and roses. "At first sight there appears to be some cleverness involved," stated the *Melody Maker*'s Lynne Barber. "The music slots together in jigsaw fashion, leaving plenty of space and clean air . . . but there seems to be little purpose to their constructs, a dearth of aesthetic sensibility. Japan's music is pre-fabricated, built from an architect's well-laid plans, yet not sculpted with an artist's passion or insight."

One musician who disagreed with the notion that Sylvian's music was "all surface, no feeling" was *Tears For Fears'* Roland Orzabal. In fact, according to Orzabal, *Tin Drum* proved positively inspirational while he and musical partner Curt Smith were cutting their own début LP. "When we were making our first album, *The Hurting*, there were various records around at the time that hugely impressed me," he said. "The Talking Heads' *Fear Of Music*, *Peter Gabriel* and *Tin Drum*. . . . *Drum* was always on my hi-fi. We were using the same equipment as Japan, synthesisers and such, but the mind truly boggled at how they got those noises out of them. It was the way everything hung together. I was always struggling to get a similar approach – not that I ever could. Our subsequent success was built on more down-to-earth hooks."

Orzabal also offered a possible insight into why Sylvian attracted such harsh criticism from the press at times. "I think the reason he hasn't been so popular with the music press is there aren't many people who turn pop music into art. And he always had a knack for doing that. Sylvian's approach had more to do with painting and sculpture than it did with four guys just picking up guitars and making some rock music. *Tin Drum*", he concluded, "was an absolute conceptual masterpiece from lyrics to artwork . . . just *everything.*"

Orzabal was surely right in his assertion that the conceptual aspects behind *Tin Drum*'s artwork were of equal importance to the music itself – at least in sales terms. Whereas the sleeves for *Quiet Life* and *Gentlemen Take Polaroids* presented Sylvian as an almost spectral figure, with the feminine aspect of his looks played up to encourage curiosity from potential record buyers (his make-up artist and hairstylist both received a cover credit on *Gentlemen Take Polaroids*), *Tin Drum*'s cover photography portrayed him as an assiduous member of the worker state – one hand clasped around a bowl of rice, the other manipulating a pair of chopsticks. Chairman Mao smiled graciously from a poster on the wall behind the singer. "It's a very simple concept," Sylvian told *Smash Hits*' Ian Birch at the time. "Steve said, 'If you made an album about China, what would you do? As a joke, you'd sit on the cover with a rice bowl, chopsticks and a picture of Chairman Mao.' It's the most pathetic idea, but because of the way it's done, I think it works."

The image, captured by respected rock photographer Fin Costello, did draw attention to one potentially uncomfortable aspect surrounding the release of *Tin Drum.* Specifically, whether the band's rapid embrace of Oriental sounds and culture was little more than a contrivance on their part, a way of generating capital from their name and ensuring success in the Far East. Sylvian's countering of such charges was nothing short of inspired brinkmanship. "*Tin Drum* wasn't 'a record about China'," he told Paul Morley. "It was a state of mind being presented, thoughts and moods pushed forward as bare as possible to not even reach the place where confusion enters into it. I want to achieve that state of mind where what I write doesn't refer particularly to time or place, but goes beyond that. Something words can't touch. I'm achieving that, I think, whether I like it or not. I make the *truth.*" The remark, with some essential modifications here and there, would prove endemic to the philosophy behind Sylvian's subsequent solo career.

In the end, it mattered little at the time whether *Tin Drum* was cod-Orientalism or one of the first successful examples of 'World Music'. The album and its accompanying imagery swiftly caught the imagination of the British record buying public who placed it at No 12 in the charts in December, 1981. The LP stayed in the Top 75 for a further 50 weeks, achieving gold and silver discs for sales rendered. It should have been a time of great joy for the band, vindication for three years of hard work. Unfortunately, Japan were too busy breaking up to notice.

7

A Penance Must Be Exacted

In the months leading up to the release of *Tin Drum*, Japan were slowly acquiring a reputation as veritable renaissance men within the fields of both art and pop. Inspired by the multi-dimensional work of French playwright/novelist/filmmaker Jean Cocteau, David Sylvian was making cautious statements about using the group's name as an umbrella title for all sorts of music/media related projects, with film scoring at the top of his personal list of ambitions. His brother, Steve Jansen, was showing a distinct gift for photography (a discipline Sylvian would later dabble in), his formative camera work displayed in various style and fashion magazines. Richard Barbieri was also far from idle, spending much of his time immersed in the "marvels of studio technology".

By far the most active member of the band was Mick Karn, who aside from being hailed as a world-class bassist was also forging a creditable alternative career as a restaurateur and sculptor. In fact, his recently opened Penguin Cafe – then located behind The Octopus Gallery on London's Gloucester Road – had gained a sterling reputation for its continental/Japanese food. Additionally, Karn's foray into clay sculpting was well received by critics, with his work exhibited in Japan in September, 1981. "I just bought some clay and started," he later told the *NME*'s Lynn Hanna. "I always wanted to try it at school but I never got around to it. People are always telling me (my work) reminds them of Bosch, but I know absolutely nothing about art."

When *Tin Drum* achieved mainstream commercial success then, all the pieces were in place for the band to unify their interests and collectively expand into areas previously unexplored by pop musicians. Therefore, it came as something of a surprise when the group announced their intention to take a break from each other following a 14-date tour of the UK in December, 1981. "Everything we do is instinctive," Sylvian told *Smash Hits* at the time. "Changes shouldn't be calculated. That's why when people ask why we're taking a break when everything's going so well, all we can say is that it's instinctive to do this. I don't know how long the break's going to be – maybe three or four months, or longer. You see, everyone is growing up and having aspirations about what they want to do other than Japan . . . now we're all at a certain creative point, it's time to take it in four directions."

Karn offered a similar response to questions regarding Japan's sudden need for a sabbatical. "Over the years, there have been things we've all wanted to do. It seems to everyone else that this is the worst possible time to do it, but we've decided to do it now – whatever the consequences. The record company are very unhappy about it . . . it sounds like the band has split up and don't want to work with each other, but it's not like that at all. We still do want to work with each other, but in different fields."

At the time, these statements made some sense. Japan had acquired a reputation as chance-takers within the rock industry, always trying to remain two steps ahead of the game. Therefore the group's decision to pull back just as everything was falling into place, though contrary to good business practice, was more or less in keeping with their eclectic image. However, there were one or two important details missing from Sylvian and Karn's optimistic testimony. "Mick's girlfriend left him and went to live with David," said Japan manager Simon Napier-Bell. "That's not an easy thing to live with. And Mick couldn't stand it."

The girlfriend in question was Yuka Fujii, who first spun into

Japan's orbit a year or so before *Tin Drum* was released. After briefly dating Steve Jansen, she bonded with Karn and the pair subsequently became an 'item'. A talented photographer and something of a singer, Fujii actually contributed backing vocals to *Tin Drum*, her winsome voice used to great effect on the track 'Still Life In Mobile Homes'. Nonetheless, sometime after recording sessions for the album finished, Fujii and David Sylvian became romantically involved, prompting her to leave Karn and settle in at Sylvian's Kensington flat. Unsurprisingly, Mick was less than enthralled with their new domestic arrangement. A series of arguments between the bassist and his best friend ensued. "Chaos," remarked Napier-Bell. "The group just couldn't function together in any way at all."

Unfortunately, Japan had already committed themselves to a comprehensive tour of the UK in support of *Tin Drum*. If cancelled, it would cost the group thousands of pounds in lost revenue. Faced with no alternative they hit the road, playing to sold out houses at Portsmouth's Guildhall (December 8), Liverpool's Empire Theatre (12) and Birmingham Odeon (17), amongst others. While all appeared well under the stagelights, the atmosphere behind the scenes was less than comfortable. "David was being a prick," remarked Napier-Bell. "He was bringing Yuka to the dressing room. All he had to say was, 'Would you mind staying at home?' Mick just had to sit there . . ."

According to Japan's manager, the situation brought out Sylvian's penchant for confrontation. "David was always confrontational," he said. "When he first wore make-up, he told the group, 'You've all got to wear make-up too.' It was nothing to do with image. He hadn't even thought about it in terms of image. It was the *challenge.* He was saying, 'If I can do it, get on a train with make-up on, you've got to do it.' It was simply leverage."

Following the UK tour, which concluded with two shows at London's Theatre Royal (December 21/22) and a further date at Hammersmith Odeon (23), a summit was called by

Napier-Bell. In short, the group wanted to split and the manager begged them to reconsider. After all, they were currently enjoying their greatest ever success, and if handled right, they might even break into the American market. A reluctant compromise was reached. The band would take a prolonged sabbatical, during which time they were free to pursue various solo projects. If things cooled down in the interim, they could always reactivate their group interests. The American angle was not to be pursued. Hence Sylvian and Karn met with journalists to spread the news, if not the gossip.

In the meantime, the hits were piling up. In January, 1982, Hansa Records finally released Japan's all-weather disco anthem 'European Son'. It reached a semi-respectable No 31 on the charts. Not to be out-done, Virgin let loose the triumphal 'Ghosts' from *Tin Drum.* Against all expectations, the song provided Japan with their biggest hit single yet, reaching No 5 in the UK in March. To this day, Sylvian remains shocked that such a stark and questioning ballad as 'Ghosts' actually charted at all. "You can be subversive with arrangements," he told *Raygun*'s Josef Woodard in 1993. "You can take away a lot of things, and it's still accessible. That was (probably) the reason for the success of 'Ghosts' . . . if I listen to that track now, I'm still amazed it did as well as it did. It's a little oblique, to say the least. But I think the signposts were still there."

They certainly were. 'Ghosts' Top Five success firmly consolidated Japan's appeal with adolescents as well as older audiences, ensuring them blanket coverage in teen-beat magazines like *Smash Hits,* where they ranked highly in the 1982 'Readers Poll'. Unfortunately, Great Britain's 'Second Best Group' were no nearer finding a solution to their internal problems, with statements, counter-statements and record company press releases regarding Japan's "current status" appearing every other week. Things took an even more surreal turn when they crashed into the charts at No 24 at the end of June with the single 'Cantonese Boy'. Since declaring themselves "on a sabbatical", the band had managed more hits than at any other time in their career.

June, 1982 also marked the first appearance of Mick Karn as a solo artist, though Virgin Records were keen to point out that his single, 'Sensitive', in no way interfered with Japan's "probable future". Whatever the case, 'Sensitive' was pleasant enough, showing a distinct Jaco Pastorius/Weather Report influence, but its jazz-inflected groove and strange melodic chord changes were hardly radio-friendly. The song subsequently failed to chart. Karn could at least take some consolation from the fact that his recent exhibition of sculptures at London's Mayflower gallery had picked up decent reviews in some of the broadsheets.

By July, Japan were back again, this time with a Hansa re-release of their 1980 single 'I Second That Emotion'. To no one's great surprise, the song climbed to No 9 in the UK charts. Yet, the band still showed no signs of reuniting. In fact, all members were actively engaged elsewhere. Richard Barbieri had turned his hand to production, working with a relatively unknown Swedish act called Lustans Lakejer, and Steve Jansen and Mick Karn were collaborating with Japanese artist Akiko Yano. David Sylvian, in the meantime, was set to release a collaborative single with the Yellow Magic Orchestra's Ryuichi Sakamoto, entitled 'Bamboo Houses/ Bamboo Music'.

As its title suggested, the double A-sided single was peppered with Oriental influences, from Sakamoto's gently pulsating keyboards to Sylvian's earnest lyricism: "All the children, too young and thin, singing bamboo music." Released at the start of August, 1982, 'Bamboo . . .' reached No 30 in the UK charts. "I couldn't say I was 100% pleased with it," David later told *The Face.* "But that was partly because of the circumstances. We were only together for six days, and it took me ages to finish it after Ryuichi left." Though the single's chart placing was somewhat of a disappointment after the Top Ten success of Japan's 'I Second That Emotion', 'Bamboo

Houses' did help draw attention to the subtle, yet persuasive influence Ryuichi Sakamoto had exerted on the sound of *Tin Drum.* Whilst Sakamoto hadn't actually appeared on the LP, his innate gift for updating traditional Far Eastern melodies had certainly provided a guiding light for Japan throughout the recording of the album.

Shortly after the release of 'Bamboo Houses/Music', Japan surprised even themselves by announcing details of a comprehensive tour of both the UK and the Far East. Aside from the odd appearance together on *Top Of The Pops* and *The Old Grey Whistle Test,* it was the first time in nearly six months that the band had acted as a collective unit. Hansa Records celebrated by re-releasing their 1979 single 'Life In Tokyo'. It charted at No 28 on October 9, some two weeks before the group were due to begin the UK leg of their expedition.

Joined by guest guitarist/keyboardist Masami Tsuchiya (David Rhodes had filled in for the absent Rob Dean on the group's winter 1981 jaunt), and supported on all dates by Japanese pop act Sandii and The Sunsetz, Sylvian, Karn, Barbieri and Jansen kicked off their longest ever road-trip with two nights at Portsmouth's Guildhall on October 20/21. Beginning with the sci-fi strains of 'Burning Bridges', Japan covered all bases of their post-*Obscure Alternatives* career, from the Bowiesque tones of 'Quiet Life' to the immaculate swing of 'Still Life In Mobile Homes'. Not once in a two-hour set did they look anything but happy.

Dates in Brighton, Glasgow, Leicester and Birmingham all went equally well, with the group picking up excellent reviews along the way. By the time they got to London's Hammersmith Odeon for a three night stop-off on November 17/18/19, many were convinced that the band had finally put whatever problems they were facing behind them, and were now looking towards the future. However, following their last UK show at Hammersmith Odeon on November 22, Japan confirmed they were breaking up. The group's final concert was subsequently performed in Nagoya, Japan on December 16, 1982.

Though they had played to mostly packed houses, their earnings remained minimal.

"When they went out on their last tour," Simon Napier-Bell recalled. "They were horrified I took my management commission. It meant they made no profit. But you had to look at it on the basis that I'd worked for six years and they'd broken up. If they hadn't broken up, I wouldn't have done it. I'd figured that once they got on that tour – working together, huge crowds, sold out venues – they'd get back together. Of course, they didn't. So I thought 'Fuck it'. I've done everything I can and these bloody stupid, pig-headed people can't see they're killing their career. So I took my commission."

To mark the group's passing (and extract a commission of their own, one suspects), Virgin Records released a 'commemorative' single, the winsome 'Nightporter' in December, 1982. It subsequently charted at No 29.

Over the years, there has been much speculation regarding Japan's demise. Some believe that if the band had allowed themselves more time to sort through their personal problems, they still might be around today. Given the evidence, it seems unlikely. According to their manager, Simon Napier-Bell, Japan were on a "disastrous" course for some time, with musical differences, internal squabbles and David Sylvian's domination on the songwriting front all causing resentment within the ranks. Napier-Bell also believed that Sylvian was starting to show definite signs of wanting to pursue a solo career before matters came to a head with Mick Karn. "I really don't think he needed Japan at all by that stage," he says.

Sylvian himself has stated many times that *Tin Drum* felt like a natural end to things. "When I finished *Tin Drum*," he told *Sounds'* Richard Cook, "I felt I'd written my ideal pop song and I didn't want to explore it any further. It was enough. As musicians we were incapable of improvising, we were a studio band, and we put everything together piece by piece. Nothing was left to chance. I wanted to move away from that."

His remarks to the *NME*'s Biba Kopf also confirmed his

displeasure with what Japan had come to represent. "With Japan, it was a matter of ironing out all the faults," he said, "so people didn't look at you as a character, a personality. They only had the music as a reference to discover anything about you. To present an ideal image does that, I think." Personal growth had also been a major consideration in his refusal to fight for the group's future. "My existence at the time," he later said, "was so based around the band I wasn't allowing any new experiences to reach me. I was sheltering myself far too much."

In the end, like all history, the exact truth behind Japan's split remains a matter of perspective, with 'the benefit of hindsight' often replacing the facts as they were. It seems most likely, however, that Yuka Fujii's romantic defection from Mick Karn to David Sylvian simply activated a virus of dissatisfaction that had long laid dormant. It is perhaps also worth remembering that even the most enduring of school gangs have to disband at some point.

At their best, Japan were very good indeed. All glistening melodies, immaculate image and clever, if dispassionate lyricism, they represented something quintessentially English – an art-school set to music. And if they occasionally sounded a little too clever or emotionally manicured for their own good, it was a largely forgivable offence. After all, given the era in which they existed, they were head and shoulders above most of their competition. The rock magazine *Q* summed up their appeal better than most: "It all ended in tears, but for a time Japan were the knees of highly chic, beautifully made-up bees. They looked like a match for anyone . . . alas, alas, alas."

Within months of Japan's break-up, Mick Karn re-established himself as both a solo artist and in demand session player. His first album, *Titles*, though disappointing, had at least charted (No 74 in December, 1982) and studio collaborations with the likes of Robert Palmer and Midge Ure ensured his trademark 'slippery' bass guitar style would continue to exert an influence on the pop scene. Richard Barbieri and Steve Jansen were also active, the duo forming close musical ties with Japanese act Ippu Do (led by sometime Japan guitarist/keyboardist Masami Tsuchiya) and Yellow Magic Orchestra's Yukihiro Takahashi. By the summer of 1983, both Jansen and Barbieri found themselves working with David Sylvian on his first solo album.

Sylvian himself also remained busy. After Japan's last tour, he chose to end his long-term association with manager Simon Napier-Bell (who went on to handle Wham!) and establish a new business enterprise called 'Opium', through which both his music and lyrics could be published. The company's name was a direct homage to the work of French renaissance man Jean Cocteau, with whom David was becoming increasingly fascinated. However, a potential problem arose when he tried to register the name 'Opium' for commercial purposes. Somewhat unsurprisingly, his lawyers pointed out that the epithet sounded more like a thinly-veiled drug reference than a sound financial endeavour. The name was duly changed to Opium (Arts) Ltd.

The man chosen to run the company, and indeed manage Sylvian's solo affairs was Richard Chadwick. A soft-spoken, yet extremely effective businessman who would see his charge through the best and worst the Eighties and Nineties had to offer, Chadwick was actually a long-time associate of both Simon Napier-Bell and Japan. In fact, when Napier-Bell became increasingly more involved with grooming Wham! for future pop stardom, Chadwick took on many of the administrative duties surrounding Japan's break-up. Within the space of ten years, he had expanded the managerial roster of Opium (Arts) to include the talents of Robert Fripp, Bill Nelson, Michael Brook and perhaps most interestingly, Led Zeppelin's former bass/keyboard player, John Paul Jones, now best known for his production/arrangement work with R.E.M., Heart, Diamanda Galas and The Mission.

Away from the world of commerce, Sylvian was also settling into a very happy relationship with Yuka Fujii, who besides providing the singer with a much-needed stabilising influence, began to exert a benign yet still important effect on the path of his solo career. In the coming years, he would praise her often, not only for introducing him to different musical forms (Fujii was the woman responsible for activating David's interest in jazz), but as importantly, for her advice and support on how he represented himself artistically – from cover artwork for his solo LPs to stage design for his tours.

With the detritus of Japan more or less behind him, David Sylvian began to talk of the future. His tone remained hesitant, but optimistic nonetheless. "Clues are a great fascination," he told *NME*'s Paul Morley, "and it's your curiosity that leads you to follow these clues as you move along. I know – I see the clues that I'm right at the beginning of my state of learning. If I presume what the end will be then I'm stupid. I'm just bringing things together . . ."

According to Mick Karn, Sylvian was headed for a fall. "I think he's incapable of carrying on himself," he said. Ultimately, it would prove to be an ill-judged remark.

8

Growth

By the spring of 1983, the dust storm kicked up by Japan's untimely dissolution had largely settled. Whereas only a year before, it was impossible to escape the band's features on the news-stands, they were now relegated to the odd snippet in the gossip columns of the music press. Even the teenagers responsible for helping push 'Ghosts' into the Top Five in 1982 seemed to have lost interest. When the 1983 *Smash Hits* Annual Readers Poll was published, Japan were nowhere to be found, with 'Best Group' honours going to Duran Duran and Culture Club. As the band had polled Number Two position as 'Best Group' only the previous year, it was a somewhat ignominious fall. David Sylvian, too, seemed out of favour with Britain's pre-pubescents, descending from No 3 to No 10 in the 'Best Male Singer' category. Even his looks were apparently failing him: in 1982, he'd been voted second 'Most Fanciable Male', a close runner-up to the sea-faring Simon Le Bon. Now he couldn't even get a look in, with Duran's "alpha male", John Taylor, the object of every girl's affections. Sylvian must have been devastated.

Although Japan's public profile was rapidly diminishing both Hansa and Virgin Records continued to churn out band-related product. On March 12, 1983, Hansa tried their luck with the old *Quiet Life* chestnut, 'All Tomorrow's Parties'. Sounding a little dated, but serviceable enough, the single made a brief appearance on the charts at No 38. Virgin (undoubtedly the more irritated by Japan's decision to throw in the towel) laid more ambitious plans with the release of a live version of the *Tin Drum* instrumental 'Canton' on May 21, 1983. Though the single was marketed as a tribute to their flagship act, it actually served as a clever advertisement for the forthcoming *Oil On Canvas* – a live double album culled from Japan's Hammersmith Odeon shows of November, 1982. 'Canton' subsequently charted at No 42.

In truth, *Oil On Canvas* proved a fine swansong for the group, capturing much of the static perfection of their live shows. All the hits, from 'Quiet Life' through to 'Nightporter' were present and correct, as well as three recently recorded studio instrumentals: the sweet-natured and bell-like 'Voices Raised In Welcome, Hands Held In Prayer' (written by Jansen and Sylvian), the cinematic and imposing 'Temple Of Dawn' (the LP's final track, written by Barbieri) and Sylvian's latest homage to Satie, the melancholy 'Oil On Canvas' itself. Jointly produced by Japan and John Punter, the album made a surprisingly strong showing in the charts, débuting at No 5 on June 18, 1983, and sticking round for a further thirteen weeks. An accompanying live video – bearing the same name as the LP – was simultaneously released, with footage drawn from the band's final dates at Hammersmith Odeon contrasted against images of rural and inner city China.

For David Sylvian, by far the most important aspect of the live album was its cover, a striking, almost spectral painting by German-born artist Frank Auerbach. Entitled 'Head Of JYM II', the image had been responsible for opening his eyes to the possibilities contained in art: "I never appreciated art to any great extent," he told *Melody Maker*'s Steve Sutherland, "I just saw it as paintings on a wall, and I couldn't open up. Then I saw the painting by Auerbach that eventually appeared on the cover of *Oil On Canvas* and it just went straight to me. It was a shock because I'd never felt anything from a painting before, and since then, I've learned quickly, going from one painting to another, being able to experience something."

The encounter proved so inspirational that it led Sylvian to experiment with painting himself. It was only a matter of time before he connected the dots to the creation of music: "[It] came out of a conversation with Yuka, really," the singer recalled to journalist David Toop. "We talked about painting, which we both love – mainly in reference to Frank Auerbach. We were talking about that sense of spontaneity, that presence that exists in his work. We wondered what would be the nearest equivalent in terms of music. One conclusion we came to was that jazz and improvisation in many ways came closest in style and application." The conversation would have a profound and lasting effect on the course of Sylvian's subsequent musical career.

Nonetheless, there were several hurdles to overcome before he could test the validity of his theory, the first arriving before *Oil On Canvas* was even in the shops. On May 12, 1983, on the way to a photo-shoot, the singer was involved in a relatively innocuous car-crash, in which he sustained only minor injuries. However, by the time the press got hold of the story the following day, Sylvian was apparently at death's door: "World's most lovely man in scar horror," exclaimed the *Sun* in typically understated fashion. For David, it was 1982 all over again: "What happened was *this*," he gruffly stated after the incident, "I was meant to do a photo session for one of the magazines – I can't remember which one – but then I had a minor car crash and got a couple of scratches. It was impossible to do the session and the magazine was informed . . . the next day it came out in the *Sun* as a major accident. They made up so many things that were blatant lies, I threatened to sue them."

Having considered himself largely free of the inanities that came with pop stardom, the incident consolidated a wish for more permanent escape: "After the car crash thing went in the paper," Sylvian told the *Melody Maker*, "I wanted to separate myself from that image but whereas most people can get away from it, I couldn't because it was *me*. It wasn't a pretentious image that I'd built up so trying to get away from it – it was just like trying to run away from myself. In the end I just had to stop doing the interviews." Though Sylvian was content enough to disappear from the public eye following his brush with Fleet Street, a complete withdrawal from the cameras was never on the cards, principally due to the impending release of 'Forbidden Colours', his latest single collaboration with friend Ryuichi Sakamoto.

The song had grown out of the soundtrack Sakamoto was writing for the film *Merry Christmas, Mr Lawrence*, a moderately entertaining World War II drama set in a Japanese prison camp, and starring pop star turned thespian David Bowie, British character actor Tom Conteh and in a supporting role as a prison officer, Ryuichi himself. While composing the music for the movie (based on the novel *The Seed And The Sower* by Sir Laurens Van Der Post), Sakamoto hit upon a gentle, circular piano riff he felt might act as the film's central theme. As he developed the piece, he was struck by the idea it might also work as a single. Knowing Sylvian was twiddling his thumbs following the break-up of Japan, he rang the singer and proposed he write lyrics to the melody. David requested a tape and a brief explanation of what the film was about.

Picking up on the homo-erotic sub-text that ran throughout *Merry Christmas, Mr Lawrence*, and the fact the writers of the screenplay (director Nagisa Oshima and Paul Mayersburg) had been heavily influenced by the novels of Japanese author/patriot Mishima (himself a tortured homosexual), he set to work on the lyrics. The end result was nothing short of startling. Instead of writing a covert and dispassionate treatise on 'the love that dare not speak its name', Sylvian chose to pursue a completely different tack, marrying the concept of homosexuality with more elevated notions of spirituality and suffering: "The wounds on your hands never seem to heal . . . I thought all I needed was to believe." He also managed to intertwine within the lyrics a sense of his own doubt about the concept of Christianity: "I'll go walking in circles whilst doubting the very ground beneath me . . . trying to show unquestioning faith in everything . . ." When finished, he christened the piece 'Forbidden Colours', in honour of the Mishima novel of the same name.

Recording of the track moved quickly, mainly because Sakamoto had already laid down much of it in the studio before David's arrival. To give the tune a more majestic feel, the duo brought in string arranger Ann O'Dell, who last worked with Sylvian on Japan's third LP *Quiet Life* : "David must have liked what I did on the Japan album because he called me in," recalled O'Dell, "but all I was really doing was extending what Sakamoto had already done on [the] synths." By all accounts, it was a lonely session: "I didn't meet Ryuichi at all," she said. "His synths were already on the track, so I just worked round that. But that's very often the case, especially with synth and brass overdubs. You get called in at almost the last minute, before the lead vocals go on. You just get given a tape of what's already recorded, and have a short briefing with the artist. Then you go away and write it!"

Released on July 2, 1983, 'Forbidden Colours' clambered into the charts at No 16, marking Sakamoto's first – and last – entry in the UK Top 20. The soundtrack to *Merry Christmas, Mr Lawrence* also fared well, helping him establish a creditable career as a film composer as well as pop performer. In fact, within five years, Ryuichi went on to win an Oscar for his scoring of Bernado Bertolucci's *The Last Emperor*, a marvellously vivid account of the fall of Imperialist China to Communism. Nonetheless, he always remained fond of his work on . . . *Lawrence* : "Bertolucci . . . is the most demanding director I have ever worked with," confirmed Sakamoto, "especially compared to Mr Oshima (the director of *Merry Christmas, Mr Lawrence*). [He] just let me work on my own for two months. He visited me once. He listened, he liked it and he left!" For Sylvian, 'Forbidden Colours' had been equally rewarding: "I thought it was such an important step for me that I said, '*now* I'm ready to do something'. The lyrics weren't as disguised as I'd done before. This was so obviously about myself and I achieved it in a way I'd never done before. Yes, I did it, and I did it right . . ."

The commercial success of 'Forbidden Colours' also acted as a buffer of sorts for Sylvian, allowing him to keep his hand in the charts while simultaneously working on the songs that would constitute his first solo LP. After a brief visit to New York in the summer of 1983, that work began in earnest, with the singer transferring the four-track demos he'd recorded at his West London flat to Hansa Studios in Berlin, Germany. Though security was tight around the project, enough news leaked out to suggest that his début album would be an elaborate affair, with several surprise guests involved – all of whom had little or nothing to do with the pop world. These rumours only intensified when he arrived back in Islington, London to start adding overdubs to the songs at Mickie Most's RAK Studios. Here, a number of faces from the international jazz scene were seen coming and going at odd hours of the day and night. If nothing else, it made for delicious gossip.

With recording more or less complete, Sylvian fulfilled a long-term ambition by setting off on a round-the-world trip. Accompanied by Yuka Fujii, and armed with a recently acquired camera to document the journey (more of that later), the couple made stop-overs in the South of France and Switzerland before venturing on to the Far East. After spending the Winter in Japan (where Sylvian and Fujii attended Yellow Magic Orchestra's farewell gig at Tokyo's Budokan Theatre on December 22), they moved onwards to India and then Nepal. Though the terrain was sometimes rocky – "dirt track[s] full of wooden and mud huts" according to David – the country's big skies and rolling vistas seemed to trigger something in him: "I think Nepal did it," Sylvian later told *Smash Hits'* Ian Birch, "because the feeling there was so strong and my enjoyment of it so positive. It's hard to pinpoint but you feel an affinity with the environment that you're in." This new-found fascination with nature came to a crescendo just outside the city of Kathmandu: "I can't remember why we stopped – maybe it was a temple – but we walked along a hillside and there was an extraordinary view that commanded the whole landscape . . . it's just a feeling which is indescribable . . . a total peace within." Like his experiences with the art of Frank Auerbach, Sylvian would soon find a way of incorporating this interest with environmental textures into his music.

After a chilly visit to Nepal's Nagorkot region for a view of the Himalayas (David captured much of the area's essence in a poem called, somewhat unsurprisingly, 'Nagorkot'), Sylvian and Fujii returned to London, where Virgin Records were firing up the promotional campaign for his forthcoming solo album. By May, details had been announced of Sylvian's first single as a solo artist. By June 2, 1984, said single was in the shops.

Entitled 'Red Guitar', the song encapsulated much of the forward momentum Sylvian had gained since breaking up Japan. Best described as 'an existential call to arms', David's opening lyrical gambit spoke volumes concerning future intent: "I recognise no method of living that I know, I see only the basic materials I may use . . ." As the track unwound on the back of a jazzy, undulating piano riff and sly, harmonically astute bass guitar, one was struck by the sheer energy present in its groove. The effect was consolidated when a slinky, X-rated trumpet break signalled 'Red Guitar's impending finale: "If you ask me, I may tell you," sang Sylvian as the song faded to black, "It's been this way for years . . ."

'Red Guitar's single release was accompanied by a promotional video, directed by up-and-coming photographer/film-maker Anton Corbijn. A surreal, illusory affair, featuring black and white images of Sylvian melting into an ever-changing background of flowers and sky, the video was inspired by the work of renowned British photographer Angus McBean – famous for his portraits of cinematic icons Laurence Olivier, Vivian Leigh and Audrey Hepburn, among others. However, it was McBean's study of Forties character actress Flora Robson that initially stirred Sylvian's interest, leading him to contact the man behind the camera. The pair got on so well that McBean made a brief cameo appearance in the video itself.

Backed by a gorgeous, acoustic rendering of 'Forbidden Colours' (and housed in a sleeve that honoured Sylvian's continuing fascination with Jean Cocteau), 'Red Guitar' climbed to No 17 in the charts, temporarily diverting attention away from the runaway success of Frankie Goes To Hollywood's summer fire-storm 'Two Tribes'. "It's quite a good commercial for the album," David confirmed at the time, " 'Red Guitar' symbolises art in a way, and art is my means of expression. The chorus just says this is my vice and this is my virtue. It's something that will preoccupy my life and give it the most pleasure and the most pain. It's that simple". His words would prove eerily prophetic.

9

Corrective Surgery

"If you cut the rope from below your feet, you're more apt to submit than retreat"

– A climber's saying.

On July 7, 1984, the result of David Sylvian's labours was finally released. Intriguingly titled *Brilliant Trees,* the record sleeve alone bore enough evidence to suggest that a transformation of sorts had taken place. Instead of presenting the now familiar image of Sylvian looking suitably cool and aloof, the cover photography for the new album (courtesy of Yuka Fujii) was much more subtle and impressionistic. Set in soft focus against a sparse, pastoral background, the singer appeared at ease, downright vulnerable, in fact. The dandified style that typified his days with Japan was also absent from view, with a sober, double-breasted suit replacing those old box jackets and grey pegs. The mystery only deepened when one delved into the inner sleeve. No fey Hollywood portraiture, no awkward smiles, just a pair of hands clumsily placed upon a glass table. The customary rules of engagement, it seemed, were being rewritten in order to prepare his audience for the music.

And what a surprise that music was. In stark contrast to Sylvian's previous work, *Brilliant Trees* breathed with life. Gone were the clever, yet frosty compositional elements that characterised (and indeed, sometimes suffocated) Japan's sound. Instead, the listener was being asked to enter into a richer, more emotionally complex world where elements of jazz and atonal improvisation wrestled with lyrical themes of self-control, internal deceit and ultimately, shy hopefulness.

The record began with the jump start of 'Pulling Punches', a jarring, and at times barbed funk work-out, much at odds with the seamless lines that wove together *Tin Drum.* Unlike 'Visions Of China' or 'Still Life In Mobile Homes' for instance, 'Pulling Punches' pecked at its own melody line, with Sylvian seemingly content to let chords hang in the air before resolving them with a brass stab or lush keyboard flourish. The lyric, too, was ambiguous, see-sawing between naïve optimism and the perils of such blind faith: "A better world lies in front of me, a sketch of life in the books I read. Then as I walk where heaven leads, why am I the last to know?"

There was little doubt that these lines referred directly to Sylvian's own preoccupations, a search for spiritual closure. Frustration, it seemed, was at the heart of the song: "Yes," Sylvian later confirmed, "the desire to understand, then a kind of anger at the inability to understand . . . the idea that you're living your life and think you know what you're doing, [yet] you're sleeping on your feet, you've got no idea, you're *not* in control. That comes out in anger and frustration sometimes – which is just what 'Pulling Punches' is."

If 'Pulling Punches' retained at least something of Japan's mutant funk sensibilities, then *Brilliant Trees'* next track set out to well and truly sever all ties with the singer's musical past. 'Ink In The Well' was awash with acoustic jazz influences, from its lazy, behind-the-beat drums to the gorgeous swing of its double bass. Yet, though the music was light and agreeable on the ear, the words that accompanied the melody were not. Inspired by his feelings on viewing Pablo Picasso's controversial portrait of the Spanish Civil War – 'Guernica' – Sylvian offered images of frightened animals running through "fields of fire", while tired peasants warmed their hands on the smouldering ruins of their former homes. "Fire at will," his voice bitterly intoned, "in this open season . . ." Though 'The

Ink In The Well' took its blueprint from Picasso's vision of a divided Thirties Spain, Sylvian was at pains to point out that his lyrics were impressionistic in nature, and neither a commentary on the painting itself nor the war that inspired it: " 'The Ink In The Well' is not based on the painting," he stated at the time, ". . . it's based on the feeling I get from the painting."

The feeling that inspired *Brilliant Trees*' next tune was perhaps easier to translate, the clue to its origins firmly embedded in the title of the song – 'Nostalgia'. Again, 'Nostalgia' saw the singer moving further away from his pop past, this time in the direction of a more ambient, atmospheric sound that relied as much on the space between chords as the chords themselves. As guitars leapt and flugelhorns soared over a spare, droning keyboard line, Sylvian's mournful vocal cut right to the quick: "I'm cutting branches from the trees, shaped by years of memories to exorcise their ghosts from inside of me . . ."

Though the imagery evoked in 'Nostalgia' retained the darker hues of later Japan material such as 'Ghosts', there was a much more satisfying feeling to be had from the song. One at last felt that Sylvian was actually opening up to his audience, letting them share in his own sense of spiritual restlessness. 'Forbidden Colours' had led the way, sure enough, but the floodgates were now well and truly open. Whatever the case or cause, this newborn self-confessional aspect was much easier to tolerate than the distant, glacial nature of his former meditations.

After 'Nostalgia's melancholic tones faded into the distance, it was left to the already released single 'Red Guitar' to close side one of *Brilliant Trees*. The real test, however, still lay ahead. If the previous four tunes had required listeners to put aside some of the preconceptions they held towards Sylvian's music, then side two of *Brilliant Trees* asked that they make a leap into new, more demanding territories. As the singer later admitted, those unwilling to follow his lead might be forever left behind clutching worn copies of *Quiet Life* and *Gentlemen Take Polaroids*: "Buying *Brilliant Trees*, a lot of people would have related side one of [the] album to the work I had done previously, but they'll have to work to get through side two. Eventually, I hope that they would have enjoyed side two more than side one. I wanted to lead people on with me in the way I'm going . . ."

The challenge was thrown down quickly with 'Weathered Wall', a sad-eyed ballad that revelled in its own lyrical ambiguities. Here, a sense of loss was being addressed, but Sylvian seemed content to allow the listener to make up their own minds as to whether that loss was personal or ethereal: "You were someone to believe in, giving life where there was a will to learn . . ." The puzzle was mirrored in the music of 'Weathered Wall'. With no bass guitar to ground the melody, the song's swaying synths and tribal trumpet calls lurched forward with only the most skeletal of drum patterns to give them shape. The approach was fiercely consolidated on *Brilliant Trees*' penultimate track, 'Backwaters'. Again, the traditional verse-chorus-verse-chorus approach of earlier endeavours was abandoned in favour of atmosphere and the conveyance of mood. Over a rolling, atonal synthesiser line, vocals clashed uneasily with pianos, French horns and serrated orchestration. The lyric was also troubled, hinting at a man who had grown tired with "trying so very hard to please".

However, the questioning and at times paradoxical nature of the two previous numbers had subtly paved the way for the revelation of the album's title track. Announcing its arrival with a legion of trumpets, 'Brilliant Trees' was a clear confirmation of Sylvian's blossoming skills as a songwriter, an uplifting and mature anthem of personal hope. Steeped in rich lyrical motifs that echoed the philosophies of the German Romantic movement of the late 1800s/early 1900s, the song captured its writers' search for peace of mind with a fearless honesty: "Every plan I've made's lost in the scheme of things, within each lesson lies the price to learn."

By directing his words to an unknown source (as with 'Weathered Wall', it is never made quite clear whether he is actually addressing a lover or a higher power), Sylvian neatly side-stepped any potential charges of religious intoxication. Instead, a delicious universality of sentiment was established throughout the song, allowing the listener to bond with his words rather than feel excluded from them: "My whole life," he sang, "stretches in front of me, reaching up like a flower, leading my life back to the soil." As the title track faded out on a leisurely wave of organic synth sounds and reedy, Oriental sounding percussion, one could almost forgive him for the first Japan album . . .

A deeply personal and, some would say, even courageous record, *Brilliant Trees* marked a major perceptual shift in the world view of David Sylvian. It also rightly afforded him an opportunity to escape the glamorous constraints of his previous life and go in search of new possibilities. Nonetheless, the LP was by no means a one man show, with several worthy collaborators invited along to help him transform a personal dream into a public reality.

Aside from the obvious abilities of David's co-producer Steve Nye, who also contributed synth and piano parts to the album, ten other musicians wove their own particular magic into the grooves of *Brilliant Trees.* New York jazzers Wayne Braithwaite and Ronny Drayton were responsible for the funked-up guitar and bass on 'Pulling Punches' and 'Red Guitar', whilst veteran session guitarist Phil Palmer lent six strings to several tracks, most noticeably on 'The Ink In The Well'. That particular song also featured a grand performance from double bassist Danny Thompson, of whom Sylvian had become aware through his work with Nick Drake and John Martyn. The soaring flugelhorn parts that graced both 'The Ink . . .' and 'Nostalgia' came courtesy of Canadian jazz trumpeter Kenny Wheeler, best known for his tenure with fusion group Azimuth. Establishing a direct link with the past (but never abusing it) were David's brother, Steve, who handled the lion's share of drum and percussion parts on the LP, and Japan keyboardist Richard Barbieri, who once again wrestled with the limits of synthesiser technology to create the queasy textures present on 'Red Guitar' and 'Weathered Wall'.

In addition to this wealth of supporting talent, Sylvian forged strong alliances with two experimental composers whose input proved crucial to the overall sound of *Brilliant Trees.* The first of these was trumpeter Jon Hassell, whose 1980 collaboration with Brian Eno, *Fourth World, Volume 1: Possible Musics,* raised many an eyebrow through its sterling command of Asian and African rhythms. After adding some distinctly tribal horn arrangements to the Talking Heads' breakthrough LP *Remain In Light* – produced, co-incidentally by Eno – Hassell redefined the perimeters of world-music with his own *Fourth World Volume 2: Dream Theory In Malaya.* A clever and complex record that married breathless trumpet excursions to indigenous Javanese music, . . . *Dream Theory* established John Hassell as a major player on the ethnic jazz-fusion scene. Eager to inform his own compositions with a little of Hassell's magic, Sylvian invited the native Canadian to Berlin to participate in the sessions for *Brilliant Trees.* The partnership worked so well that Hassell eventually ended up being credited as co-writer on 'Weathered Wall' and the album's title track.

A more enduring connection, however, was established with Sylvian's main collaborator for *Brilliant Trees,* the inimitable Holger Czukay. A former student of avant-garde composer Karlheinz Stockhausen (whose stark, wintry compositions had inspired Japan's most successful single 'Ghosts'), Czukay was best known for his work in the Seventies with German experimental group Can. Weird, wonderful and paddling furiously against the tide of the time, Can's strange brew of clattering rhythms and compositional madness ensured a small, but devoted cult following that stuck with them like glue until the group disbanded in 1976.

Having already pioneered the use of sampling techniques with Rolf Dammers on the 1969 album *Canaxis 5,* Holger's subsequent solo work saw him delving further into the unconventional by adding short-wave radio broadcasts to his music –

a technique his former teacher, Stockhausen initiated – as well as continuing his own investigations into tape splicing. The results, heard to stirring effect on the LPs *Movies* and *On The Way To The Peak Of Normal*, entranced Sylvian so much that he sent a letter of introduction to Czukay. A friendship was duly formed: "[When I met David], I could see he was a very sensitive person," Holger confirmed, ". . . with a lot of sensitivity towards art. He was interested in somehow getting connected with mood and atmosphere, and so I could help him . . ."

That help came, in David's words, in the form of "Someone to bounce ideas off," or more expressly "In [allowing me] to create a sense of space, a sort of unspecified aural landscape". Czukay also made sure Sylvian didn't escape his vocal duties on *Brilliant Trees*. "David always tried to avoid singing," chuckled Czukay. "He tries to hide. He used to say to me 'Holger, could you sing something?' You see, when David is singing, somehow for him, it's a sacred thing . . . it's not an everyday job. It's about giving *birth* to something."

When Sylvian finally took up the challenge, Czukay was impressed: "I'm never interested so much in lyrics, especially when lyrics become pretentious. But with David, I could immediately feel something. The words, the way he was pronouncing them, singing them, interpreting them . . . it got me. It could touch me. Only later [did] I ask what these songs were about. But this is always the way with me. I'm always grasping these things by a pure sense of music."

Aside from coaxing Sylvian to sing (a problem that would escalate alarmingly in the coming years), Czukay was also responsible for adding a satisfying, exotic lustre to *Brilliant Trees*, whether in the form of gentle French horn interludes, plaintive guitar or Dictaphone samples. "I was going to the undertaker," he said somewhat curiously, "and found he had a bunch of old Dictaphones, and with this machine I found I had the first analogue sampler in the world."

"On 'Pulling Punches', there are a lot of brass things played on the Dictaphone," Sylvian later confirmed. "We ran through the track and he played the tape, and they all fell into the places they are on the finished piece. That kind of thing is an improvisation of tape which I'd never heard of before I'd worked with Holger." Those Dictaphones were also inadvertently responsible for introducing Sylvian to another future collaborator – jazz trumpeter Mark Isham: "David had been working with Holger, who had this strange little Dictaphone machine that had some trumpet parts recorded on it, and there were some bits David wished were different. So the engineer said, 'I just happened to work with [a trumpeter] the other day . . .' and that happened to be me."

Coming to prominence in the late Seventies as part of Irish soul maverick Van Morrison's much lauded touring band, Isham subsequently moved onto fronting his own group in the early Eighties, enjoying critical success with his début album *Vapour Drawings*. Though his field of expertise was jazz, he was fully aware of Sylvian's work with Japan when he got the call: "I knew the later Japan records," he recalled. "They were artistically very intriguing. Like Brian Eno, and in America, David Byrne, [Japan personified] the concept of the art student becoming the musician. I think that's tremendously valuable, because they came in with none of the considerations . . . the predisposed notions that trained musicians have." Finding David "a serious fellow, but charming . . . absolutely charming", Isham ended up contributing some tasteful trumpet fills to 'Red Guitar'. The session marked the beginning of a mutually beneficial four year association.

The final musician to indent their personality on *Brilliant Trees* was Sylvian's old partner-in-crime, Ryuichi Sakamoto, whose breezy synth and piano work graced 'Weathered Wall', 'Red Guitar' and the album's title track. As usual, Sakamoto's innate flair for melody and space perfectly complimented the warmth present in Sylvian's voice. "You know, with Sakamoto and David," said Holger Czukay, "they are not so far from each other. Somehow, they are brothers in mind."

With the benefit of hindsight, and given the pedigree of the musicians involved, *Brilliant Trees* seemed almost predestined to succeed on an artistic level. Yet, at the time of recording, Sylvian had absolutely no idea whether such a collaborative effort would work. It was to his credit then, that a vague hunch paid off so well: "When I recorded *Brilliant Trees*," David told journalist Kathleen Galgano, "I started the album in Berlin, out of necessity, out of a low budget and it being the cheapest studio I could find. But I [also] found that going to a strange place, [meeting] all these musicians for the first time – some of whom I'd never even spoken to prior to meeting them – created a sense of adventure about the whole project. I didn't just feel it, I noticed it in the other musicians. They (gave) more of themselves in that environment than in their natural environment, their hometown or whatever."

The response accorded the LP by the British music press must have finally laid to rest any nagging doubts the singer had regarding the viability of a solo career: "Sylvian has grown up," declared *Sounds*' Carole Linfield. "He's left art school, gone through the grey and come out in a spectrum of pastel shades that entrance and enthral. Gone is the clichéd imagery that once haunted Japan . . . in its place is a solo artist who deserves more respect than his beautiful face often allows."

The *Melody Maker* were equally enthusiastic with their praise, with former Japan detractor Steve Sutherland now positively championing Sylvian's cause: "*Brilliant Trees* is David Sylvian's cautious re-emergence from private meditations to public observations . . . and if he still draws too copiously from this century's great depressives, Jean Paul Sylvian isn't reference dropping but, on the contrary, still formulating the necessary vocabulary to tackle his perennial problem, and hence impose peace of mind through music. In trusting his instincts, instead of courting affection," Sutherland concluded, "*Brilliant Trees* inadvertently attains the stature Sylvian's always sought. It's a masterpiece."

Kind words indeed. But Sutherland also rightly drew attention to the number of literary references Sylvian used to form the lyrical backbone of the album. For instance, on 'Pulling Punches', 'The Ink In The Well' and 'Red Guitar', he had name-checked three of French existential philosopher Jean Paul Sartre's fictional works – *Nausea, The Age Of Reason* and *Iron In The Soul.* 'Ink . . .' and 'Red Guitar' also made clear reference to the output of French renaissance man Jean Cocteau, with lyrical nods to his extended essay *The Difficulty Of Being* and film *The Blood Of A Poet.* As Sutherland deduced, drawing on such erudite sources was more about the conveyance of appropriate imagery than rampant literary plundering. Yet, it could also be frustrating when trying to figure out what exactly David was trying to convey to his audience.

After all, Sartre's existentialism was primarily a Godless philosophy, wherein man was free to act in accordance with his own nature provided, of course, he accepted the consequences of those actions. Such objective detachment sat uneasily alongside the more spiritual essence of songs like 'Backwaters' or the title track itself, where transcendental notions of Heaven and Earth prevailed. Sylvian later acknowledged these lyrical dichotomies, implying that the creation of the album had actually led him to challenge the nature of his own beliefs: "When I wrote *Brilliant Trees,*" David confessed, "I was becoming more and more interested in the spiritual life. I hadn't come across the Kabbala and the Tree of Life, but I was on the brink of discovering it. When I did, I found that's what *Brilliant Trees* related to – but I had no concept of that at the time. I've found that happens a lot, even when I first started writing. I think you anticipate your next stage of changing, [sub]-consciously."

Notions of spirituality aside, the glowing press reviews and air of positive anticipation generated by the single 'Red Guitar' ensured that *Brilliant Trees* entered the UK charts at No 4 in the second week of July, 1984, one position higher than Japan had ever achieved. After years of hiding his emotions behind a façade of clever lyrical props, it seemed the simple act of expressing his own feelings – no matter how ambivalent or confused they might be – had freed him both critically and commercially. "Maybe I wasn't equipped to write about myself before," Sylvian told *NME* writer Biba Kopf. "Even 'Ghosts' was an outside observation. You don't feel the person singing the song is experiencing those emotions. [Yet], 'Brilliant Trees' – the song – is obviously something genuine. It doesn't say anything in particular, which is something I'd hitherto always found difficult to do, to work towards something with no particular result . . . maybe that comes with being a little more confident about my work. With Japan," the singer added, "I felt that I got to the top of the ladder and there was nowhere else to go. But now, I feel I'm at the bottom of a new ladder of creativity that has so many possibilities . . . I want to keep working and climbing."

The next step on that ladder towards artistic freedom brought Sylvian considerably less critical acclaim. In fact, more a critical mauling. At around the same time that *Brilliant Trees* cast its melancholic shadow throughout many a British bedsit, the singer's first photographic exhibition was taking place at London's Hamilton Gallery. The photo-montages on display dated from 1982, and captured David's recent voyage around the globe as well as more intimate portraits of girlfriend Yuka Fujii, collaborators Ryuichi Sakamoto and Holger Czukay, brother Steve Jansen and faithful Siamese cat Oppi. "A lot of the pictures were taken during my travels," he said, "and I do spend a lot of time in Japan, in Kyoto especially. Japan has a quality to it I like. I feel an affinity with the people and the places." Sylvian's choice of camera for his experiments was an unusual one, but totally in keeping with previous incarnations: namely, the Polaroid Sun 600. "It appeals to me because it's so fast, it's all there in five minutes," David told journalist Anton Rush. "I never had any real cameras, I mean I had those idiot-proof ones, but I never had the film developed. I'm very lazy like that."

To his credit, Sylvian worked hard to convey an interesting sense of mood and texture with the photos, using montage/

cut-up techniques, surface scratching and hand-painted framing devices to enhance the images. But unfortunately, someone had got there before him and done it, in many a mind, a hell of a lot better. The previous year artist David Hockney, hitherto noted more for his contemporary paintings, won considerable acclaim with his own exhibition – 'Cameraworks' – at London's Hayward Gallery. The similarities between Hockney's groundbreaking use of Polaroid pictures linked together to form a collage and David's more recent efforts were uncomfortable, to say the least. Inevitably, the cognoscente cried "Rip-off". Very loudly. Backed into a corner, Sylvian had little alternative but to come out fighting: "I find it all very narrow-minded," he protested. "I mean, if you've got any credibility as an art critic, you should be able to see the difference straight away . . . Hockney's photos are about movement, mine are more static. Anyway," David continued, "people come up with similar ideas all the time. One person didn't create Cubism, it was created by a group of people, but everybody now associates it with Picasso. The times inspired people to come up with the same ideas as him."

One had to feel a degree of sympathy for Sylvian. After all, he'd only sought to follow in the footsteps of his role model Jean Cocteau, and break free of being pigeonholed in just one area of artistic endeavour. Sadly, like Jagger and Bowie before him, Sylvian had fallen foul of that old critical adage: pop stars should stick to what they're good at – being pop stars. Still, the exhibition was healthily attended (mainly by Japan fans, it has to be said) and the book that collected his photographic works – *Perspectives: Polaroids 82-84* – (limited to 5,000 copies) sold moderately well despite its hefty price tag. "The Polaroids and drawings served as an education," he later confessed. "It was a naïve pleasure to move into other areas. I'm not so sure I was justified in thrusting it on the public. I was weak at the time."

The critical reaction accorded Sylvian's venture into alternative art forms served to highlight the potential difficulties he faced in shedding the skin of his former pop life. Like many performers in his position, his success thus far had been built on courting the affections of two distinctly separate markets: the student/adult brigade that took their listening cues from the serious rock press, and younger, less critically discerning fans who became aware of him through teen-focused magazines like *Smash Hits* and *No 1*. This duality was mirrored in the very marketing of *Brilliant Trees*. On the one hand, the promotional rounds for the album saw the ex-Japan frontman fend off difficult questions about the nature of his art from canny journalists at the *NME* and *Melody Maker*. Yet on the other, his features were still being plugged mercilessly (if somewhat less frequently) in the poster section of less discriminating teen mags. In fact, to mark Sylvian's breakthrough as an artist/photographer of note, *Smash Hits* ran a "Win your very own David Sylvian Polariod" competition, with a copy of his book (dedicated to Jean Cocteau, by the way), LP, 'Red Guitar' video and snappy Polaroid camera offered as potential prizes. While there was nothing inherently wrong with such a competition, it was unlikely to improve his chances of being invited round to Henry Cartier Bresson's house for tea and biscuits.

The world of pop was responsible for cultivating his current image and Sylvian knew it. He was now 26, and the frothy attractions that first brought him to music were being replaced in his mind with more progressive notions of spirit and rigorous self-examination. To engineer a healthy (and still wealthy) escape from the dewy gaze of teenage girls and capitalise on the more serious themes present on *Brilliant Trees*, he would have to move still further towards the very fringes of the music scene.

10

Sahara Bound

August 18, 1984 saw the release of David Sylvian's second single from *Brilliant Trees*, the lovely 'The Ink In The Well'. Yet, unlike 'Red Guitar' before it, 'Ink . . .' failed to break into the Top 20, stalling instead at a disappointing No 36. Though no one knew it at the time, the song's lack of commercial success was an arbiter of things to come. In fact, 'The Ink In The Well' would mark Sylvian's very last appearance in the Top 40, with the final single gleaned from *Brilliant Trees* – 'Pulling Punches' – tanking at No 56 in November, 1984. Given his seeming desire to escape from the pop mainstream, he must have been secretly delighted.

The autumn of 1984 also marked the re-emergence of Sylvian's former Japan colleague Mick Karn. After his break-out 45 'Sensitive' and album *Titles* met with critical sniffs and poorer sales, Karn had been largely absent from the music scene, save for a one-off single with Ultravox's Midge Ure – 'After A Fashion' – that peaked at No 39 on the charts in July, 1983. Now he was back as one half of the portentously titled duo Dali's Car. His vocal foil this time round was ex-Bauhaus singer (and Maxwell tape poster boy) Pete Murphy, best known for his gravelly, sunken-throated performance on 'Bela Lugosi's Dead', a song that encapsulated the gothic movement of the early Eighties. With Karn's rubbery bass playing and Murphy's high-cheekboned charm, one might have expected great things. However, the duo's début single 'The Judgement Is The Mirror' and subsequent album *The Waking*

Hour failed to engage the public's interest (they stiffed at No 66 and No 84 respectively), and Dali's Car were gone in a wisp.

With the benefit of hindsight, the duo's quick demise was perhaps for the best. After all, given their surreal, overblown lyrics, spurious image and complete lack of any discernible tunes, Dali's Car are now principally remembered by the music press as 'the world's most pretentious collaboration': "Suffice to say, if Peter had his way it would have been a lot more pretentious," Mick later offered, by way of defence.

Still, Karn's re-emergence did help answer certain questions for old Japan fans, the most pressing of which was whether he was on speaking terms with Sylvian after the shenanigans of 1982. "Oh, it's amicable between me and David," Mick confirmed. "I can't wait to hear his new stuff to see what's going on in his head. We still see each other when we can . . . [but] I can't listen to *Brilliant Trees* that often . . . just because modern music interferes too much." Sadly, Mick never intimated what exactly modern music was interfering with . . .

As Karn stepped back up to the musical drawing board in the UK, Sylvian was busy in Japan taking part in a film documentary about himself. "The idea didn't appeal particularly, but I was extremely short of money!" he would later reveal. Nevertheless, what started out as a relatively straightforward venture soon transformed into something much more involved. Unlike most film biographies, the creative reins on the shoot were actually handed over to Sylvian. "At the end of 1984, I went to Japan to make a documentary about myself. I was supposed to write and direct everything, which I thought was really strange. [Consequently] there was only one section I wrote which was documentary. The rest I tried to make up with more interesting things."

Guided by on-site technical director Yasuyuki Yamaguchi, Sylvian eventually captured 40 minutes of useable film, which he then cut into two parts: an opening documentary section loosely based around his career, and a second, more innovative piece that, thanks to manipulative camera technology and careful editing, transformed Tokyo's industrial spires into a watery landscape of quicksilver and sand. The inspiration for part two's more abstract approach came from Sylvian's growing fascination with the work of German artist Joseph Beuys. "The kind of thoughts and emotions he provokes by using certain materials are very odd," said David. "It's stimulating to relate to those materials in that unorthodox way. Some of the objects he uses – whether it's a car battery or a printing press – if he's able to instil into that image something otherworldly, relating to unseen energies, something 'magical', then think of the potential with something as abstract as sound."

To advance his theory, Sylvian set about composing the accompanying music to the film. As with the video itself, the soundtrack was divided into two separate parts, the first of which David recorded quickly with Tokyo based tape engineer Seigen Ono. This composition – entitled 'Preparations For A Journey' – was distinctly Oriental sounding, with native Japanese voices giving way to an undulating synth pattern that circled around before fading off into the distance. To capture the more ethereal feel of the second half of the film, Sylvian called on the services of Ryuichi Sakamoto. In two days, the duo had created an eerie, nomadic piece that fused the background hum of Tokyo's streets to a spare, but compelling tribal beat. They christened it 'Steel Cathedrals'. On both tracks, Sylvian's vocals were conspicuous by their absence.

Believing more could be done with the music of '. . . Cathedrals', he flew back to London with the tape and arranged a supplementary recording session. As usual, the roll call of session musicians was top-notch: Kenny Wheeler on flugelhorn, brother Steve Jansen on percussion, ex-Japan guitarist Masami Tsuchiya on 'abstractions' and Holger Czukay on short-wave radio and anything else that came to hand. Yet, the real surprise was the additional presence of guitarist Robert Fripp.

A semi-mythical figure, Fripp announced his presence on the music scene in 1967 with the engaging trio Giles, Giles

An early publicity shot of Sylvian. "David was just extraordinary - a cross between Mick Jagger and Brigitte Bardot" - Japan manager Simon Napier-Bell. (LFI)

David Sylvian on stage 1978. (LFI)

One of Japan's earliest publicity photos from 1976. L-R, back row: Richard Barbieri, Steve Jansen. Front row: Mick Karn, Rob Dean, David Sylvian. (LFI)

Richard Barbieri, David Sylvian and Rob Dean backstage in 1978. (LFI)

Lewisham's answer to The New York Dolls. Mick Karn (left) and David Sylvian captured live. (LFI)

Mick Karn and David Sylvian experiment with an early version of the 'new romantic' look, circa 1979. The image was quickly dropped. (LFI)

Giorgio Moroder (left) and Sylvian in the studio recording the single 'Life in Tokyo' in 1979. (LFI)

A change of emphasis. Japan return with a new look and musical style for their third LP, Quiet Life. (LFI)

Sophistication at last. Japan in 1980. L-R: Mick Karn, Rob Dean, Richard Barbieri, David Sylvian and Steve Jansen. Dean soon left the group. (Rex)

"Great Britain's cleverest pop group". (LFI)

Yuka Fujii and Mick Karn celebrate the opening of his new restaurant, The Penguin Cafe in 1981. The couple parted in less than ideal circumstances, bringing about the end of Japan.(LFI)

David Sylvian contemplates his new solo career in1984. (Peter Anderson/SIN)

Sylvian caught on camera at his first photographic exhibition - Perspectives - at London's Hamilton Gallery in June, 1984.(Rex)

Seeking to escape his pop past, Sylvian replaces dyed hair and make up with long locks and a beard. (Yuka Fujii/Retna)

David Sylvian with contemporary dancer/ choreographer Gaby Agis in 1987. Sylivan wrote the score for Agis's 1987 ballet The Stigma Of Childhood (Kin). (Rex)

The Road to Graceland tour in 1993. Though Sylvian has often expressed his displeasure with live performances, he greatly enjoyed this tour. (Brian Rasic/Rex)

The Last Romantic. (Yuka Fujii/Retna)

Ingrid Chavez. (LFI)

and Fripp, before gaining greater notoriety as the musical brains behind King Crimson, an avant-garde/prog rock combo whose deviant anthem '20th Century Schizoid Man' established them as darlings of the progressive rock movement. After a stream of well received albums – *In The Court Of The Crimson King*, *Larks In Aspic* and *Red* – Fripp disbanded Crimson in 1974, and moved on to a series of increasingly eclectic collaborations with David Bowie, Peter Gabriel, Daryll Hall and The Police's Andy Summers. By 1981, he had reactivated King Crimson, only to shut them down again after three more LPs in 1984.

With his King Charles haircut, gold granny glasses and studious attitude, Fripp cultivated the image of rock's most cerebral guitarist, but for many his most interesting work was recorded with ex-Roxy Music keyboard player and general art-terrorist Brian Eno. Their first album together, 1973's *(No Pussyfootin')* saw Fripp's already deformed guitar tones mutilated beyond belief by Eno's penchant for studio experimentation. Amassing an army of Echoplexes, distortion units and tape loops, Brian created the now famous 'Frippertronics', the mesmerising wall of noise that eventually became Robert's signature guitar sound. Subsequent releases from the duo – 1975's *Evening Star* and 1977's *Before And After Science* – only consolidated their reputation for creating musical anarchy. Professorial in demeanour, mercurial in wit and always ready to confound expectation, Fripp was destined to become a welcome and lasting addition to Sylvian's growing arsenal of artistic polymorphs. "At the time [of our first collaboration], I wasn't a performing musician," recalled Robert. "I hadn't been performing since 1984. [But], I thoroughly enjoyed the session with David, so we stayed in touch."

After Fripp et al added their contributions to 'Steel Cathedrals', Sylvian took the tape to Virgin Records to see if they were interested in releasing it as a separate item to his forthcoming film. As the piece featured no vocals, and would, therefore, appeal only to a select (World Music) audience, the record company passed. By way of compromise, Sylvian agreed to record additional material in an effort to push the listening time up to album length. An agreement was struck. In the meantime, to keep fans happy (and presumably protect their investment – after all, *Brilliant Trees* had cost over £100,000 to produce), Virgin released a Japan retrospective, *Exorcising Ghosts*, in December, 1984. With a wealth of material culled from the band's latter years, and the inclusion of some of their best known singles – 'Quiet Life', 'Visions Of China' and 'Ghosts' – the LP managed a semi-respectable No 45 on the charts.

With financial backing secured, Sylvian set about writing his complementary piece to 'Steel Cathedrals'. To aid him in the task, he reunited with Jon Hassell, the trumpeter so important to the realisation of *Brilliant Trees*, as well as usual suspects Steve Jansen and Holger Czukay. The line-up was completed with the inclusion of Mick Karn's childhood hero, Percy Jones, on fretless bass. The music eventually created by the ensemble was both instrumental and impressive. Cut into three distinct parts – 'Ancient Evening', 'Incantation' and 'Awakening (Songs From The Tree Tops)' – the emphasis was again on the conveyance of image and mood, this time with desert plains and Sahara skies coming clearly to mind.

Nonetheless, when Sylvian ran the new tracks back to back with the music of 'Steel Cathedrals', he remained unimpressed. As separate pieces, they worked well. As an album, less so. Cap in hand, he returned to Virgin Records, explained the dilemma and suggested a possible solution: "What if I do another vocal side to back up 'Steel Cathedrals'?" Faced with little alternative, Virgin stumped up some cash for additional studio time, though this time Sylvian had to dig deep into his own pockets to make up the remaining balance. Sadly, the results of further experimentation proved equally fruitless. While the demos David recorded with vocals were strong, they didn't sit well with the ethereal charms of 'Steel Cathedrals', or for that matter, 'Words With The Shaman'.

With much money spent, and everyone keen to see a return on their investment, a quick decision was called for.

The solution offered, whilst by no means perfect, was at least equitable for all concerned. As contractually agreed, Sylvian's two-part documentary, *Preparations For A Journey*, was to be aired (with accompanying music) exclusively on Japanese television. However, the second part of the feature – the otherworldly *Steel Cathedrals* – would be made available to his British audience in the form of a 25 minute video, replete with infamous soundtrack. The three songs Sylvian recorded with Jon Hassell – now collected under the umbrella title *Words With The Shaman* – were also to be released as an EP. And finally, the music created for 'Words . . .', 'Preparations . . .' and 'Steel Cathedrals' would be amassed on a limited edition cassette, and again, released commercially in the UK. The title of this collection was *Alchemy: An Index Of Possibilities.* The only exclusion to this frenzy of commercial activity were the vocal tracks David recorded – they would be held back to form the backbone to his forthcoming album, due for release in the unspecified future. One felt only pity for Virgin's marketing department.

When *Steel Cathedrals, Alchemy: An Index Of Possibilities* and *Words With The Shaman* did finally hit the shops on December 14, 1985, critical reaction was good, though *Sounds*' Ronnie Randall used his review to draw attention to the complexities that came with such a blanket release: "Velly Intelesting, but shurely shome mistake? An EP that's really a twelve inch single and an LP that's a mere EP only available on cassette. Added to which – nowhere can the golden larynx of the former 'world's most beautiful man' be located." Yet, when it came to the music itself, Randall was more effusive with his praise: "Whichever way round you listen to them, the whole is a beautifully gentle and hypnotic experience, full of warmth and tingling atmosphere. I've always admired Sylvian's willingness to take chances and never opt for the easiest commercial option. I have one word for this shy, retiring young man. Banzai! . . . I mean Bonza!"

The relative success of David Sylvian's first real foray into instrumental music (*Words With The Shaman* subsequently charted at No 72 the week before Christmas, 1985) was not only crucial for the purposes of establishing artistic growth, but also in forging an alternative career as a creditable composer of ambient/New Age styles. Still, he remained keen to point out that there was danger in such easy compartmentalisations: "I was aiming for something between pop music and avant-garde music," Sylvian told *Record Collector*'s Mark Prendergast. "My approach was to build up layers and layers of sound until something was working for me emotionally. I'm interested in unease in music, and instrumentals, if they are to work, must convey a sense of fascination. 'New Age' music, to my mind, is a marketing term for record companies and an uncreative solution by musicians to the problems of making instrumental music."

Despite his protestations, Sylvian's recent experiments had taken him one step closer to defining the possible nature of his craft. Eager to capitalise on that forward movement, he headed still further into the soil.

11

Look Not To The Heavens

By early 1986, David Sylvian's escape from previous pop responsibilities was almost complete. His tentative move into instrumental waters had been critically well received, and there was enough interest from old fans to still keep him afloat as a commercial entity. Such enduring loyalty was just as well, as by now Sylvian had completely dropped the image that sold him in the first place. In place of the snappy, new romanticised threads was a wardrobe largely comprised of plain shirts and unobtrusive cardigans. Those ivy-league ties were also a thing of the past, with silver chains and polo necks now the preferred option. Most telling, though, was the additional abandonment of the old make-up/blond wedge combination that defined his years with Japan. The 28 year old who greeted the press circa 1986 was brown haired (Sylvian's natural colour), pale of face, and by all accounts, a lot more comfortable.

"I always thought I looked pathetic," he told *Blitz*'s Jim Shelley. "[The image] was never as important to me as people thought. It was always a disguise to avoid confronting myself. In the area I was brought up in, I knew it wasn't acceptable and that was why I did it. I accentuated the feminine part of my nature, because of an ideal of myself. At one point, I was very confused about what I was, and what Sylvian was as a public image. I've come to terms with that now. I know what I am. I exist as David Sylvian."

While the rationale behind Sylvian's remarks was sound

enough, in the eyes of many critics he had simply supplanted one image with another – cannily moving from pop dandy to Eighties renaissance man by way of various flirtations with art, photography and, of late, ambient music. Such charges took on greater validity when one looked at his track record. When the public rejected Japan as a viable British alternative to The New York Dolls, Sylvian moved the goalposts and reinvented the group as a youthful Roxy Music. When that incarnation proved restricting to his ambitions, he simply modified his approach to success by the appropriation of Ethnic/World beats. Presented with such evidence, there was a compelling argument to suggest that existing "as David Sylvian" simply meant shedding skin as and when necessary.

The case for the defence, however, was strong. Unlike many of his contemporaries, Sylvian had always readily admitted his mistakes, not so much for the effect of distancing himself from them as seeking public penitence. Therein lay a certain honesty in itself. Additionally, he had always been the most reluctant of stars. Even at the height of Japan's fame, the singer was renowned for avoiding interviews and photo shoots, preferring instead the comforts of an old book to the opportunities of self-promotion. His recently declared policy of 'no live dates for three albums' also pointed towards a performer heartily sick of the tour-record-tour-record cycle required to sustain commercial interest. And there was confirmation from his old manager, Simon Napier-Bell, that spoke volumes regarding the real nature of Sylvian's quest: "He came to me once and said, 'I want to be a minor rock star. I want to be like a left bank poet.' . . . I said, 'I don't know how to do that – I only know how to go flat out until you become a major rock star, and all you can do then is back off it."

If anyone required proof that David Sylvian was actively seeking to back off his pop responsibilities, it came in splendid form when his new single 'Taking The Veil' was released on August 9, 1986. A stuttering beat, moody bassline and only the most occasional of vocals (beautifully sung, nonetheless) all conspired to render it relatively harmless as far as chart action was concerned. The best that 'Taking The Veil' could manage was a weedy No 53. Yet, when one investigated the song, some of the old trademarks that granted Sylvian his stardom were still apparent: an impressionistic lyric that toyed with images of longing and anticipation – this time a young child's innocent dream of one day becoming a nun . . . "In dresses white, all set for sail, little girl dreams of taking the veil." There were also those familiar hints of dissonance at the edges of the tune that had worked so well for Japan – courteously provided on this occasion by Robert Fripp's asymmetrical guitar lines.

But where 'Taking The Veil' differed vastly from some of Sylvian's more popular tunes was in its conveyance of musical unease. Unlike 'Quiet Life' or 'Gentlemen Take Polaroids', there was no real hook present, just a cluster of notes cycling uncomfortably around a sparse kick-drum – hardly the stuff No 1s were made of in the mid-Eighties. To Sylvian though, it was all in keeping with a greater plan: "People aren't that simplistic, are they? Even at the height of joy, there's an underlying current. I think to create . . . music successfully, there must be these dark elements."

The duality to which he referred was much in evidence on *Gone To Earth*, the singer/songwriter's second solo LP released on September 13, 1986. An ambitious double album recorded at Virgin boss Richard Branson's own studio, The Manor in Oxfordshire, as well as West London's Town House, *Gone To Earth* again found Sylvian testing his own boundaries, though this time with more mixed results.

The record itself was split into two parts, the first disc consisting of seven vocal cuts, and the second a purely instrumental affair, comprising six more atmospheric pieces. Kicking things off was the already familiar (and somewhat disappointing) 'Taking The Veil'. Yet, the LP took an almost immediate upturn with the engaging charms of 'Laughter And Forgetting', a delightful piano-driven ballad with redemption through love as its central motif: "Running like a horse between the trees, the ground beneath my feet gives me something to hold onto . . ."

As with 'Brilliant Trees' and 'Weathered Wall' before it, 'Laughter And Forgetting' used lyrical themes of outstretched hands and open hearts to make its point – the religious overtones obvious to all but the most casual listener. But before one could level charges at Sylvian of trawling his own past for inspiration, he silenced all dissent with *Gone To Earth*'s centrepiece, the evocative 'Before The Bullfight'. Funereally paced, with Spanish sounding flugelhorn and guitar flourishes providing only the slightest sense of relief, '. . . Bullfight's self-lacerating honesty was uncomfortable to hear, but difficult not to be entranced by: "When all's forgiven, still every fault's my own, I will take my turn to fight the bullfight . . ." A song that this time dealt with the dissolution of love, and the fight to regain one's sense of self-control in the aftermath, 'Before The Bullfight' illustrated Sylvian's growing knack for channelling the most disturbing of personal experiences into fine musical drama.

The next tune (if it can be called that) was the title track itself, a strange but compelling piece which saw the singer contest the validity of organised religion with more holistic notions of faith. Though the lyric was ambiguous, the suggestion that acquiescence to dogma serves only to constrict man rather than free him was undoubtedly clear. The 'Gone To Earth' of the title then, was more about finding enlightenment in the ground beneath one's feet, than in any man-made creed. David tried to capture some of the song's essence in an interview with the *Melody Maker*'s Steve Sutherland: "I think a lot of the elemental aspects in the lyrics . . . have their spiritual equivalents, and there are two reasons . . . my affinity with nature in the physical sense – and the feeling I get from it – and on another level, (its overall) spiritual properties, like the way being near water can affect people. Of course, living in an urban environment, you're drawn to nature in a different way . . . If I was living in the country, I probably wouldn't need to write this kind of music, but living in the city, it's quite a different thing . . ."

The music of 'Gone To Earth' was as complex to define as the lyrics themselves, with Sylvian's mellifluous vocal literally attacked by a barrage of distorted guitars. Peace from the cacophony came only once, when the song hit its middle stride. Here, the wall of noise parted for a moment to allow a tranquil voice to utter the words, "The soul goes beyond being and enters this divine world . . ." After this brief respite, chaos again ensued.

The voice that calmed the musical seas belonged to J G Bennett, a contemporary philosopher who'd begun his studies into mysticism under the auspices of legendary Armenian seer George Ivanovitch Gurdjieff. Following his teacher's advice to "Take the understanding of the East and the knowledge of the West and then seek", Bennett subsequently left Gurdjieff's tutelage to instruct his own group of students at Sherbourne House in Dorset. One of his more noteworthy pupils was Robert Fripp, the man responsible for the caterwauling guitars on 'Gone To Earth'. Due to his subsequent friendship with Fripp (who used spoken word snippets of his teacher's voice on many of his own LPs), Sylvian made the decision to include Bennett's views on the passage of the soul on the album's title track.

In comparison to the heady charms of 'Gone To Earth', the next tune, 'Wave' seemed somewhat laboured. Though Sylvian's lyric was strong – the last line "I'd tear my very soul to make you mine" particularly effective – the music itself rumbled along like an over-stacked hearse, never evolving beyond the studio jam that inspired it. David himself later admitted the song was a pale shadow of what he'd originally intended. Of much more use was *Gone To Earth*'s penultimate vocal track, the captivating 'River Man'. Again, spirituality was the key, with the singer bouncing images of earthly escape against a suitably hypnotic two-note bass pattern: "So I keep running, falling, till I reach the water, run with me holy man". Side two ended with the singer's most traditional song in years, the even-tempered 'Silver Moon'. Beautifully understated, the track might perhaps have been written for Sting in one of his reflective moods.

The instrumental pieces occupied sides three and four of the album. If one had, by some act of God, missed what Sylvian was trying to convey on the vocal section of *Gone To Earth*, the titles of three of the six pieces that made up the remaining disc left few doubts. 'The Healing Place', 'Answered Prayers' and 'The Wooden Cross' all carried obvious religious connotations, predominantly of a Christian nature. Even the remaining tracks 'Where The Railroad Meets The Sea', 'Home' and 'Upon This Earth' communicated some notion of spirit. The music itself reflected the titles, with only a gentle guitar or acoustic piano interlude interrupting the overall aura of church-like silence. Like the work of painter Joseph Beuys (whose views on the destruction of nature were voiced on 'The Healing Place'), these pieces were about suggesting a mood – never intended to be intrusive per se – more a soundtrack for one's thoughts: "It's not to make a representation of nature or to bring the countryside into the home," David confirmed, "it's . . . to create a mood that's comfortable to work in, to think in, to bring yourself closer to your inner self, or, at least, at its highest level anyway."

As a follow-up to *Brilliant Trees, Gone To Earth* worked well enough. Wisely, Sylvian had chosen to abandon his previous fascination with Far Eastern musical forms in favour of a more ambient/jazz-orientated feel. That decision alone had encouraged real compositional growth. But there were a few quibbles. For one, the album's production style (courtesy of Steve Nye and David) was discouraging, the music sometimes sounding thick and muddy in places where lightness should have reigned. Another fault was that certain tracks felt rushed, unfinished even, with 'Wave' a particularly bad offender. While some of the blame could be apportioned to budgetary restrictions, Sylvian's decision to get ideas down on tape quickly had compromised the promise of several songs. On this point, he remained defensive – especially when it came to the instrumental pieces: "The instrumental half lends itself to the way people don't sit down and listen to music anymore. They aren't as rewarding as vocal songs, no, but they're not meant to be listened to in the same way. I wrote hundreds of them, and recorded them very quickly, randomly, because Virgin weren't really interested in them. I paid for most of them myself."

One thing that Sylvian couldn't be faulted on was his choice of musicians for the project, all of whom gave exemplary performances. Aside from Robert Fripp, whose guitar work graced five tracks (and who was credited as co-writer on 'Gone To Earth' and 'Upon This Earth'), ex-Be Bop Deluxe man Bill Nelson also contributed guitar to several songs, his emotive solos on 'Before The Bullfight' and 'Answered Prayers' just two highlights worthy of mention. As usual, Steve Jansen and Richard Barbieri were present on percussion and keyboards respectively, with Jansen even turning his hand to bass guitar on 'River Man'. And another old face, Canadian Kenny Wheeler, returned to blow some distinctly Miles Davis-like flugelhorn on the aforementioned 'Before The Bullfight', as well as providing a breath-taking solo on 'Laughter And Forgetting'.

Some new arrivals also made their presence indelibly felt throughout *Gone To Earth.* Top soprano saxophonist (and occasional King Crimson member) Mel Collins lent 'Silver Moon' and 'River Man' some ghostly shades of blue, while respected Barbadian trumpeter and mainstay of the Sixties British jazz scene Harry Beckett almost saved 'Wave' from itself: "[David's] a quiet guy, not all that talkative," recalled Harry. "But his identity is all in his compositions and arrangements. You'd think he would have been a bigger name – I know he's a cult figure and all of that – but he's certainly not as big as he should have been . . ." From a man who had worked with Charlie Mingus, Ronnie Scott and Graham Collier, this was high praise indeed.

Another "first timer" was classical/jazz improviser John Taylor, a pianist of extraordinary technical facility, whom Sylvian knew of through his work with Kenny Wheeler in Azimuth. Though Taylor's seamless piano parts allowed David's voice to soar to new heights on the ballad 'Laughter And Forgetting', it was the first time he'd actually crossed paths with a 'pop' musician: "I'd not really worked with anybody, shall we say, in the world of more popular music," remembered John, "so I had very little comparative information . . . [yet] I was very aware that David was a seriously involved musician that realised using improvisers was something that could be of benefit to his music."

Perhaps one of the bigger surprises on *Gone To Earth* was the presence of "The Paganini of the pedal steel", Mr B J Cole. A renowned sessioneer, whose deft touch had graced records by everyone from Andy Fairweather-Low to Long John Baldry, Cole was brought in by producer Steve Nye to add some slinky tones to 'Silver Moon'. However, his initial encounter with Sylvian proved a little frosty: "He's a very private man," said B J, "quite . . . aloof. I think lots of people have found him that way. I've worked with Scott Walker on a number of occasions, so I know the sort. But then again, when you've only worked with someone [for a short time], you can quite easily just get the mood." Asked if there were similarities between David and Scott – two performers who, besides sharing a similar vocal range, are often lumped together by the music press as two of 'pop's great melancholics' – Cole was emphatic: "Not in my experience. Strangely enough, I found Scott very open and communicative." As far as the music was concerned though, B J was more enthusiastic: "If it wasn't for people like David and Brian Eno, Jon Hassell and Harold Budd, what would this business be worth?"

One musician who formed a more lasting association with David Sylvian through his work on the album was bassist/

percussionist Ian Maidman. A veteran of the rock wars, who had seen action with Joan Armatrading, Murray Head and Lloyd Cole in the early Eighties, Maidman was perhaps best known for producing two of Irish folk artist Paul Brady's more critically acclaimed albums – *Back To The Centre* and *Primitive Dance.* However, his introduction to the Sylvian camp came via producer Steve Nye, the man responsible for recruiting Maidman into The Penguin Cafe Orchestra in late 1984. By 1985, Ian found himself working on a side project with Sylvian and Nye: "I did something with David, featuring John Taylor, Steve Jansen and Steve (Nye), though it never saw light of day," he recalled. "It's wafting around somewhere . . . probably in David's attic. [But] my memory of it was very good."

That session (an early version of the doomed 'Wave') led to Maidman being called in to participate in the making of *Gone To Earth,* an experience he found nerve-wracking at times, but ultimately rewarding: "(It was) enjoyable, interesting, inspiring. I think working with David . . . it pulls something out of you. You can't just go in and be Mr Session Bass Player. He wants something different – ideas. He was one of the first people I'd worked with where it's all about innovation." Ian eventually ended up working on three tracks in all – 'Taking The Veil', 'Silver Moon' ("I was quite proud of my bassline on that one!") and the entrancing 'River Man', where he added a bizarre pattern of bass harmonics to give the track its spooky feel. "The songs were all completed in terms of chord changes, but how they were treated was pretty much open. They just evolved in the studio." Aside from enjoying the relaxed working environment, Maidman credited Sylvian with perhaps the highest honour one musician can bestow on another – a genuine love of their material: "I loved the songs. There's something about David's songs that are really timeless. They could have been written at any time. In the Twenties even. They just have that feeling."

Entering the charts at No 24 in the third week of September, 1986, *Gone To Earth* stuck around for some five weeks on the Top 100, before finally disappearing into the ether. Compared with *Brilliant Trees*' Top Five success and robust shelf-life (the album stayed in the charts throughout the summer of 1984, before dropping outside the Top 75 in Mid-October), *Gone To Earth* was a commercial disappointment. Yet, given David's seemingly wilful sabotage of his own public profile, one could hardly expect platinum discs.

The critics remained kind, however, with *Sounds*' Chris Roberts leading the praise: "This is the record he's been gliding towards since 'The Tenant'," wrote Roberts, "and it's the perfect realisation of artist converting image to mood, subverting fantasy to super-reality. Delicate, but with the strength of legions, it's an Eighties masterpiece and conceivably his finest approximation of distilled beauty *ever*. And always stepping out from behind the rocks is *the voice*. It's the coolest voice in the world. [*Gone To Earth*] is almost as breathtaking as it is life giving. The Last Romantic."

NME's Dede Fadele was equally forthright in her praise towards Sylvian. Yet, she sounded a rightful note of caution concerning the LP's instrumental pieces: "Initial apprehension with regard to the 'ambient' LP is justified. It all too readily coalesces into an air-conditioned hum: pleasant and evocative of cactus country, mountain ranges and assorted foliage – but too distant somehow."

Complex, quixotic, serene and beguiling, *Gone To Earth* represented David Sylvian's most direct challenge to his audience yet. If one had worked hard to understand the more transcendental notions present on *Brilliant Trees*, or fought with the desert storms of *Words With The Shaman*, then the arcane cryptography that formed the backbone of *Gone To Earth* might be just too high a summit to climb. The only way to crack the code, or seek a demystification of sorts, was to turn to the artist himself. And even then, there was no guarantee answers would be forthcoming.

12

Spirituality, Literature, Sex And Self-Doubt

In many ways, *Gone To Earth* symbolised a form of closure for David Sylvian, a natural end to the cycle of ideas he'd begun exploring with *Brilliant Trees*. It was certainly the last time he would be so open in addressing his own notions of spirituality. Yet, for his audience, the album represented a game of "catch-up". To appreciate the themes Sylvian raised, one had to make the effort to understand them, and that took work. The essence of spirituality, after all, was purely notional. To comprehend, evaluate and either embrace or reject another person's beliefs often meant putting aside one's own views – never the easiest of tasks. The task was made even harder then when the views in question were as intricate as Sylvian's. Such potential ironies were not lost on him: "It just becomes very abstract. Everybody has a different idea what 'the spirit' is. My own experiences," David conceded, "probably wouldn't enlighten anybody in any way. I can only emphasise how important it is to me: it's my major interest and it sets my values and morals. That hopefully reflects in my work."

The singer also understood the pitfalls of making any definitive statement regarding the nature of his beliefs: "I could use the word faith, but it might be misleading. But faith is definitely something I have," Sylvian confirmed to *Blitz*'s Jim Shelley. "[Yet], I can't be too specific, and in a way, I don't want to be. By talking about it, it loses some of the power it has. If you say the occult . . . or certain philosophers . . . or magic or mysticism, everyone reacts in different ways – usually negative ways. They look at it as if it must be a weakness if I said I needed it." He did, however, drop some broad hints as to where his inclinations lay during the making of *Gone To Earth* at a later date: "Most of the things I read are rather factual books on various forms of religious belief from Buddhism to Christianity to the Jewish Kabbala, and even certain kinds of magic like Rosicrucianism. Just an assortment of things really, that throw more light on my own experience. Through the music, it's possible for me to show an appreciation of life and nature – but I don't think one should preach."

If one added Sylvian's interest in the teachings of J G Bennett and Gurdjieff to the above list, then he must also have been more than 'passing familiar' with the concepts behind Sufi, Taoism, Vedanta and The Bhagavad Gita – an impressive palette of spiritual colours from which to draw ideas. Still, it was the emotion generated by such ideas, and not the intellectual philosophy behind them that mattered most to him: "My work is primarily based on my own feelings and experiences and not intellectual understanding. For me, the latter is the secondary thing."

Where David Sylvian had been most successful in crystallising these feelings alongside notions of spirituality was in his ability to introduce transcendental themes to otherwise simple love songs. On one level, ballads (and the term is used loosely) like 'Weathered Wall', 'Brilliant Trees' and 'River Man' all worked well as naked expressions of emotion, passionate entreaties to an undisclosed source. Nonetheless, the lyrics could also be read as invocations to a higher power – prayers, in effect. It was a dichotomy Sylvian readily acknowledged. In fact, he seemed to revel in the creation of such ambiguities: "Yes, they operate on two levels, one a one to one level – a man to woman level – and then on a higher level too. Both are relevant and both are intentional."

A fine example of this two-tier approach was witnessed on one of *Gone To Earth*'s stand-out tracks, the torch-like 'Laughter And Forgetting'. Taking the title of Czechoslovakian author Milan

Kundera's 1979 satire of politics and hedonism as his template, Sylvian crafted a beautifully realised parable of salvation through love. Yet, as one peeled back the layers of the song, a more complex interpretation came to light: "I certainly wrote it in that way," Sylvian told *NME*'s Don Watson. "They were intended to be satirical lyrics, rather than romantic as they appear at first. But as time's gone on, I've seen different levels of integration to it. Laughter is the lightness to be able to stand back and say, 'This is all worthless', and in that sense you can stand away and see clearly what you're trying to do – not just in music but in life. Forgetting is the ability to not dwell in the past on things you've done which are wrong, or things inside you which are wrong – it's a kind of overcoming of yourself, of the fear of failure."

The song also drew attention to another of Sylvian's gifts – the ability to appropriate information from a whole host of literary sources and successfully assimilate it into his own material. Book titles were a particular favourite: Mishima's *Forbidden Colours*, Sartre's *Nausea, The Iron In The Soul* and . . . *Age Of Reason*, Cocteau's *The Difficulty Of Being* – all turned up as song titles or lyrics in one form or another. Even the central themes of 'River Man' strongly echoed the great German romantic novelist Hermann Hesse's spiritual odyssey *Siddhartha*. In keeping with his tendency towards public penitence, David readily acknowledged such thefts with the telling line "Guilty of stealing every thought that I own" on *Gone To Earth*'s 'Before The Bullfight'. "In a lot of ways . . . everything you produce is just an intersection of what you've perceived," he said later. "But there's a line at the end (of 'Before The Bullfight) – 'When's all forgiven, still every fault's my own.' Your faults, I believe, are the only thing you learn from."

One area where it was becoming increasingly difficult to track David's more obvious influences was in the actual music he produced. With Japan, connecting the dots was laughably easy – The New York Dolls, David Bowie and Roxy Music all clearly referenced at one time or another. Even *Tin Drum*, the group's most original record, doffed its cap in the direction of

Stockhausen and The Yellow Magic Orchestra. Yet, since striking out on his own, Sylvian had managed to neatly blur the lines between initial inspiration and final product. Signposts still existed, with *Brilliant Trees* recalling the work of Miles Davis, Brian Eno and Joni Mitchell, but as the eclecticism of *Gone To Earth* proved, he'd also made real steps towards establishing a musical identity all his own. While the judicious use of jazz improvisers like John Taylor and Kenny Wheeler was undoubtedly a factor in allowing the music to grow, he also seemed to be tugging at his own intellectual boundaries: "I'm very interested in myself in the way I'm growing, and where my mind is leading me. It's into a territory I'm really enjoying exploring, and (subsequently) the work is coming easily to me. I don't struggle over writing anymore. With Japan . . . I'd really struggle to get eight songs ready for an album. It doesn't happen like that any more."

Sylvian's more confident approach to life circa 1986 also saw him dispense with one of his less publicised creative tools – cocaine. Having first dabbled with the drug in his Japan days, he'd become increasingly reliant on it as a way of combating fatigue: "I had this illness, a mental problem, which meant I was always exhausted . . . the doctors couldn't do anything so I used coke." The alliance had proved mutually beneficial throughout the making of several albums, up to and including part of *Gone To Earth,* but now all bets were off. "I'm feeling more comfortable with myself," he confirmed. "I've come to terms with aspects of myself which, on *Brilliant Trees,* I was still struggling with a great deal."

Another aspect of Sylvian's life that he chose to make public at this time was his rather unconventional view of sex – or more expressly, the lack of it. "I never enjoyed sex," David told Jim Shelley. "It never interested me. Do I know why? No, I've never bothered to explore why. I'm quite happy that it doesn't. I've tried sleeping with men, but it didn't interest me – just as sleeping with women didn't interest me. Sexual energy," he continued, "is a form of creative energy: the lowest form. If you can use that energy . . . for a higher creative purpose, it gives you more power for the creative side of you." While such a statement was unusual for a 'pop' musician still in his twenties, it did cast more light on Sylvian's spiritual explorations. Abstinence from sex for the purposes of creating a 'higher state of being' had long been a central tenant of mysticism, with the father of modern physics Sir Isaac Newton allegedly a firm believer in 'sparing the seed' for the purposes of purifying thought. The theory had also been linked to the science of Alchemy and Shamanism – two belief systems Sylvian had name-checked on the instrumental releases *Alchemy: An Index Of Possibilities* and *Words With The Shaman.*

Alchemy. Shamanism. Kabbalism. Buddhism. Rosicrucianism. Christianity. All separate roads to one thing perhaps, but each offering a different mode of spiritual transport for getting there. In truth, though Sylvian had expressed an interest in them all, he remained reluctant to commit: "Religion is a very important thing for me – to find out what and why and give my life a positive direction. So often you sense what you're doing is right, but I want to *know* what I'm doing is right . . . in a universal sense. I'm at a stage," he continued, "where I have to make a decision about what doctrine to follow and I haven't made it yet. It's not something I should talk about until I have made that decision." On this point, he was as good as his word for several years.

A more pressing concern regarding Sylvian's musical future also reared its head towards the end of 1986: to wit, the singer's growing dissatisfaction with his own voice. A problem that had been brewing since his days with Japan (and had seriously bucked the production of *Brilliant Trees)* Sylvian was now publicly decrying what many considered his most bankable asset: "I feel I can convey what I'm trying to put over in music more successfully without vocals. Maybe it's because I'm not that good a singer and my vocals will always be mannered to a certain extent, whereas the instrumental work won't suffer from that." To him, it was a matter of conviction. "I don't have a lot of confidence in my voice," he later admitted. "I sing the songs because nobody else could sing them the way they *have* to be sung."

The paradox was obvious. While Sylvian may well have been irritated by the sound of his own voice, it remained the only instrument he possessed for conveying his lyrical ideas. Should he choose to retreat into a purely instrumental world, then he denied himself a side to his nature that had always been important – the simple act of self expression.

Trumpeter Mark Isham, who had worked with David on *Brilliant Trees,* and was about to cross paths with him again, acknowledged the singer's dilemma: "Yeah, I've had that conversation with him," laughed Isham. "He gets tired of just the singing aspect of it. But I don't know . . . he doesn't stop writing lyrics . . . there's a part of him that's just very interested in expressing himself that way. He's one of those songwriters who's an interesting poet and an interesting musician together. You have the Dylans of the world, who are poets first, and the song is a simple vehicle that the poem floats upon. Then you have other writers, who are very much into the complexities of the music and the words are just secondary. [But] the greatest songwriters are the ones who have an equal balance. I think David is one of those who puts equal creativity into both."

Sylvian's ambiguity towards his own voice was understandable. After the howls and shrieks of *Adolescent Sex* and *Obscure Alternatives*, he'd struggled to find a more suitable vocal range, eventually settling on the Bryan Ferry/David Bowie approximation that carried him through to Japan's final curtain call, the engaging *Tin Drum.* However, since embarking on a solo career, his voice had become progressively stronger, much more his own invention. That it remained mannered or derivative was neither here nor there. The deep and sinuous quality that it projected was still the perfect accompaniment to his music. Additionally, if he ever chose to fall silent, many critics and supporters might have to don mourning suits: *Sounds* journalist Chris Roberts had already acknowledged

Sylvian as possessing "The coolest voice in the world." And *The Sunday Times'* Robert Sandall wasn't far behind: "His voice, particularly in its lower reaches, is an extraordinarily resonant instrument, capable of communicating an almost somnambulant quality of unconscious purpose amid superficial indirection. He sounds," reasoned Sandall, "as if he is meditating to music." To the great relief of somnambulists everywhere, Sylvian decided to persevere with his vocals a little while longer. Suffice to say, the results were rather splendid.

13

Pleasant Diversions

With *Brilliant Trees* and *Gone To Earth,* David Sylvian had joined a long and illustrious line of performers whose success had seen them reject material excess in favour of more spiritual pastures. In the field of popular music, soul-searching of one form or another was almost a prerequisite, the trend beginning in earnest with Thirties bluesman Robert Johnson and continuing through to The Beatles' flirtation with Eastern transcendentalism in the late Sixties and beyond. Yet, what seemed to separate the nature of Sylvian's quest with the more fleeting dalliances of other artists was the sheer ardour of it all. Once renowned as "the prince of surface", he was now in danger of disappearing between the cracks altogether due to a complete unwillingness to play the pop game. "I've always thought being anonymous was very attractive," he once offered, by way of defence.

Such a stance was noble enough, but his diminishing public profile brought its own set of problems. Increasingly difficult to market, and constantly short of cash (by 1986, Japan's back catalogue sales had declined alarmingly), Sylvian's position as 'balladeer to the masses' had also been largely usurped by a slew of young, hungrier acts. The London-based trio Talk Talk, led by the talented Mark Hollis, had scored major chart success in 1986 with the mournful single 'Life's What You Make It' and subsequent hit album *The Colour Of Spring.* And waiting patiently in the wings was Colin Vearncombe's sad-eyed creation Black, who were destined to add a bitter-sweet note to

1987 with the corpse-like singles 'Wonderful Life' and 'Everything's Coming Up Roses'.

Even former punk/agit rocker Green Gartside had come in from the cold with the soulful hues of Scritti Politti's 'The Word Girl' and 'Wood Beez (Pray Like Aretha Franklin)'. While Green could never have been classified as a pop melancholic, the image that accompanied his recent success was 100% pure Sylvian circa 1982 – carefully coiffured blond tresses and more than a hint of make-up. He'd even taken to citing artist Joseph Beuys as an influence on his work. Duran Duran's Nick Rhodes must have been green with envy. As always, Sylvian cocked a snook at it all: "[Dropping the image] was like opening a door, removing that superficial element that lies on top of the music."

Though an air of ambiguity now marked his dealings with the pop world, Sylvian summoned up considerably more enthusiasm for his next three projects, one of which was a collaboration with former Ravishing Beauty and current pastoral songwriter Virginia Astley. A solo artist who scored a fair degree of critical success with her 1983 début album *From Gardens Where We Feel Secure,* Astley had come under fire for the sin of under-producing her music. To alleviate the problem, and create a commercially more tenable sound, her new record company, WEA, suggested bringing in Ryuichi Sakamoto to produce her latest endeavour. As the project got underway, Sylvian was invited by Astley and Sakamoto to sing on one of the tracks, the hymnal 'Some Small Hope'. Mild and meditative, the song recalled a far gentler age than the one in which it had been written. Sadly, with David on board (and potential crossover sales in the offing), someone had the bright idea to release the song as a single. Never a chart-topper to begin with, it subsequently bombed. Still, it was pleasant to hear Sylvian's voice back to back with a woman's – a rare event – and with any luck, it may have introduced Virginia's music to a few new fans. (Perhaps not as many as she might have hoped for though, as the album on which 'Some Small Hope' appears, *Hope In A Darkened Heart,* has long since been deleted.)

Interestingly enough, David's brief alliance with Virginia Astley marked the third time within a year or so that he found himself working with Ryuichi Sakamoto. Along with 'Some Small Hope' and the soundtrack for the video 'Steel Cathedrals', the duo had also found time to join forces with one of Japan's more refreshing pop bands, Sandii & The Sunsetz, in the spring of 1985. The alliance began when Sakamoto presented Sandii with an instrumental track, 'Rachel', feeling it might be a potential single for the band. Sensing a hit, Sandii then took the demo to Sylvian with a request that he write lyrics to the tune. With a little help from Ryuichi, David actually ended up presenting her with a whole new song instead, the sublime 'This Is Not Enough'. The original point of focus, 'Rachel', was left to Sandii herself to finish.

Revisiting his past was unusual for Sylvian. After all, the last time he'd had anything to do with Sandii and her Sunsetz was when they supported Japan on their farewell tour of 1982. Now he found himself writing songs for them. In some ways then, his next move was perhaps unsurprising. In the autumn of 1986, it was announced that David had recently collaborated with old adversary Mick Karn on two tracks for the bass player's forthcoming album, *Dreams Of Reason Produce Monsters.* In truth, the reunion had been a long time coming. Though Yuka Fujii was still an integral part of Sylvian's life, any real animosity between Sylvian and Karn had long since ceased. They were even seen on the town together occasionally, usually with a glass or two of wine in their hands. "Mick always makes me laugh a great deal," admitted David. "He's a very funny character."

Nonetheless, if some old fans saw the team-up as a clear sign that a full blown Japan reunion was on the cards, they were to be sorely disappointed. "As a romantic idea it would be nice," Sylvian told journalist Tim Goodyer at the time, "but I can't see it. The idea of working in a group is enticing after working on your own for so long . . . but there (isn't) enough conviction. I'm sure it'll be talked about in another five years, but I hope it'll only be talk because I don't think it would be a good thing." He was, of course, right. With four years having passed since the band originally folded, any reformation would be seen by the press as little more than a cynical money-making exercise. Additionally, it was unlikely that a reactivated Japan would have anything new to say. Both Richard Barbieri and Steve Jansen had continued to work with David on and off since the break-up, and now that he and Karn were collaborating again, there were few musical questions left to answer.

The first fruits of Mick and David's reunion eventually arrived on January 17, 1987 in the form of 'Buoy', a neatly crafted single that fused vintage elements of Japan's trademark sheen to a more contemporary production style. Allegedly a paean to homosexual love – though there was little to support such an analysis aside from Sylvian's cheeky line "There's more to this than meets the eye" – 'Buoy' popped into the charts at No 63, only to fall out again after one week. Yet, despite the cool commercial reception accorded it, the song did whet the appetite for Karn's new album, which dutifully appeared on 28 February, 1987.

Considerably better than his first solo effort (the wisely forgotten *Titles), Dreams Of Reason Produce Monsters* was creditable enough, if a little under-developed in places. The bassist had certainly lost none of his talent for snake-like string manipulation, as 'The Three Fates' and 'First Impression' showed, but other tracks such as 'The Language Of Ritual' and 'Land' still found him languishing in the same Far Eastern/African areas that typified his previous musical life. That David abandoned such themes with *Brilliant Trees* only served to heighten the potential irony. However, there was real progression apparent on the remaining Sylvian/Karn collaboration, the seductive and charming 'When Love Walks In'. Built around a vaguely French sounding melody, and featuring an inspired bass-line from Mick, the gentle air of melancholy the song conveyed was streets ahead of anything else on the record. Co-produced by Karn and Steve Jansen (who also played drums on the LP), *Dreams Of Reason Produce Monsters* managed a fleeting appearance on the charts at No 89.

In keeping with this flurry of ex-Japan activity, July 1987 saw the first LP release from the newly formed Dolphin Brothers, a duo comprised of Richard Barbieri and Steve Jansen. The record, *Catch The Fall*, was surprisingly good, with Jansen acquitting himself admirably as a lead vocalist. Unlike Karn's latest endeavour, where the emphasis was placed firmly on chordal experimentation, The Dolphin Brothers seemed doggedly in pursuit of a good old fashioned tune. On this count, they were more than successful, with 'Pushing The River', 'Real Life, Real Answers' and the title track itself all radio-friendly enterprises. Unfortunately, due to a lack of willingness on Virgin Records' part to actively promote their signing, *Catch The Fall* failed to make any real commercial impact in the UK. Thankfully, however, the LP made a dent in the Japanese market (always a fail-safe for Japan related product), thereby allowing Barbieri and Jansen an opportunity to continue with the project.

As Karn, Jansen and Barbieri struggled to reassert themselves in the marketplace, Sylvian moved further into the realms of the avant-garde by writing the score for dancer/choreographer Gaby Agis' modern ballet *The Stigma Of Childhood (Kin)*, a work concerned with "Information, living in London – the physicality of that". A fairly recent convert to the world of dance, David had been contacted by Agis (and partner/sculptor Kate Blacker) about the project via letter: "She wrote to me out of the blue asking if I'd be interested," confirmed Sylvian. "I'd seen clips of her stuff on TV, read enough about her to be intrigued, so we arranged a meeting." For Agis, Sylvian was an obvious choice from the start. "I had become frustrated with the limitations of very structured dance [and] had got increasingly into improvised situations. It seemed to me, through listening to David's music, that he was in a similar situation – a feeling of wanting to move beyond the structures that pop music was forcing on him".

Following their first meeting, and a visit to Sadlers Wells Theatre to see Agis perform, Sylvian agreed to write the score: "I liked the idea of working with a choreographer more than say doing a soundtrack to a film," David enthused, "because music and dance are both very abstract forms. Sensual, fluid. It [doesn't] have to be rhythmic, but . . . humane, hypnotic." In the end, the composition Sylvian provided Agis for . . . *(Kin)* was all of these things. A lilting combination of mournful cello sounds and Celtic tinged guitar, the piece was the best instrumental David had written since *Words With The Shaman* some two years before. *The Stigma Of Childhood (Kin)* subsequently premiered at London's Almeida Theatre on September 8, 1987, running for some two weeks. Obviously satisfied with his interpretation of her work, Agis asked David to contribute to the score of a later show, the oddly titled *Don't Trash My Altar, Don't Alter My Trash,* to which he dutifully agreed. That show eventually found a home at Hammersmith's Riverside Studios in November, 1988.

All in all, Sylvian's various guest appearances and collaborations provided him with a much needed opportunity to cool his jets and replenish energies. However, they represented little more than pleasant diversions from the real task of writing his next LP. In stark contrast to the perpetual round of delays and excuses that David usually offered in lazy defence, he set about the task of creating solo album number three with an almost youthful gusto.

14

Penumbra

The world saw little of David Sylvian in the early months of 1987. In fact, he rarely strayed from the confines of his West London flat. However, this was less to do with a Greta Garbo-like wish "to be alone", but more a serious need to write songs for his new album. Working with the bare essentials of a four track tape-recorder, guitar and piano, Sylvian eventually surfaced from his dug-out in March with enough ideas to merit a call to producer Steve Nye. After a positive response from Nye to the material, recording studios were duly booked.

In keeping with the "foreign climes lead to interesting records" approach of *Brilliant Trees,* Sylvian and Nye descended on Chateau Miraval Studios, in sunny La Val, France, where general manager Patrice Quef insured an atmosphere conducive to hard work. At this point in the proceedings, David was joined by the small band of players that would be so important in realising the songs he'd written earlier in the year. "The idea," said Sylvian, "was to create a looseness among the musicians involved because everybody's meeting in a strange place for the first time. It just opens people up a bit more."

As usual, he had chosen his supporting cast with the utmost care. Aside from the now perennial presence of Ryuichi Sakamoto, double bassist Danny Thompson – the man responsible for the irresistible "twang" behind 'The Ink In The Well' – also returned to the fold. A cheerful and infectious Cockney, Thompson was semi-legendary in muso circles for turning up to gigs on a push-bike, double-bass precariously strapped to his back. Folk-rocker John Martyn, who with Danny created one of the early Seventies most critically acclaimed albums, the masterful *Solid Air,* once recalled a story that summed up much of Thompson's appeal: "I was with Danny years ago and we were doing a studio gig at the BBC, where there was this poor little apprentice engineer, and he said, 'Mr Thompson, we're getting a strange buzz on the bass'. Danny put down the bass and went into the control booth. 'That,' he said to this bloke, 'is *tone* and it's taken me 20 years to get it.' "

Sylvian's new recruits this time round were no less impressive. Filling in on rhythm for an otherwise engaged Steve Jansen was acclaimed percussionist Danny Cummings, best known for his work with Dire Straits. And taking on guitar duties for the project was the inestimable David Torn. Brought on board following a recommendation from Mick Karn (who toured with the native New Yorker early in 1987 in support of his first solo LP), Torn was already a well established figure on the jazz scene before hooking up with Sylvian. Beginning his career with the critically acclaimed (but completely unlistenable) Everyman Band in 1979, he had gone on to record with Don Cherry and Jan Garbarek, before striking out on his own with the otherworldly LPs *Best Laid Plans* and *Cloud About Mercury.* Highly regarded, Torn brought with him a musical pedigree to equal that of Robert Fripp or Bill Nelson.

Players in place, recording went both quickly and well, allowing Sylvian to return to Angel Studios in Islington, London within a month or so to add orchestral arrangements to the material. In this process, he was assisted by Ryuichi Sakamoto: "I knew (Ryuichi) to be a good arranger and wanted to work with him in that capacity for some time," David later told Kathleen Galgano. "He has a fantastic grasp of many different forms of music. He immediately latches onto what you want and what you need, and tries to stay as true to your original ideas as possible." To add more class to the proceedings, Sylvian also invited trumpeter Mark Isham along to the London recordings. It was their first reunion since *Brilliant Trees*: "[I noticed] he'd left a lot of room for instrumental solos. [The music] was a little more open than before," said Mark, "leaning more towards a jazz direction." Isham added trumpet parts to three of the songs before heading back to the States to begin work on his own album.

With backing tracks completed, Sylvian journeyed to Wisseloord Studios in Hilversum, Holland, to lay down vocals and a few remaining piano overdubs. Again, no delays were incurred, and he was back at The Wool Hall in Bath within two weeks to mix and master the tapes. Producer Steve Nye joined him at the controls: "I could trust him . . . with the orchestral ideas I had in mind," David later confirmed. By mid-May, said tapes were in the can. From start to finish, the recording had taken only two and a half months. By Sylvian's usually laborious standards, this was nothing short of miraculous.

Some four months later, David's sixth single as a solo artist arrived in record stores. Entitled 'Let The Happiness In', the song was initially something of a shock for those who enjoyed the more optimistic grooves of *Gone To Earth.* For a start, no drums were present, just a thick cluster of brass and synth sounds that seemed to ascend and descend endlessly, creating a dirge-like atmosphere. Sitting on top of the orchestral soup was a positively suicidal sounding vocal from Sylvian: "I'm waiting for the agony to stop, Oh, let the happiness in . . ." Yet, as the track progressed, a hymn-like optimism began to invade from all sides: the dense brass and mournful trumpet (courtesy of Mark Isham) that sounded so despairing but a moment ago began to exude a real sense of joy. As a sparse percussive figure picked up the beat, Sylvian's lyric succinctly nailed the song's striking emotional turnaround: "I'm waiting for the skies to open up, and let the happiness in . . ." A beautifully realised tune – though never the right choice for a single – 'Let The Happiness In' crawled into the charts at No 66 in the second week of October before promptly disappearing.

Following fast on the heels of the single, David's third solo album, *Secrets Of The Beehive,* was released on November 7, 1987. A splendid effort, conveying the same sense of joy and sorrow as an old blues record, . . . *Beehive* portrayed an artist at the top of his form. Breaking with established tradition, Sylvian's songs this time round were almost entirely acoustic in setting, with only an odd synthesiser or electric guitar sprinkled into the mix. When ornamentation was needed, it came in the form of Ryuichi Sakamoto's stirring but never intrusive string arrangements. By taking such an approach, Sylvian's voice was allowed to truly govern his songs, instead of fighting against a tide of electrification. In short, *Secrets Of The Beehive* was an album all about the space between melody and vocal. Or as David might have it, between "darkness and shadowy light".

High points on . . . *Beehive* were hard to spot, mainly due to the sheer quality of material on show. Yet, the opening vignette, 'September', was indicative of just how far Sylvian had come from his lowly musical origins. A wistful tune, based around three or four sparse piano chords, its real strength lay in the ability to deceive the listener through the simplicity of its approach: "We say that we're in love," Sylvian sang, "while secretly wishing for rain, sipping coke and playing games . . ." An ambiguous line, that summed up the artifice behind many a love affair, it was a glowing example of the songwriter's abiding fascination with expressing sinister themes in the most innocuous of places.

While Sylvian had roped in many of the overtly spiritual references that peppered the lyrics of *Gone To Earth,* Angels, Devils and old Gods still ran riot throughout the album. 'The Devils Own', for instance, invoked images of "The howling of the stray souls of Heaven" over a ticking piano figure. 'When

Poets Dreamed Of Angels' was equally fervent in its summoning of seraphs and demons. As two Flamenco guitars (played by David and top sessioneer Phil Palmer) battled for supremacy, Sylvian pitted disturbing images of domestic violence against more metaphysical notions of conflict: "When poets dreamed of angels, what did they see? Bishops and knights well placed to attack."

Violence, in one form or another, was one of the more dominant themes of *Secrets Of The Beehive.* Aside from the wife-beating of 'When Poets Dreamed Of Angels', 'Mother And Child' also offered a disturbing spin on its seemingly harmless title: "Blood is drawn up from the well . . . an innocent guilty as hell . . ." Even the doe-eyed musical charm of 'The Boy With The Gun' drew its inspiration from bloodshed. An avenger's tale, told from an embittered teenager's perspective, Sylvian's words were uncharacteristically blunt. Some might even call them lascivious: "He'll free the sinners of deceit, they'll hear his name and run, his justice is his own reward, measured out beneath the sun."

Lyrically at least, moments of relief proved few and far between. Though the pungent 'Maria' and aforementioned 'Let The Happiness In' did offer vague remission from love amongst the ruins, tracks such as 'Waterfront' brought any romantics listening back down to Earth with a bump: "On the waterfront," David wearily intoned, "the rain is pouring in my heart . . ." That the music of *Secrets Of The Beehive* was so light and meditative only heightened to serve the sense of contrast he was undoubtedly looking to convey. Nonetheless, the LP's centrepiece, 'Orpheus' (its title a subtle nod to the work of Jean Cocteau), did offer hope of sorts. Though Sylvian confessed to wrestling with "an outlook on life that shifts between darkness and shadowy light", as the song ventured towards its end, he allowed himself a critical degree of optimism: "When this joke is tired of laughing," he sang, "I will hear the promise of my Orpheus sing . . ."

Iridescent yet acerbic, open yet obscure, *Secrets Of The Beehive* finally crystallised the duality of approach Sylvian had been actively seeking to capture since *Brilliant Trees.* "[The] whole album was written instinctively," David offered. "It wasn't premeditated in any way. For the first time, each track was written in one sitting. Usually I carry them around for months . . . it's a wonderful feeling, because I know it didn't come from me – it came *through* me . . ." By all accounts, the process of lyric writing had also been markedly easier: "The lyrics are more important than before," he confirmed. "Before they were like keys to help listeners into the landscape of the music, whereas [now] they are more straightforward. I just tried to make the lyrics more accessible to people, so they weren't alienated."

Where Sylvian had also been undoubtedly successful was in allowing his songs to breathe. Unlike *Gone To Earth,* where thick walls of sound threatened to overwhelm things at times, . . . *Beehive*'s overall groove remained minimalistic and elegant. Trumpeter Mark Isham, who played on 'When Poets Dreamed Of Angels', 'Let The Happiness In' and the gorgeous 'Orpheus' attributed the change to Sylvian's growing fascination with all things jazz: "For me, the main difference was the sense of space . . . and for lack of a better word – and don't take this the wrong way – a real jazz influence. The way he opened [things up], you do [think] of Miles Davis. Davis was behind that notion of slowing things down a bit . . . that was one of the most general things Miles did for music as a whole. David's approach to *Secrets Of The Beehive* was also orchestral – dealing in colours. That [recalls] Gil Evans." Isham's assessment of the sound of . . . *Beehive* was right on the mark. While the album was never wholly derivative of jazz magus Miles Davis' groundbreaking 1961 LP *Sketches Of Spain,* it did echo similar musical themes: flamenco sounding trumpets, sparse orchestration and the use of silence as a subliminal (yet critically important) weapon.

Over the years, many have come to regard *Secrets Of The*

Beehive as David Sylvian's most fully realised work. However, reviews at the time swung wildly between glowing praise and howling criticism. The *NME*'s Jack Barron sat in the blue corner: "Nowadays," said Barron, "one gets the impression that Sylvian doesn't sleep well enough to dream . . . [yet] *Secrets Of The Beehive* is a fabulous and mercurial record. If Sylvian ever smiled the magic would be broken, the narcissistic mirror he stares into would lie in splinters."

In the red corner, with gloves off, was *Sounds'* Peter Kane: "More mood music. And the mood is just short of abject misery and self-pity. David paces a lonely room, waiting for phones to ring and friends to drop by just so he can remind them what a terrible time he's having. Now I know of people out there who find Mr Sylvian's music quite ravishing," Kane conceded, "but there's something so dank, depressing and po-faced about the whole enterprise that reduces this to a solitary listening experience of the most pained order. Sensitive souls only need apply."

Refereeing the bout was *Q*'s Anthony Quinn: "Sylvian's mannered croon isn't everyone's idea of a great voice," reasoned Quinn, "but it suits his material pretty well, and there are one or two pieces here ('Orpheus', 'Waterfront') which I feel better for hearing."

When presented with charges (and there were many) that his music was maudlin, miserablist or downright bloody depressing, Sylvian offered an interesting defence: "[My music is like] being alone in a room with yourself, or even a step worse than that. [It's] introspective in a way that makes some people really nervous. The kind of people who immediately turn on a television when they are alone don't enjoy my music – it makes them terribly uncomfortable." That many of his critics believed the singer would greatly benefit from flopping down in front of a TV set himself on the odd occasion remained an argument for another day.

A natural form of closure to four years of self-exploration, *Secrets Of The Beehive* proved to be Sylvian's last solo album for twelve years. "I knew the path I'd been pursuing since *Brilliant Trees* had been exhausted. It had come to a conclusion of some kind or another. I knew I had to do the next thing." Fulfilling a promise he made as far back as 1983, the "next thing" he decided to do was take the music on the road.

15

Preaching To The Converted

With *Secrets Of The Beehive,* David Sylvian largely realised his long-time desire to create a sense of jarring unease in the most opulent of musical surroundings. However, if the album represented a triumph of sorts for its creator, its performance in the charts was sorely lacking. In fact, the LP barely grazed the UK Top 40, achieving only a paltry No 37 on the charts in November, 1987. Such a poor showing was undoubtedly the result of the singer's increasingly selective appeal within the pop market.

There was a clear argument, of course, to suggest that the music Sylvian now created was nothing to do with pop at all, and any level of commercial success he attained might be more realistically compared with the record sales of avant-garde artists like Brian Eno and Harold Budd. Yet, he still remained wary about siding with any particular cause. "If you think of the avant-garde as the bottom of the ladder and pop as the top, then I tend to work somewhere in the middle," he said. "[In fact], I don't think I could [ever] work completely in the avant-garde, because most of them are extremely proficient musicians, and I'm not." Even though his actions sometimes suggested otherwise, he remained ever loyal to the concept – if not the execution – of the pop myth. "I hope I've never given the impression that I'm trying to remove myself from pop music. Because I'm not. I love it . . . I think there's great value in popular music. Sometimes I want to work in that field, and sometimes I want to explore something a little more abstract. It's just a choice."

Truthfully, Sylvian circa 1987 was neither avant-garde or pop. Instead, he was becoming that most curious of cultural phenomena: a cult. In many ways, it had been a seamless transition. By hermetically sealing Japan at the height of their fame in 1982, he'd managed to escape the ignoble decline most pop performers are subjected to when a sea change occurs in musical tastes. Equally, by his refusal to align himself with the fringe elements that orbited the musical mainstream, he avoided disappearing into the nebulous regions of "muso territory". What he had done, however, was carve his own particular niche – that of the romantic pop outsider. The world-weary voice, darkly introspective lyrics and sorrowful, yet spiritually uplifting music all conspired to present Sylvian as a man on the outskirts of society, captivated by what he sees, but unable (or unwilling) to join in all the same. "A lot of my songs," he once conceded, "have to do with a desire for acceptance, a desire to belong, whilst at the same time, there's always this sense of isolation, of not being able to belong. The ideal society can exist, but it has to be based on universal laws. In some ways, that's why I feel my isolation. I'm an anti-social person because I can't respond to the society I live in."

In literature, this notion of 'outsiderdom' was nothing particularly new. The theme of the artist struggling to "conform to the patterns of everyday existence" had been a central tenet of the 19th/20th Century German Romantic movement. Writers such as Goethe, Hesse and Mann all created characters who forever remained on the periphery of life – longing for assimilation, but due to some schism of personality, finding themselves rejecting the invitation when it came. Novelists as diverse as Hemmingway, Camus, Lawrence and Tevis also added much to the form. French author/playwright Jean-Paul Sartre even based his philosophy of existentialism around such notions of psychological dislocation.

Yet, the concept of the outsider wasn't just confined to literature. It was also intrinsic to the appeal of rock'n'roll.

Since the Sixties, performers such as The Who's Pete Townshend, The Doors' Jim Morrison and David Bowie had all made great capital from the idea of emotional and societal disaffection. Bowie had even taken it as far as becoming an alien for a while. However, what Sylvian brought that was new to the party was a straddling of both worlds. As a poet, he worked well, his self-doubt and introspection never too obtuse or distant to alienate his audience. And as a songwriter, his compositions – while presenting a challenge – were still accessible enough to inspire both joy and sorrow in the listener. In short, to his fans David Sylvian represented an eloquent fusion of old-fashioned romantic and new-age seer, or as one writer would have it, "an existential tour guide for the Eighties jet-set". Whether by accident or design, it remained an alluring image. And one he was about to put to the test.

As the world and his wife knew only too well, Sylvian had never been fond of touring. Even at the height of his obsession with rock'n'roll imagery in the late Seventies, the idea of hitting the road remained more a chore than a treat. The problem, in his mind, was a lack of enthusiasm towards live performance. "When I'm performing, I feel I'm just too casual," he said in 1982. "I don't get nervous. I just get up there and do it. I don't feel like I'm giving that much a lot of the time, and I feel I ought to be. There's only one or two songs that I'll actually get into . . . it's a weird state of affairs. The audience is misguided into believing that I'm giving them something I guess." Such was his distaste for the live medium, that when he branched out as a solo artist in 1983, Sylvian made a solemn promise not to tour until he had three albums worth of material under his belt. While some took the decision to be indicative of a desire not to rely on old Japan songs to formulate a set, it was perhaps more to do with avoiding all gigs for the foreseeable future.

Nonetheless, soon after *Secrets Of The Beehive* hit the shops, Sylvian kept to his word and announced dates for a world tour, starting in the North American city of Minneapolis on March 23, 1988. Inevitably, rumours began to circulate regarding the line-up of musicians that would accompany him on the jaunt – the fans' wish list comprised of names like Mick Karn, Robert Fripp, Ryuichi Sakamoto and Holger Czukay. Realistically, however, such a dream team was never on the cards. Fripp, Sakamoto and Czukay all had busy solo careers (and would cost too much money), and Karn was eagerly pursuing his own muse. Still, when Sylvian's backing group for the tour were confirmed, the musical pedigree involved was no less thrilling.

Reprising their roles in Japan, Steve Jansen and Richard Barbieri came on board to back Sylvian on drums and keyboards respectively. Taking on bass and additional percussion duties was The Penguin Cafe Orchestra's Ian Maidman, who worked with David on *Gone To Earth.* All brass parts were to be handled by Mark Isham, a mainstay of the Sylvian camp since *Brilliant Trees.* And on guitar came recent *. . . Beehive* recruit David Torn. The only new face was that of additional guitarist/keyboard player Robby Aceto, a New York born experimental composer, who besides scoring for both ballet and theatre productions, fronted his own band, the intriguing Red Letter. Though all the musicians (bar Aceto) had contributed at various times to Sylvian's records, for many of them it would be the first time they had actually met face to face. "It was good casting, I think, on David's part," recalled Ian Maidman. "Though I wasn't aware of David Torn, I sort of knew Mark Isham. Robby Aceto was a complete wild card. I think he was a recommendation from Torn. Ultimately, we were all there to do justice to the music." Trumpeter Mark Isham confirmed Maidman's analysis: "I think David put together a very clever band . . . it contained a lot of disparate elements, but they were all well-balanced. That would make for a very good show."

Though rehearsals for the tour – now officially titled *In Praise Of Shamans* – were due to begin at Nomis Studios in the first week of March, 1988, a last minute switch of location saw the band end up at John Henry's studio complex in North London's Caledonian Road. "Quite scuzzy," remembered Maidman, "but it's a bit of an institution." Here, songs were put through their paces, while lighting and production design were also developed and tested. By mid-March, everything was in place.

Unfortunately, the tour got off to a rocky start before a note was even played, with the plane scheduled to take the group from Gatwick Airport to the USA not bothering to turn up. The rescheduled flight from Heathrow fared little better, with a three hour delay incurred before take-off due to engine trouble. Many of Sylvian's entourage were well used to such hiccups. "The whole thing with planes and delays becomes a kind of blur," recalled Ian Maidman, himself a veteran of several Joan Armatrading tours. "You just kind of go where you're put. It's like [you're] in the flight-case, pushed around, and then wheeled out for the gig!" After several false starts, the group finally found themselves in Minneapolis, where pre-tour rehearsals continued at the site of their first concert, The Guthrie Theatre.

On March 23, 1988, Sylvian finally returned to the stage after an absence of nearly six years. His new show was nothing if not ambitious. On the production side, the performers were surrounded by a solid mesh of honeycomb prints, a direct nod to the imagery of *Secrets Of The Beehive* – itself inspired by the work of painter Joseph Beuys. Adding to the intoxicating feel of this nest-like backdrop were a series of hexagonal reliefs, suspended from wires in the ceiling, and presumably there to add extra depth and colour. As far as lighting was concerned, tastefulness reigned. Unlike Japan's latter days where neon and blue blazed from the stage, this time musicians were soaked in red, orange and green hues, giving things a sedate, serious feel. And then there was Sylvian himself: a surprisingly slight and anonymous figure, with his newly grown long hair bunched into a dishevelled ponytail. Dressed in what looked like an Oxfam cardigan, he spent most of the concert obscured from view behind a bank of industrial keyboards, or jumbo-sized acoustic guitars, straying only briefly to centre-stage as and when the vocals required it. Rock'n'roll this was not.

In such deliberately composed, low-key surroundings, there was little to do but concentrate on the music itself. Thankfully, it didn't disappoint. Playing a selection of material from all three solo albums plus various EPs, the band juggled complex instrumentals like 'Incantation', 'Ancient Evening' and 'Steel Cathedrals' alongside more accessible songs such as 'The Ink In The Well' and 'When Poets Dreamed Of Angels'. Wherever possible, Sylvian allowed the music to be extended or improvised – giving new shape to previously formulaic pieces, while also highlighting the skills of the musicians on stage. For some though, David's omission to perform some of his better loved songs proved an irritation: 'Laughter And Forgetting', 'Red Guitar' and the seminal 'Forbidden Colours' were all conspicuous by their absence. Still, as first gigs went, it made for an impressive (if different) return.

From Minneapolis, the *In Praise Of Shamans* tour wound its way into Chicago, before veering sharp right towards Canada, and two nights at Toronto's Massey Hall on 25/26 March. After a well received show at Montreal's St. Denis Theatre, the group found themselves back in the States for a date at Washington's Lisner Auditorium. On April 1, the Sylvian entourage ventured onwards to New York for a prestigious date at the city's Town Hall. In the audience that night was one of America's more distinguished songwriters, Suzanne Vega. "[I'd] spent quite a few months listening to his music," Vega recalled, ". . . mostly because of Anton Sanko . . . the co-producer of my third album, and my keyboard player at the time. [He] was a major fan, with an unusual perspective on Sylvian."

Sanko, who besides working with Vega has also found considerable success in scoring films (as well as collaborating with New York's greatest living poet, Jim Carroll), confirmed Suzanne's remarks: "*Secrets Of The Beehive* is one of the greatest records ever made. The first time I heard it, I couldn't take it off. [Usually], I'm not that kind of obsessive listener, but I played it over and over again. I just wanted to know how he did it. I was trying to get in between the music – just trying to understand it. That hadn't happened to me since The Beatles." For Sanko, it was Sylvian's use of mood and texture that mattered most. "When I think of Sylvian, it's not as a specific songwriter, lyricist or singer, [but] more as an artist. It's the way he contextualises his ideas . . . the whole environment he places himself in that to me is so exciting, idiomatic and iconoclastic."

After the warm reception accorded them in New York, the group fulfilled further obligations in Boston, San Diego and Los Angeles before finishing the Stateside leg of the tour at Berkeley's Zellerbach Hall on April 6. Sylvian was both surprised and delighted by the positive response towards his music from American audiences. Never having cracked the country sales-wise with his former group, the fact that his fan base extended so far – and so healthily, if attendances were anything to go by – boded well for future excursions. Interestingly, David's cult status in the US market had been sealed only a year before his visit, when his image was used by artist Jon J Muth in the DC comic book series *Moonshadow*. Written by mainstay of the comics industry J M Matteis, *Moonshadow* concerned a young man's metaphysical voyage into adulthood, with Sylvian's features representing the book's main character as a man. If nothing else, it proved the singer's influence turned up in the most unlikely of places.

The tour's next stop was Japan, the sight of Sylvian's last stand with his former group, and where he still commanded the profile of a pop-star. The band were due to perform six dates in all, beginning with appearances at Tokyo's Kanihoken Hall and Nakano Sun Plaza between April 11 and 14, before moving to Osaka's Archaic Hall on April 15. After this, they would return to Tokyo for two further concerts, culminating with a final engagement at the Nakona Sun Plaza on April 17. Suffice to say, tickets for all concerts were sold out well in advance, with touts asking upwards of 15,000 Yen (approximately £70 at the time) for a half-decent view. Though David's band were aware of the following he commanded in the Far East, the age of some of the fans still surprised them: "In America," said Ian Maidman, "the audience was old – not ancient – but older, whereas in Japan there were lots of kids, mainly teenage girls. The gigs were just so packed out."

By the Japanese dates, the group were well into their stride, with certain songs coming to the fore as real show-stoppers. 'Let The Happiness In', 'Weathered Wall' and 'Brilliant Trees' all took on a life of their own within the concert hall, their hymnal qualities enhanced by the subtle lighting and intimate production design. *Gone To Earth*'s 'Riverman' was another song that shone like a beacon live. Always a funky little track, its sly combination of pulsing bass guitar and hypnotic percussion provided both band and audience a rare opportunity to step away from the show's more austere elements and let their hair down a bit. The previously lack-lustre 'Taking The Veil' also benefited from its transition from LP to stage. Slower and more sedate than the original recording, '. . . Veil' now gave Sylvian a grand opportunity to flex his vocal cords, as well as allowing guitarist David Torn to let rip with a fierce Fripp inflected solo.

By all accounts, Torn was largely responsible for keeping spirits high on the tour, mainly due to his keen sense of humour. "Torn's a natural comedian," confirmed Ian Maidman. "He just makes you laugh at the most stupid things. He's a joker with a really lateral mind. [At one point] he'd taken to describing himself as an octagonal tuna fish. Why? I don't know . . . but it lightened things up a lot!" Mark Isham, while a little more cautious with his words, confirmed Torn's propensity for the odd joke or two: "Tour joker? I don't know about 'tour joker' . . . let's just say he's got an outlandish sense of humour . . ."

The other member of Sylvian's touring party to establish a flamboyant reputation throughout was guitarist/keyboard player Robby Aceto. "Robby was great fun," said Maidman. "He had a nickname – The Monster – but I can't for the life of me remember why. (Anyway), Robby always wore black, but he had a turnaround halfway through the tour. One morning, he just appeared in this white pin-stripe suit. He looked . . . amazing. He said he wasn't going to be the monster anymore – he'd grown tired of being dark . . ."

Haute couture aside, Japan saw some of the most technically accomplished shows of the tour, with several dates recorded for a proposed live album. But just like the long-form Sylvian video documentary completed by cinematographer Nigel Grierson in 1987, the concert tapes never officially saw the light of day. Reaction from the crowd to David's unusual choice of material may have been a factor on this shelved release: "In Japan," Sylvian confirmed to *Record Collector*'s Mark Prendergast, "I remember the audiences were less emotional, less expressive and possibly bewildered by the choice of material and its presentation. The performances were quite intense . . . we chose to improvise on the longer pieces, the heavyweight stuff like 'Steel Cathedrals' and 'Words With The Shaman', for example." However, some bootleg copies of the band's Tokyo shows did escape the net, continuing to circulate at extortionate prices even to this day.

With Japan behind them, the Sylvian entourage – who aside from band and crew, comprised David's manager Richard Chadwick and girlfriend Yuka Fujii – journeyed onwards to Europe, with dates in Italy, Germany, Holland, France and Belgium. For Sylvian, the Italian leg of the tour proved particularly enjoyable, offering him the additional benefit of being able to soak up some of that Mediterranean spring sunshine. Nonetheless, after some notable gigs in Bari, Rome (where the group did a three day stint on Italian TV show *DOC*), and Milan, the singer's health gave out while performing the song 'Orpheus' at Turin's Teatro Colosseo on May 11.

After abandoning the show in search of a doctor, he was subsequently diagnosed with a combination of upset stomach and general fatigue. The next day was spent in bed, catching up on lost sleep. "I'm afraid I'm not a very healthy person," David later offered. "My worst habit – well I'd say it's smoking. As for food, I can survive on very little. After all, I'm a useless cook!"

The tour's tight schedule was certainly a factor of Sylvian's temporary brush with ill-health. "I actually got quite spaced out myself on that tour," said Ian Maidman, by way of explanation. "The schedule, the music . . . the whole package." However, the bassist remained unsure as to whether it affected Sylvian's enjoyment of the remaining dates. "I was having such a good time myself I wasn't as aware of it as I might have been. Maybe he was disappointed . . . I don't know. Everybody has bad nights . . . he had a few. I certainly did."

Medicine of a sort arrived for Sylvian when his old friend Holger Czukay attended one of the band's gigs in Cologne, Germany. By all accounts, it was an eccentric visit. "He came on the tour bus one day," said Maidman, "with a video tape of the Pope giving mass to ten thousand people. He'd actually added music to it – a soundtrack – lounge jazz, I seem to remember. He's a very funny man . . . funny ha ha . . . mad professor type." The soundtrack Ian referred to actually made up part of the album *Rome Remains Rome*, with snippets of Pope John Paul II's said mass appearing on the track 'Blessed Easter'. Though Czukay undoubtedly meant little by it, the Pope's first appearance on a rock record stirred up some controversy at the time.

After fulfilling European obligations, the band finally arrived in England on May 28, for the first of three highly anticipated shows at London's Hammersmith Odeon. In many ways, the performance represented an opportunity to assess how far Sylvian's faithful had come since their last meeting with him in 1982. Whereas before, his audience was largely comprised of immaculately turned out teenagers, resplendent in frilly shirts and carefully applied make-up, the crowd that attended

Hammersmith that night in May, 1988 were older, wiser and genuinely appreciative of the music. No screams, no tears, just hushed silence and polite applause when required. Truthfully, the concert marked the passing of an era, a bitter-sweet reminder of the youthful innocence that inspired the new romantic movement.

That said, Sylvian and the band's performance was largely excellent. Particular highlights included a thrilling take on 'Boy With The Gun' (sadly topical at the time due to the Hungerford massacre), an optimistic reading of 'Orpheus', a jaunty run-through of Mark Isham's 'Grand Parade' and a sublime rendition of 'Before The Bullfight'. That the singer managed only three or four sentences to the audience the entire night was to most a minor quibble. "He takes his work seriously," said Mark Isham of Sylvian's at times solemn demeanour. "He takes educating himself seriously, his whole aesthetic experience seriously. He's not just out to be a rock'n'roller." Ian Maidman concurred: "There's a very serious side to him, but conversely there's a very light side to him. I don't think the two things are mutually exclusive. When it comes to getting on the bus in the morning he's just the same as everyone else. However," Maidman concluded, "he's not as serious as people think."

After the Hammersmith shows, the band took on 12 more dates throughout Great Britain, including notable stop-offs in Manchester (June 3), Portsmouth (June 7), Poole (June 10) and Newcastle (June 14), before the tour finally ground to a halt at Edinburgh's Playhouse Theatre on June 15, 1988. Aside from the hiccup in Turin, Sylvian had completed 80 dates in just under four months. For the musicians involved, the overall reaction had been immensely gratifying. "To me," said Mark Isham, "it was about seeing music of that sophistication – not traditionally commercial music – being taken around the world, and receiving such a glowing response. It was just very gratifying. You have to admire David for creating such a thing."

That the shows had been atmospheric, mood-enhancing

affairs was beyond doubt. Yet, many fans and critics had alluded to an almost "otherworldly" quality to the music at times. It was a view the band were aware of. "I think the reason we all came together," said Isham, "was [that] we had an interest in communicating something special in the music, and that does start to rub shoulders with the notion of spirituality. It just depends on how you define that notion . . ." Ian Maidman agreed: "I don't think it was ever explicitly discussed – it certainly wasn't calculated – but even the name of the tour, *In Praise Of Shamans* . . . [I think] David chose individuals that were going to be sensitive to those kind of ideas. I did feel it was something Shamanistic we were going for. We live in a time," he continued, "when much of that quality of life has deserted us . . . it's leaked away. What the music was about, maybe, was trying to raise those spirits . . . trying to evoke something. That (Shamanistic) metaphor was very powerful for me. It kind of shook up my logical frame of mind."

For many of the musicians, the tour marked the last time they actually worked with Sylvian. However, they remain glowing in their assessment of his abilities. Mark Isham (who has since gone on to forge a career as one of Hollywood's most in-demand film soundtrack composers) offered the following: "David's absolutely charming, very bright. He has a vision that bypasses genres, the mainstream. He has an ability to ride on top of all of that." Ian Maidman (now a producer, and a prominent face on the British jazz scene) was equally kind: "He's truthful, inspired . . . driven. Driven from an honest place. You can't say that for many people in the pop industry. I think life is very paradoxical, and David embraces that. Of course, that [philosophy] has attendant problems, but he never runs away from that. He's an edge-walker, always slightly ahead . . . always looking for something." Guitarist David Torn compared David to Miles Davis: "I think Sylvian's got . . . Miles Davis' sense for assembling really interesting, even provocative, constellations of musicians . . . he really knows how to get the best playing out of them."

Despite *Secrets Of The Beehive*'s less than stellar performance in the charts, *In Praise Of Shamans* conclusively proved that Sylvian could still pack them in at the box-office. However, whether he'd actually gained any pleasure from the tour itself was another thing. For instance, when asked in 1988 if he'd enjoyed it, the most positive response he could muster was "sort of". By 1990, his assessment of the experience had grown somewhat kinder: "I really enjoyed that tour . . . it was worth it." Yet, when asked for an opinion of the dates in 1994, the milk had well and truly soured: "*In Praise Of Shamans* was a mess," he told journalist Craig Peacock. "I was a mess at the time. The whole entourage was beset by problems."

That Sylvian and his manager Richard Chadwick had encountered difficulties behind the scenes throughout the tour was no secret. In fact, one story has it that the singer went into an emotional meltdown outside an (unnamed) American hotel due to unforeseen administrative *difficulties*. Whatever the truth or level of enjoyment (and it seems to change from year to year), the dates did at least have the effect of re-establishing Sylvian's profile at a critical juncture in his career. Yet, in typically obstinate fashion, he chose once again to cut and run.

16

Little Epiphanies

In the spring of 1988, it had been difficult to get away from David Sylvian. Besides the *In Praise Of Shamans* tour, he also had two new records in the shops. The first of these was the single 'Orpheus', lifted from *Secrets Of The Beehive* by Virgin Records to mark his return to the road. Sadly, despite the song's undoubted quality – and blanket rotation of its accompanying video on both *MTV* and *VH-1* – it failed to make the charts. The public were a little more forthcoming, however, towards the LP *Plight And Premonition,* his latest collaboration with Holger Czukay. Although the album was an all-instrumental affair, it still managed a brief appearance at No 71 in the UK charts on April 2, 1988. Given the difficulties Sylvian and Czukay encountered just trying to get the album released, even this most modest of chart placings could be seen as a vindication of sorts.

Things had started well enough, with Holger inviting David to Can Studios in Cologne, Germany in the winter of 1986, to contribute to his forthcoming album, *Rome Remains Rome*: "He came to the studio, which is a very moody place," recalled Czukay. "You could say it resembles a live environment with recording facilities. It's huge – about 200 square metres, 6 metres high – it was an old cinema. It has different types of landscapes." After Sylvian had laid down a vocal on one of Holger's songs, the pair began playing around with some new musical ideas: "David wanted to get out of just singing," said Czukay. "He wanted to create some environmental music. We understood this about each other very well." What started as a rough studio jam soon became something more involved, with Czukay calling in friend/journalist Karl Lippergaus and former Can drummer Jaki Liebezeit for added inspiration: "I asked Jaki to come over," confirmed Holger. "He's a very good person to just listen . . . to fit into something without killing the music."

Within three days, the quartet had completed two separate pieces, which Sylvian duly christened 'Plight' and 'Premonition': "The titles have a double meaning," said Czukay. "It gives the attitude of what the music means to us." Beautifully realised, each composition conveyed both a sinister and tranquil quality, the music drifting along in complex spirals rather than traditional chord patterns: "For David," recalled Holger, "*Plight And Premonition* was one of the biggest surprises of his life. The way we produced it together was something he didn't expect at all." The singer readily agreed: "It was quite new for me to work in that manner. You go into the studio with no preconceived ideas and you just improvise material onto tape, and then work with that . . . develop that composition, and put some kind of shape [to it] at a later stage." To Sylvian, much of the appeal of working with Czukay was the scant regard he had for established recording techniques: "Holger works in a technically wrong way – that's what makes it so exciting . . . people learn from Holger. [He] breaks the rules."

Unfortunately, the problems began for the duo when they approached their respective record companies with a view to releasing the improvisation. Due to the nature of their contracts (they were both signed as solo artists), any collaborative release would be legally difficult to administrate. Until a suitable compromise could be found, the tapes would remain in the vaults. The dilemma was eventually solved with the advent of Virgin Records' new instrumental off-shoot, Venture Records. Under this subsidiary label, *Plight And Premonition* could be released without legal ramifications to either party. In short, three days work in the studio had taken over seventeen months to see the light of day.

Still, the experience didn't seem to put Sylvian and Czukay off. After a four month break following the *In Praise Of Shamans* tour, David returned to Cologne in December 1988 to begin work with the German composer on two new instrumental pieces, 'Flux' and 'Mutability'. This time, the duo extended their musical line-up to include ex-Can guitarist (and former Czukay student) Michael Karoli, Japanese vocalist Michi, and Karlheinz Stockhausen's son, Markus, on flugelhorn. "He's a great trumpeter," confirmed Holger. "David already knew of his qualities. Markus immediately fitted in with what David was looking for. He's a little like Mark Isham." Can's Jaki Leibezeit also returned to the fold to handle both percussion and African flute.

As usual, both Sylvian and Czukay made no attempt to "write a song", preferring instead to just play with ideas, as and when they came. "[The creation of] *Flux And Mutability* was very interesting, something special," recalled Czukay. "It came out of (tape samples of) Korean words and orchestration. I was looking for something that would fit into David's guitar – he was playing so much guitar at that point – and somehow I started to accompany him with these foreign (Korean) words. Yet, when we listened back to the tracks, we saw we didn't need the words, so we took them out completely and left David's guitar parts in." Whilst *Mutability* literally composed itself (the piece took only a day to complete), *Flux*'s birth proved a little more fraught, with David insisting on reworking the composition time and time again to capture a more spacious feel. After much wrangling (and numerous guitar and flugelhorn overdubs courtesy of Michael Karoli and Markus Stockhausen) Sylvian was finally content. "*Flux* conveyed more of David's intentions," said Holger. "It reflects his stronger attitudes. It's sort of a spiritual music. You know, it's not often you find people like him . . ."

The results of the Cologne sessions were subtly impressive,

with *Flux*'s ethnic rhythms, razor-like guitars and breathtaking flugelhorn excursions recalling the same desert plains present on Sylvian's 1985 effort *Words With The Shaman. Mutability*, on the other hand, was a far more serene piece, with a circular, almost hallucinogenic feel to it. Of the two, its pastoral quality remained, perhaps, the more persuasive. However, when released (with a striking cover design by Yuka Fujii) in September, 1989, *Flux And Mutability* divided the critics. While US jazz magazine *The Wire* described the album as a "sound poem", the British rock press seemed a little less sure of the LP's charms. "This is a low-key affair," reasoned *Q*'s Richard Scott, "sleepy even. Like last year's *Plight And Premonition*, these two 'ambient' instrumentals drone along pleasantly/pointlessly in a doomy, gloomy sort of way. Both [Sylvian and Czukay] seem to have lost their way of late, especially if you remember . . . *Brilliant Trees* and the remarkable *On The Way To The Peak Of Normal* and *Movies*. Hear one of those instead."

While it remained debatable as to whether Sylvian and Czukay had lost their way, the release of two similarly themed instrumental albums within the space of a year did seem to try the patience of fans. Whereas *Plight And Premonition* had at least nudged the charts at No 71, *Flux And Mutability* sank without noticeable trace. Perhaps it was the 'New Age' aura surrounding the LP that served to alienate the public. "It's a stereotype which is convenient for the record industry," David told *The Sunday Times*' Robert Sandall. "What they're trying to say is, 'This is the modern equivalent of easy listening. Buy this and it won't offend you'. It's laziness. [New Age] is one of the four different racks that chain stores put my work in, hoping somebody will recognise me." What Sylvian's record company specifically wanted, of course, was a hit – something their ever more irascible signing hadn't provided them with for over four years. It came as something of a surprise then, when Virgin announced news of a forthcoming single – allegedly 'in the pop vein' – from the singer.

Nevertheless, if anyone had built up hopes of David Sylvian returning to the charts on the back of a pleasant, inoffensive pop-like ditty, they were duly crushed when the single was actually released in October, 1989. Entitled 'Pop Song', it was the most biting and acerbic thing Sylvian had yet committed to plastic. The musical equivalent of a nervous collapse, 'Pop Song's melody – and the term is used loosely – meandered like a drunken sailor, its clattering drum pattern (lovingly provided by Steve Jansen) and jarring, quarter-tone synth flourishes creating a decidedly off-kilter effect on the ear. The song's lyrics were equally abrasive, with the singer simultaneously pouring acid on love, rampant consumerism and the inanities of factory work: "We'd listen to the radio," he gently sang, "it was loud and it irritated me so . . ." One could literally smell the sarcasm on his breath. Disturbing, cacophonous and at times, downright bloody marvellous, 'Pop Song' stood about as much chance of entering the UK Top Thirty as Madonna did of staying out of it. Suffice to say, it didn't trouble the charts.

Azimuth pianist John Taylor, who had last worked with David on *Gone To Earth*'s musical centre-piece 'Laughter And Forgetting' was called in (along with computer programmer Stuart Bruce) to help Sylvian realise the discordant elements of the song. "He contacted me, and we recorded it one Sunday afternoon," recalled Taylor. " 'Pop Song' was composed already, it was just a question of improvising as much as David wanted, and he would choose and arrange from there. I was very aware that he knew what he wanted from it." Taylor also appeared on the B-side of the single, adding acoustic piano to the three minute instrumental oddity 'A Brief Conversation Ending In Divorce'. The last track featured was the musical score Sylvian had written for Gaby Agis' 1987 ballet *The Stigma Of Childhood (Kin)*.

If 'Pop Song' represented a two-fingered salute from Sylvian to his record company for trying to squeeze a hit out of him (and there is much to suggest such an interpretation), then

Virgin didn't seem particularly offended by the gesture. In fact, their next move positively honoured the singer. In December, 1989, an ornately designed 5 CD box set, re-packaging all of Sylvian's work since leaving Japan was issued to stores. The collection, entitled *Weatherbox*, included *Brilliant Trees, Gone To Earth, Secrets Of The Beehive* as well as a first time CD release of *Alchemy – An Index Of Possibilities* (including *Words With The Shaman*). The score for *The Stigma Of Childhood (Kin)* and the recent instrumental piece *A Brief Conversation Ending In Divorce* were also present. With the production of *Weatherbox* limited to only 30,000 copies, it has subsequently become a highly desirable (and definitive) piece of Sylvian-related ephemera.

The artist responsible for *Weatherbox*'s baroque design was long-time Sylvian collaborator Russell Mills. Their association had actually begun as far back as 1984, when one of Mills' paintings was used for the cover of the Japan retrospective, *Exorcising Ghosts.* A dark and expressive piece, recalling the rusty hues present in Frank 'Head Of Jym II' Auerbach's work, the canvas so impressed David that he subsequently bought it. Mills' next project for Sylvian was the cover sleeve for his 1986 LP *Gone To Earth.* This time Russell used the zodiacal sign for Taurus as his painting's central motif, the image echoing the Flamenco overtones of the track 'Before The Bullfight'. Duly smitten with Mills' work, Sylvian again purchased the original painting for his private collection. It now hangs in the offices of David's management company, Opium Arts.

The duo's next collaboration, in 1988, was the production design for the *In Praise Of Shamans* tour. Taking his inspiration from the title of Sylvian's most recent album, *Secrets Of The Beehive,* Mills provided a strange, honeycomb-like backdrop for the shows, which actually seemed to have the effect of encasing the musicians on stage. He was also responsible for . . . *Shamans*' accompanying tour programme, a clever combination of greaseproof paper (on which a brief Sylvian biog was printed), band information and a curious fold-out section that made much of the show's beehive theme. Obviously on a roll, the artist additionally found time to illustrate the front cover of *Trophies*, a slim, but beautifully presented, book collecting David's lyrics and poems from 1982's 'Ghosts' to 1987's 'Waterfront'.

Aside from his work with Sylvian, Mills also designed album covers for the likes of Brian Eno, Harold Budd and Talking Heads' David Byrne, his artwork for Budd's 1986 LP *Lovely Thunder* particularly effective. In addition to these efforts, Russell's images were used as front cover illustrations for novels by Milan Kundera (*The Unbearable Lightness Of Being*) and Samuel Beckett (*Murphy*). But for many, Mills' work on Sylvian's *Weatherbox* was rated as amongst his best yet. Looking more like a bookcase than a CD set, the rusty yellow hues of the outer box design and alchemical symbols that encased each disc (Earth, Water, Trees, Stone and Light) created a perfect accompaniment for the music inside.

The partnership was officially sealed when Sylvian and Mills announced their intention at the start of 1990 to collaborate on a joint project based at the Temporary Museum on Tokyo's Shinagawa Bay. The presentation, christened *Ember Glance: The Permanence Of Memory*, was to be a celebration of memory in all its forms, ("Personal, social, historical, and the collective unconscious" as Sylvian put it) and was to utilise light, photography, sculpture and music to make its point. In addition to Sylvian and Mills, English painter Adam Lowe was also on hand to provide artwork for the exhibition, which would be lit by Japanese designer Haruki Kaito.

Ember Glance: The Permanence Of Memory eventually opened to the public in September, 1990, as part of the Tokyo Creative '90 art festival. Best described as a "gallery installation", the exhibition was a sprawling work barely contained by the building that housed it. Along with various sculptures and wooden boxes hung at random points from the warehouse's high ceilings, the presentation also used sundry objects such as bone shards, mirrors, coins and broken violins to invoke a sense of recollection in observers. The final area of the array housed a partitioned wall, though what it actually represented was anyone's guess. To accompany the myriad images on display were two eerie, Eastern inflected, instrumental pieces composed especially for the occasion by David – 'The Beekeeper's Apprentice' and 'Epiphany'.

For Sylvian, the creation of such an elaborate combination of light, image and sound had been a real challenge. "(It was) a new experience for me, and something I enjoyed enormously. We could use the space in any way we wanted to. There was a large degree of sponsorship involved because it was part of an art festival, so we managed to conjure up something that was quite extraordinary." Nonetheless, because the installation was site-specific, there was little chance of it being shown elsewhere. In fact, when *Ember Glance: The Permanence Of Memory* finished its allotted run in Tokyo, many of the set pieces were subsequently destroyed. Still, the installation was comprehensively photographed before being dismantled, with the images captured making up a 95-page booklet. This memento – along with the instrumental music Sylvian composed for the project – was duly released in December 1991 as a limited edition (20,000) book/CD box set. *Q* magazine's Martin Aston summed up much of its appeal: "Mills illustrates his full-colour coffee-tableish tome with photo-montages of the installation, its composite elements (gauze veils, mirrors, 'found' objects, landscape images, lightboxes) amid various shades of expressionist art. Sylvian's instrumental soundtrack . . . is another of his lengthy (32 minutes) ambient watercolours . . . contributing sombre tones of Eastern promise."

An ambitious and well-reviewed enterprise, *Ember Glance* allowed Sylvian a brief respite from the pressures of working as a solo artist. By its temporary nature, it also represented no threat to any long-term musical plans he may have had. Yet, its wilful blending of sound and colour did raise another question: specifically, when he might try his hand at composing film soundtracks. "I'm waiting patiently for the right film," David offered, "but the proper screenplay hasn't presented itself. I've been offered some strange horror movies, and things that make me wonder why they wanted my music for those projects." Strangely enough, the singer was about to become involved in writing the soundtrack for a horror movie of sorts – its title, *Rain Tree Crow.*

17

Old Sins Cast Long Shadows

David Sylvian's association with *Ember Glance: The Permanence Of Memory* took up much of his public profile throughout late 1989/1990. Yet, behind the scenes, a much more intriguing project was getting underway – expressly, the reformation of Japan. As far back as April 1989, Sylvian had been in meetings with his former colleagues regarding the possibility of a "band improvisation". However, things had run less than smoothly at first. "[David] said, 'I may not have mentioned it, but if this does happen, it has to go out under my name'," Jansen told *Music Technology*'s Tim Goodyer. "So we backed off immediately – 'Bye, see you next year . . .' "

The ice began to melt in earnest in the summer of 1989, when Sylvian entered into negotiations with Mick Karn. Revising his previous stance, the singer put forward the idea of the group entering a studio with no preconceived musical ideas or set time limit. They would simply jam together and see what came out. To sweeten the pill, any resulting songs would be credited as co-writes, and more importantly, "politics" would be kept to a minimum. Impressed with the package, Karn spoke with Jansen and Barbieri on their return from Italy (the duo were touring with ex-Yellow Magic Orchestra member Yukihiro Takahashi at the time) and a cautious agreement was struck.

With the benefit of hindsight, the proposed alliance was odd, to say the least. Though Sylvian's career was hardly in the ascendant money-wise, he had established a solid body of work that allowed him a certain degree of artistic latitude. His collaborations with Holger Czukay and Russell Mills gave him access to both an 'ambient' and art-related audience, and another solo album would surely keep the financial wolf from the door. Yet, the concept of working with a band again seemed to intrigue him. "I began to think that the idea of a group composition would be a good thing to put myself through. I needed to work with people I knew very well, and who I thought would also benefit from the experience . . . so it was an obvious choice to turn to Mick, Steve and Rich."

For Karn, Jansen and Barbieri, the prospect of a reformed Japan may have been financially more compelling. After all, by their own admission, their post 1982 projects had been less than enthusiastically received in sales terms. Nonetheless, there were other compensations. As session musicians, they were much in demand, with Karn's rubbery bass playing currying particular favour. Before reuniting with Sylvian, he contributed to several tracks on Kate Bush's *Sensual World*, among others. Jansen and Barbieri were similarly engaged, not only with their Dolphin Brothers project, but also as part of Yukihiro Takahashi's touring band. A reunion, while fiscally sound (and Virgin's offer was very attractive), wasn't crucial to anyone's career prospects. Suffice to say, it went ahead anyway.

The quartet (neither former Japan guitarist Rob Dean nor Masami Tsuchiya were invited to join the project) began their improvisations at Studio Miraval, in La Val, France in September, 1989. The reason for picking Miraval was twofold: Sylvian had enjoyed its sedate atmosphere while recording *Secrets Of The Beehive*, and perhaps more importantly, it was cheap. In fact, Miraval's rates were "about £800 a day", saving the band at least £500 in comparison to English studio charges. After laying down bed tracks, the musicians moved onto Condulmer and Zerman di Mogilano Studios in Italy, before returning to London for a quick stint at Fulham's Marcus Studios. From there, the group ventured to Air Studios in Central London, before moving on yet again to the Tears For Fears owned Wool

Hall in Bath. It was here the recording budget ran out, and problems began in earnest.

From the onset of the project, Sylvian had been emphatic that though Japan had effectively re-formed, their old name was not to be used for the purposes of marketing new product. "I actually put it in the contract for the project that nobody is ever allowed to apply the name Japan to it," he said. "With so many bands re-forming for cynical reasons, I just didn't want it stated as such." However, after seven months, numerous locations and much money spent in various studios, the group found themselves in the unenviable position of having to return to Virgin Records for an extension on their budget. Virgin – understandably irked by Sylvian's refusal to capitalise on former glories – offered a thorny olive branch: use the name Japan for the record, and we'll give you the cash you need.

At this point things descended into farce, the real truth almost impossible to disseminate from possible fictions and even angrier words. Suffice to say, Sylvian point blank refused to have anything to do with the name Japan. As far as he was concerned, while the identity of the musicians remained the same, the intention behind their present aims was wholly different. In short, no deal. Karn, Barbieri and Jansen however, saw things a little more expansively, leaning towards the viewpoint 'what's in a name, anyway?' The solution to the dilemma was one of the more ugly incidents in the group's already potted history.

Sylvian, remaining inflexible about the band's name, yet unwilling to let the project slide, suggested paying for the mixing process himself – provided, of course, that he could assume a degree of creative control over the results. To Jansen et al such an intractable stance was nothing short of betrayal. But without the cash to match him, they were powerless to offer an alternative. Sylvian duly took the tapes, and headed back to London's Olympic Studios to begin mixing. In an unprecedented move, Mick, Steve and Richard went to the press with their side of the story. "At the end of the day, he's tried to take it away from us," Jansen told *Music Technology*'s Tim Goodyer at the time. "We [aren't] allowed to go to the mixing because he put up the money, and that for us, doesn't show respect . . . I know he believes he's right in what he's doing. He believes in himself to such a degree [he's willing] to abuse his friends. That's the bottom line."

In Sylvian's defence, his actions of April, 1990, did have a certain craggy integrity to them. Reticent to have the memory of Japan soiled by accusations that they had only re-formed for the money, he'd stood his ground (as well as opening his wallet) and seen off Virgin's bid to have the group trade on its old name. Additionally, it was no secret that he'd been unhappy with the results of some of the material the band had produced, and hoped that by overseeing the mix, he could set things to rights. However – and it's a big however – the singer supposedly entered into the reunion as an equal partner. At no time was it specified he would exert more control over the project than his fellow band members. Yet, by financially moving the goalposts at the last minute and excluding his colleagues from any further part in the creative process, Sylvian was (on the face of it) relegating three of his oldest friends to little more than hired hands. Japan's manager, Simon Napier-Bell, once made the accusation that "David was an absolute tyrant in the studio". His actions of 1990 did little to counter the claim. "(He's) an incredible manipulator," said Richard Barbieri. "Charismatic, charming . . . but he wants control over everyone, including his friends. That's wrong."

Shaken by the bust-up, but determined to salvage something from his experience, Sylvian spent eight months intermittently tweaking the tapes. After a spell at Olympic, he moved to Pete Townshend's Eel Pie Studios, before cutting said tapes to disc at the Town House in West London. Steve Nye assisted the singer at each stage of the mixing process. By February 1991, Virgin were confident enough with the results to announce details of a forthcoming LP from the band formally known as

Japan – now operating under the nom de plume Rain Tree Crow ("Guess who thought of that unassuming little name?" said a suitably irked Mick Karn). However, the record company were also at some pains to point out that the collaboration was a one-off, and no further releases should be expected from the group. It hardly made for thrilling advertising.

Preceded by the single 'Blackwater' (which put in a brief appearance at No 68 in the UK charts in March 1991), the album *Rain Tree Crow* finally arrived in record shops on April 20, 1991. Considering the circumstances behind the LP's birth, the eventual result was surprisingly good. Exuding a warm, worn character, the songs of *Rain Tree Crow* ranged from lonesome instrumentals – 'Scratchings On The Bible Belt', 'Red Earth (As Summertime Ends)' – to tough, guitar-driven rock – 'Blackcrow Hits Shoe Shine City'. In among these extremities were more traditional Sylvian/Japan fare, with the gentle balladry of 'Cries And Whispers' and 'Pocketful Of Change' recalling something of both *Tin Drum* and *Gone To Earth.* 'Pocketful Of Change' (its title lifted from the Bergman film of the same name) was particularly impressive, with David challenging his vocal range to fine, sonorous effect.

Two tracks on *Rain Tree Crow* stuck out a proverbial mile. The first was 'New Moon At Red Deer Wallow', a haunting instrumental that illustrated just how far Karn, Jansen and Barbieri had come as musicians. Awash with queasy synth patterns, rust-bucket percussion and an Aboriginal-sounding bass clarinet, 'New Moon . . .' was as beguiling as it was strange: " 'New Moon At Red Deer Wallow'," Sylvian later said, "is really exceptional. The track realises the potential that this group always had that was never realised before." As did *Rain Tree Crow*'s stand-out moment, the exquisite 'Every Colour You Are'. Brittle and tired-sounding, the song conveyed a quite magnificent sense of desolation in the span of just four short minutes. "Feel like crying," sang a weary Sylvian. "The jokes gone too far, you can be anything you want, every colour you are . . ."

Reminiscent of the work of Daniel Lanois in its evocation of big skies, barren landscapes and rocky terrain, *Rain Tree Crow* was surprisingly American in its sound, with a hint of muddy Mississippi blues on almost every track. "There are phrases and sequences that are more blues, and sometimes rock," confirmed Barbieri. "I used to like Led Zeppelin. I think it's all coming back . . ." Aside from David (who provided some tough-sounding licks on the biting 'Blackcrow Hits Shoe Shine City'), the quartet used three guitarists in all to help give the songs on *Rain Tree Crow* a harsher edge. Previous Sylvian collaborators Bill Nelson and Phil Palmer contributed tasteful fills to the mellow 'Blackwater' and husk-like 'Every Colour You Are' among others, while renowned ambient composer Michael Brook added a satisfying lustre to 'Pocketful Of Change' and 'Scratchings On The Bible Belt'. In fact, Brook was actually scheduled to produce the album, until the band decided to do it for themselves.

Though the music of *Rain Tree Crow* was undoubtedly collaborative in nature, Sylvian still ruled the roost lyrically, his words conveying a certain frailty of mind only hinted at on previous solo releases. The mournful tones of the LP's closing track 'Cries And Whispers' were indicative of the overall malaise. "A shattered dream in a bed of lies, now my love dies, cries and whispers . . ." "The album," revealed Sylvian, "is about self-reflection. The idea of the title, 'The Crow', is something that I've used as a symbol of what's been happening to me for the past four years. It's been a dark period and this music is part of the healing process. It's both a symptom and cure." What the singer didn't reveal at the time was how dark a period it had actually been. Losing much of the positive momentum he'd established with *Gone To Earth* and *Secrets Of The Beehive*, Sylvian's emotional well-being took a severe nose-dive in 1988, resulting in him turning to therapy for the first time. "I was in therapy on and off for about two years," he later recalled. "Through my analyst and talking to my parents, I've got the idea of what was missing in my childhood . . . it helped a lot."

What didn't help, of course, was the subsequent war of words that broke out between Sylvian and his estranged colleagues following the album's release. Though retaining an air of diplomacy throughout, his comments regarding the ill-fated reunion did have a taint of acid to them. "My relationship with the boys in the band has ended," he told the *NME*'s A J Barratt. "It [isn't] something I feel particularly negative about, but that doesn't mean I rejoice over it. Musically . . . we did something . . . that if we were mature enough ten years ago, we would have tackled. We've [now] done it, and I feel happy about that. If that's a way of saying goodbye to one another professionally and personally, then I can live with that."

Mick and Steve's comments on their temporary alliance with Sylvian were more down to earth, but no less effective. "Very soon [into the project]," Jansen told *Q*'s Adrian Deevoy, "we saw David change into this awful person again. Basically he was being a creep, and I told him to fuck off." Karn concurred: "He was going through this ludicrous spiritual-cum-intellectual phase . . . we'd go out to eat and it would turn into a mammoth argument about the meaning of life. Any fool knows that you can't find 'the answer' over a curry."

Perhaps the worst aspect of the fall-out was that it again brought to light the very reasons why the group should have let sleeping dogs lie. "I'm neither ashamed nor proud of what Japan did," said the very wearied Sylvian. "If people want to somehow keep that period alive . . . it's really up to them – but they're fooling themselves." He continued: "What I feel about the work with Japan is that at [its] centre, there's an emotional void. On the whole I don't think the work is that interesting, or stands up to much scrutiny. I find it irritating that they highlight an area of my work in which I place no value myself."

A serviceable, at times compelling, record, *Rain Tree Crow* brought Sylvian, Jansen, Barbieri and Karn back into the UK Top 30 after an absence of nearly eight years – the LP making its début at No 24 on the charts at the end of April, 1991. The critics were more or less kind. "Years [have] elapsed since the glam-art experimentalists' last collaboration," said *Vox*'s Max Bell, "but . . . Catford's finest have reconvened to make, er, a concept album. The recording evolves around a Red Indian dude and his quest for water. Okay, so Sylvian stills sings like a particularly bloodless Scott Walker, but his melodies satisfy even when the tunes come complete with smoke signals, red flags and a map." *Q* took an equally level-headed approach: "Not something one might play at parties, perhaps," reasoned Jimmy Nicol, "but a strange grower that should be played pretty well everywhere else. It would seem a shame if this is only a one-off project."

But one-off it most certainly was. Following the bust-up over mixing, the two factions cut all lines of communication, with even the most perfunctory of business being redirected through their individual management companies. With family involved, such intransigence was hard work. "It's no fun for our parents knowing we're avoiding each other," Jansen told Adrian Deevoy. "I guess [David] must feel guilty. But that guilt doesn't override [the] other failings he has."

An ugly end to the most undignified of reunions, the Rain Tree Crow saga did little for David Sylvian other than add a blemish or two to his reputation as an otherwise agreeable fellow. However, the LP that came out of the storm still has its fans, with Tears For Fears' Roland Orzabal a fervent admirer of its dusty charms. "I was crazy about *Rain Tree Crow*," he confirmed. "An unbelievable album. I love every track – you can tell they'd all been listening to *Spirit Of Eden* by Talk Talk." The haunting vignette 'Boat's For Burning' also provided Orzabal with his favourite Sylvian lyric yet. "When he sings, 'Strike a match, stand well back, this boat's for burning' . . . it's like . . . fuck. Incredible. Just too perfect a pop group."

Indeed.

18

The Owl And The Pussycat

The years 1988-1991 were difficult ones for David Sylvian. By his own admission, much of the positivity he'd summoned for the making of *Gone To Earth* and *Secrets Of the Beehive* had been lost in a subsequent battle against depression and self-laceration. These notions of self-doubt even extended to the work he'd been involved in throughout the late Eighties/Early Nineties. Though at the time Sylvian seemed genuinely enthusiastic about his instrumental collaborations with Holger Czukay, he later dismissed the LPs *Plight And Premonition* and *Flux And Mutability* as "harmless". His project with Russell Mills – *Ember Glance: The Permanence Of Memory* – fared little better, with the singer describing it, somewhat ungallantly, as "cluttered" and "uneven". In view of such negativity towards his own output, it was no surprise that sooner or later *Rain Tree Crow* would also get the cold water treatment. "I'm always disappointed in some respects by the work that I do," Sylvian said in 1991. "I always feel that it falls short of its original potential in some way. But maybe that's what spurs me on to try again and again."

While Sylvian was being somewhat harsh about his recent efforts, some of the criticisms he raised rang uncomfortably true. Though his collaborations with Holger Czukay and Russell Mills were pleasing enough on the ear, there was nothing remarkable about them. In fact, as instrumental pieces they added little to the themes he'd already explored with *Words With The Shaman*, the ambient side of *Gone To Earth*, or his 1987 score for Gaby Agis's ballet *The Stigma Of Childhood (Kin)*. *Rain Tree Crow*'s worn groove had proved much more satisfying, but any hope (or interest) in reactivating the project lay in ruins following his decision to seize control of the LP from his colleagues in its final stages. Aside from the acerbic bile Sylvian served up on the 1989 single 'Pop Song', his efforts since 1987's *Secrets Of The Beehive* represented little more than statements in marking time.

For critics of his work this lack of progression proved too tasty a feast not to bite into. For years, many had seen Sylvian in danger of disappearing into an abyss of his own romantic invention, his "self-absorbed and miserablist stance" eventually leading him to complete creative stasis, or worse. After all, the world of art was littered with those who'd fallen foul of challenging the extremities of their intellect. Novelists Strindberg, Stendhal, Hesse and Flaubert had all ground to a nervous halt trying to capture perfection in their work. Whilst Sylvian operated in the potentially less hazardous realms of popular music, that form too had thrown up its own distinguished roll-call of artistic martyrs, from Jim Morrison to Kurt Cobain. These age-old notions of "suffering for one's art" had been neatly encapsulated in one sentence by the dancer Nijinsky: "God at one extreme, misery at the other." Obviously for David Sylvian, he had spent a little too much time at the wrong end of the spectrum.

However, in spite of his problems, Sylvian continued to work. Though a long-considered collaboration with fellow pop melancholic Scott Walker failed to materialise (David got as far as visiting Scott in the studio, but individual schedules prohibited any further alliance), he did find time to make a contribution to Hector Zazou's tribute album honouring the centenary of French poet Arthur Rimbaud's death. The LP, *Sahara Blue*, featured Sylvian reciting one of Rimbaud's lesser known works, the atypically optimistic 'To A Reason'. However, because the album wasn't linked to Virgin Records (who held exclusive rights on David's recorded output), contractual problems arose over its release. While a few CDs escaped the net, the threat of legal action from Virgin meant the album was soon withdrawn from sale. It eventually resurfaced a year or so later. For the record, other artists contributing to *Sahara Blue* included John Cale and the ever-present Ryuichi Sakamoto.

Ultimately, it was Sylvian's friendship with Sakamoto that was inadvertently responsible for allowing him to put paid to old ghosts, and open a new, decidedly more optimistic, chapter in his life. The synchronicity trail began in earnest when David made a guest appearance at Ryuichi's show at Hammersmith Odeon in October, 1991, to perform 'Forbidden Colours' and 'Orpheus'. This impromptu reunion led Sakamoto to ask the singer to collaborate with him on his forthcoming LP, scheduled for release the following year. Sylvian readily agreed, and studios were booked. Yet, in the break between Ryuichi's offer and the actual recording date, David received a tape in the post from a young vocalist/actress by the name of Ingrid Chavez. So impressed was he by its musical content, he contacted Chavez and invited her to participate in the forthcoming sessions for Sakamoto's album.

While Ingrid Chavez's début LP was only just arriving in shops at this point, she had already made quite a splash in the media – mainly due to a writ she had recently served on the rather more famous Lenny Kravitz. In short, she collaborated with the dread-locked soul rocker on an early demo version of Madonna's subsequent 1991 hit single, the sexually charged 'Justify My Love'. Yet, though the Queen Of Pop's vocal delivery on the song heavily recalled the breathless enunciation and silky phrasing provided by Chavez on the original demo, on its release 'Justify My Love' remained credited to just Madonna and Kravitz. According to Ingrid, Lenny had originally persuaded her to relinquish any royalties from the song in return for a fee of $500. But when the single hit the top of the US and UK charts (subsequently selling over a million copies), she was forced to reassess the terms of their original agreement. After a mercifully short legal battle, Chavez received her just reward, with a full co-writing credit and substantial back-royalties awarded to her by the courts.

Though it was the Kravitz case that greatly raised her public profile, Ingrid Chavez had in fact been around the edges of the music scene for over three years, thanks to her association with wayward pop genius Prince. In fact, she began her career in earnest as an actress/singer playing the diminutive one's love interest in *Graffiti Bridge* – the third (and thankfully) last of the semi-autobiographical films 'The Artist' involved himself in during the Eighties. The link didn't end there. Her recent self-titled début album was not only released by Prince's Paisley Park record label, but more importantly, the man himself had co-written five of the songs as well as acted as producer.

Unlike previous Prince protégés Patty Kotero and percussionist Sheila E (whose solo LPs proved little more than handed down demos from their boss), Chavez actually managed to carve her own musical identity on the record, thanks in large part to a distinctive, half-whispered vocal style. Best described as a cross between Eartha Kitt and Tori Amos, the singer/rapper's decidedly feline presence set light to otherwise undistinguished funk/ambient fare like 'Hippy Blood' and 'Slappy Dappy'. It was this gift for warming the edges of a song that so appealed to Sylvian. After several phone conversations, Chavez accepted an offer to meet with the singer in New Orleans before heading on to the studio sessions for Sakamoto's forthcoming album.

The result of the trio's collaboration – 'Heartbeat (Tainai Kaiki II): Returning To The Womb' – was a neatly crafted pop song, mournful enough to appeal to Sylvian fans, yet retaining enough swing to find that all important crossover market. Aside from David's typically smoky vocal, and some clever instrumental interplay between Sakamoto and guest guitarist Bill Frisell, Chavez made her presence felt throughout as "a seductive background murmur", intertwining gentle half-spoken/half-sung passages with Sylvian's main melody line. To consolidate the teaming, Sakamoto, Sylvian and Chavez also recorded the lissom 'Cloud # 9' at the sessions. Not content to leave it there, the trio subsequently performed a short concert for the press (as part of a promotional junket), as well as making a video for the forthcoming single release of 'Heartbeat . . .' To cap it all, the song was duly played by the trio at Sakamoto's concert at the Budokan in February, 1992. By the time 'Heartbeat . . .' made the charts in June (peaking at No 58), Sylvian and Chavez had already been married for three months.

A "whirlwind" romance in the truest sense of the word, the sparks began to fly when the couple first met in New Orleans. "We spoke to each other on the phone a lot," Sylvian later recalled to *Vox*'s Jamie Kemsey, "[and] we were getting on really well, so I asked her to come to New Orleans, because I'd never been there. We started travelling together, finally did the record and fell in love in the process." Though Sylvian and Chavez had only known each other for two and a half months, they decided to make the relationship official in Ingrid's hometown of Minneapolis in late February 1992. "Yes, I'm a married woman," confirmed Chavez. "David flew into Minneapolis for one day from London. We got married in my apartment with just two cats for witnesses. And then he had to fly back the next morning."

The change in Sylvian following his marriage was marked, to say the least. After three years of very public pronouncements regarding his deteriorating mental state (Sylvian's ten year relationship with Yuka Fujii had collapsed, in part because of his depression), he made a number of remarkably quick decisions that allowed him to move on with his life. Number one on the priority list was getting out of England. "I found the UK to be cynical and downtrodden," the singer later confessed. "I could see a younger generation rebelling against that, but I (didn't) belong to it. So many relationships (I had) were coming to an end there, so I felt it was time to go."

Not surprisingly, Sylvian decided to settle in his wife's home town of Minneapolis, where the couple eventually found a house in "a nice, quiet neighbourhood". Compared with his previous doom-laden image as pop's lost poet, the thought of Sylvian residing in domestic bliss among the friendly natives of Soul City was as splendid as it was strange. The irony wasn't lost on him. "I suppose America is really an extreme case of *being*. But then in Middle America, life is easy . . . to me, America isn't born yet. It's made up of exiles . . . a nation of exiles. Anyway, that's how it seems to me."

Decision number two saw the singer reactivate his long-standing friendship with guitarist Robert Fripp. Since the two last worked together on 1986's *Gone To Earth*, Fripp had involved himself in numerous projects, the most high profile of which was The League Of Crafty Guitarists – a collection of players amassed from his newly opened Guitar Craft School. Aside from touring with the ensemble throughout the late Eighties, Robert also found time to record two albums (*Prostitute* and *Kneeling At The Shrine*) as well as tour with former pop pixie Toyah. As with Sylvian and Chavez, their musical collaboration ultimately led to marriage. "When I met my wife – dear little creature – and proposed in a week," Fripp recalled, "I had no interest in being married, but I met this wonderful little woman and I knew this was my wife. Very happily, she accepted me."

The seeds of a new musical partnership between Robert and David had been sown at the end of 1991, when Fripp contacted Sylvian about the possibility of him taking on vocal duties in a re-formed King Crimson. Though the prospect of fronting a rock band intrigued the singer, after due consideration he passed on the offer. Instead, David proposed the idea of an "improvisational" studio project between the two. Eager to get working again, Fripp accepted Sylvian's invitation. However, the nature of the alliance radically changed when David was offered a brief performance residency (above a department store, of all places) in Tokyo at the end of 1992. Burned by the negative experience of 1988's *In Praise Of Shamans* jaunt, he remained sniffy at first, but after a conversation or two with Fripp, promptly changed his mind. "I mentioned it to Robert because I didn't have any intentions of doing it. But he said, 'Well, let's use that as an opportunity to write.' So we got together two weeks prior to the actual event, which gave us a week to write the material and a week to rehearse it. That kept us on our toes."

Rehearsals began in the autumn, with the duo adding renowned stick-bass player Trey Gunn to their ranks. "We were basically working as a trio, Robert, myself and Trey," Sylvian recalled to journalist Kerry Doole. "Some of the material was very atmospheric, instrumental, kind of landscape music." After a productive (if somewhat frenetic) fourteen days, the band had amassed enough useable material to take the project live. So successful was the response accorded them by audiences, the decision was made to continue the experiment with some impromptu dates in Italy. "Because the food in Italy is always good," said a suitably famished Robert Fripp. "The business is always a problem and food is always good."

Inevitably, the songs composed for the project soon found themselves in the recording studio. Though a fair number of ballads had been written, Sylvian was content to focus on the more aggressive numbers the trio had in their hands. "It was an area we (all) wanted to cover," David told *B-Side*'s Jamie Kemsey. "I was thinking of getting involved in more rock-orientated music [anyway], because the subject matter I wanted to deal with was of a more frustrated nature." The drummer called in to help them handle "the heavier stuff" was Jerry Marotta, sticksman to Peter Gabriel and "very loud" to boot. In keeping with the Gabriel connection, David Bottrill (the engineer behind Peter's hit albums *So* and *Us*) was drafted in to co-produce the LP with Sylvian. Additional percussion duties were to be handled by Marc Anderson.

Pre-production for the record began at Applehead Studios in Woodstock, New York, in December 1992. After a suitable rehearsal period, the musicians moved just round the corner to Dreamland Studios to begin recording. From here, they headed to Daniel Lanois' Kings Way sound complex in New Orleans (a studio Sylvian particularly favoured because of its informal atmosphere). By the beginning of March, 1993 the tapes were on their way to New York's Electric Lady Studios for mixing. Unfortunately, due to a prior touring commitment with his string quartet, Robert Fripp had to cut and run at this point, leaving the mix down to Sylvian and Bottrill. However, no delays were incurred, and the finished product was with Virgin Records by April.

The resulting LP, *The First Day*, was finally released on July 17, 1993. Suffice to say, Sylvian hadn't been joking about its aggressive content. Tracks such as '20th Century Dreaming (A Shaman's Song)' and 'Brightness Falls' were chock-full of shattering drums, bad-tempered bass-playing and sonically abusive guitars. In fact, Fripp had a field day on almost every song on the album, his fleet-fingered solos tumbling over each other like towels in a dryer. The plan, it seemed, was one of 'attack or be damned'. "The record came out rather more loud than if I had been working by myself, which is rather exciting in a way," Sylvian later admitted to *Creem*'s Steve Holtje. "Despite the fact that we only used a few of the songs from the tour, [*The First Day*] reflects the intensity of the way we sounded."

Intensity was definitely the watchword on the LP's centrepiece, the invigorating 'Firepower'. Featuring a riff that wouldn't be out of place in the Black Sabbath catalogue, the song's principle appeal lay in Sylvian's embattled vocal performance (its distorted tone achieved by putting his voice through a battered Radio Shack amplifier). " 'Firepower' is the microcosm of the whole album," confirmed the singer. "It's about dealing with the frustrations of life, and eventually finding the values that will help you become more centred and focused, and be able to respond to the world around you in a much more positive manner. In a way, (that's) the journey to be made on this album. A lot of the lyrics deal with the darker nature of life or survivalist existence."

This theme of survival ran riot throughout one of the lighter songs present on *The First Day*, the hugely enjoyable 'Jean The Birdman'. "Life is a cattle farm," sang an uncharacteristically cheerful Sylvian. "Coyotes with the mules, life is a bullring for taking risks and flouting rules." Though it was sometimes difficult to discern through the furious arsenal of guitars that dominated the sound of the album, gentle satire and cautious optimism were at the heart of *The First Day* – whether in song titles such as 'God's Monkey' or the lyrical content of tracks like the funky 'Darshan – The Road To Graceland': "From flux to form, kneeling on the road to Graceland". "It's an ironic line," Sylvian confirmed to *Raygun*'s Josef Woodard, "but . . . also a very sincere one. That's why I like it. The notion of Darshan implies a kneeling, a bowing before some power greater than one's self."

Fripp mirrored the singer's comments regarding the notion of accedence to a greater good. "I have no trust in myself, [yet] I have an unshakeable confidence in the benevolence of the creative impulse. When a musician walks on stage and believes they are responsible for the music, the show is dead, unless music finds a way of acting through the egotism of this performer, who actually believes they have anything to do other than allow the music to directly address their skills. The musician doesn't play the music – the music plays the musician." And if ever a man spoke as he played, it was undoubtedly Robert Fripp.

An engaging LP that ran the gamut of musical emotions, from the clattering metallic funk of 'Brightness Falls' to the exquisite Frippertronics of closing track 'Bringing Down The Light', *The First Day* bounced into the UK charts at No 21 at the end of July, 1993. What started life as an innocent collaboration had ultimately made the best of business sense. "Rash praise corner," reasoned *Vox*'s John Gill. "Parts of this resemble the best Can record ever made without any members of Can actually being present. Following on from his *Plight/Flux* albums with Holger Czukay, Sylvian's collaboration with the Crimsotronic Fripp brings together two heavyweight influences in an, uh, flux that sometimes sparks with vision. What gives *The First Day* Sylvian's signature," said Gill, "is the voice, and his willingness to follow a fascinating experiment through to its conclusion."

The album did have its critics, however, including a certain member of Can. "Robert Fripp is a great guitarist," reasoned Holger Czukay. "He's made some flipped out things. But when I heard the record I called up David and said, 'I don't think he understands your special qualities and moods, or how to handle you.' " To Czukay, the fault lay in the LP's overtly rockist nature. "The music was more general, not so specific. I had the feeling that David was somehow forced to fight this 'rock rhythm', make something out of it with his singing. I would never do that with him. I would try to create an atmosphere so that he felt good. What's important with David is that he keeps his hand in until the last minute. That's *really important.* His influence is strong. If you don't acknowledge that, [you] make him just another . . . musician. *The First Day*," concluded Holger, "was traditional. I wouldn't have expected that."

Fascinating experiment or trad rock twiddling, *The First Day* still had the desired effect of re-establishing both David Sylvian and Robert Fripp's public profiles after an uncomfortable period in the commercial wilderness. It also spawned two highly creditable singles/EPs, the first of which was the joyfully infectious 'Jean The Birdman', released on August 28, 1993. Made available as a two CD set, with a total of four previously unavailable Sylvian/Fripp instrumentals – 'Tallow Moon', 'Dark Water', 'Earthbound (Starlight)' and 'Endgame' – added to sweeten the package, it looked like the song might put Sylvian back in the Top 40 after an absence of some nine years. Yet, despite a fair amount of air play, and blanket rotation of the (admittedly cheap looking) video by *VH-1*, 'Jean . . .' only managed to flutter his way up to No 68 in the charts, before its Icarus-like descent into the bargain bins.

The second release from *The First Day* sessions came in the form of a deluxe EP featuring two radical reinterpretations of

'Darshan – The Road To Graceland', courtesy of dance/re-mix teams The Grid and The Future Sound Of London. In the case of The Grid's Dave Ball, connections abounded with Sylvian and Fripp. As one half of the highly successful 'futurist' duo Soft Cell, he began his musical career in the early Eighties sharing the charts with David's former group Japan. "The first time I saw Japan in the flesh," recalled the immensely likeable Ball, "was at *Top Of The Pops* in 1982. They were there to do 'Ghosts', and Mark (Almond) and I were there with 'Say Hello, Wave Goodbye'. When I heard 'Ghosts', I thought 'Ah, this is interesting', so I bought it. Actually, it was the third record I'd bought by Japan. I already had 'Life In Tokyo' and 'Quiet Life'. The next thing I know it's 1993, and I get a call from Robert saying, 'Would you be up for mixing 'Darshan?' "

Like Sylvian, Ball had managed to avoid disappearing into the abyss after the break-up of his first band. After a wobble or two in the mid-Eighties with commercial non-starters Other People and English Boy And The Love Ranch, he re-emerged in 1990 with musical partner Richard Norris to form The Grid, a dance act that would eventually score ten hit singles and two well received albums in the space of five years. However, the connection with Robert Fripp came when the duo were looking for a rock guitarist to contribute to three tracks on their second album. Both huge fans of Fripp's work, they asked their manager Robert Eindhoven if he had a contact number for the owlish one. "I used to manage King Crimson," Eindhoven casually informed them. Within days, Fripp was in the studio. "Robert had done some playing for us as a sort of freebie," said Ball. "He's one of these people who doesn't charge for sessions, but says, 'When I need a favour, then I'll give you a call.' The favour turned out to be 'Darshan'."

Though the re-mix took only a day or so, Ball and Norris managed to give the song a much needed contemporary sheen, boosting the drums as high as possible in the mix to make it danceworthy. "(Darshan's) quite an odd track really, not the sort of track I'd imagine DJs would immediately pick up in a club. The main thing I remember about it was that it was about fourteen minutes long! A weird one . . . everything seemed to go into slow motion when we were doing it." As hallucinogenic as the session may have been, the duo still managed to rope in many of Robert Fripp's more serious guitar excesses. "I'm sure Robert won't mind me saying this," confided Dave, "but he does tend towards 'muso-ness'. The main thing I've always said to him is 'Robert, do it again, but with less notes'. If he can get away with playing fifty notes then he will, because he can. He's got the technical ability." Ball was equally praising of Sylvian. "Japan were great abstract pop. In David's solo career, he's gone for the abstract part of it, but retained a great pop sensibility. The guy's matured in years, but also as a musician. You do your youthful pop thing, and then you *hear* something in your music, and pursue that element. With Sylvian," concluded Ball, "it was the darker side of Japan."

Whilst The Grid's re-mix of 'Darshan' retained at least something of the track's original feel, The Future Sound Of London's interpretation of it was altogether more radical. Dumping everything from the tapes bar a few Frippertronic guitars and the odd gushing synth, FSOL chose to concentrate their efforts on bringing out the song's more ambient possibilities. When they handed 'Darshan' back to Sylvian and Fripp (re-christened 'Darshana'), it sounded more like a drunken Portishead track than anything else, with trip-hop drum patterns and Eastern-inflected keyboards replacing squeaking guitars and furious percussion. Suffice to say, David and Robert loved it – so much so, in fact, that they gave FSOL a 25% royalty on all sales of the EP. This was the first (and last) time the team received such a lucrative deal for their re-mix work.

Ultimately, *The First Day* and its attendant by-products worked the trick of re-introducing David Sylvian and Robert Fripp to the record buying public, in a new (if somewhat curious) guise. The pair even worked well as a double act for the purposes of press promotion, with Sylvian content to loiter in the background as his partner tripped the verbal light fantastic. "The difference between the play of children and the play of the artist," Robert instructed *Time Out*'s Nick Coleman, "is that in play one plays without regard for repercussions. The difference is that one is in innocence, the other, the work of the master musician, is in the assumption of innocence within the field of experience." It was a theory the two were about to put to the test in the unforgiving confines of the concert hall.

19

On The Road To Redemption

In the late summer of 1993, David Sylvian and Robert Fripp announced news of their forthcoming *Road To Graceland* world tour, scheduled to kick off in Japan's Kanni Hoken Hall on October 14. Though the previous year's live dates were relatively low key affairs, *The Road To Graceland* was to be a far more ambitious enterprise.

In addition to Sylvian, Fripp and silent partner/stick player Trey Gunn, guitarist Michael Brook and drummer Pat Mastelotto had been brought on board to help re-produce the thick rock textures present on *The First Day*. Previous Sylvian collaborator Haruki 'Ember Glance' Kaito was the man chosen to handle lighting and production design for the jaunt.

However, Sylvian's mind was unlikely to have been completely focused on the tour, principally because his wife was about to give birth. "Personal relations are bound to have an effect on one's life and work," he told *B-Side*'s Jamie Kemsey at the time. "The fact that I'm married indicates an enormous change. The fact I am about to become a father indicates an enormous change in my ability to share my life and give. I've been so wrapped up in my own experiences, my own work – everything in my life has been geared towards the work and my own development . . . meeting Ingrid was very important to me."

In September, Ingrid Chavez gave birth to a healthy baby girl, whom the couple named Ameera-Daya. The names chosen for the infant were significant: Meera meaning 'miracle', and Daya meaning 'graciousness'. After a brief initiation into the joys of fatherhood, Sylvian joined Fripp and the others for rehearsals for their forthcoming jaunt. By early October, everything was in place and the band flew to Japan for their first date at the Kanni Hoken Hall.

Compared with the sublime textures presented on the *In Praise Of Shamans* tour, *The Road To Graceland* proved a far more energetic show, both in terms of artistic design and musical content. Production manager Haruki Kaito excelled himself on the lighting front, with bursts of green, blue and orange soaking the musicians on stage at critical junctures in the set, his use of fiery red during 'Darshan' proving particularly effective. Kaito's backdrop for the show was worth the price of admission alone, with ghostly white and amber images projected onto the blank, sail-like canvas at regular (but never predictable) intervals.

The music mirrored the inherent moodiness of the production design. Songs such as show opener 'God's Monkey' and '20th Century Dreaming (A Shaman's Song)' conveyed a far more immediate impact live than on record, thanks in large part to Robert Fripp's propulsive guitar work. Though he preferred to remain seated during performances, Fripp was never found wanting for energy. Whether it was in the creation of searing false harmonics on 'Brightness Falls' or the breathtaking six-string gymnastics of 'Jean The Birdman', the owlishly bespectacled guitarist could always be relied upon to create sheer bloody pandemonium when the occasion required it. "I don't feel myself to be a jazz guitarist or a rock guitarist," he once said. "I don't feel capable of playing in any of those idioms, which is why I felt it necessary to create, if you like, my own idiom."

Fripp wasn't surrounded by slouches. Guitarist Michael Brook's combination of Eastern inflected fretwork and bluesy riffing provided a suitably tasty contrast to Robert's more star-bound excursions. Interestingly, Brook was also employed as a one man support act throughout the tour, playing a selection of material from his solo albums. "They get a guitar player, and I get to be the opening act . . . everybody benefits," he said. The band's rhythm section were equally impressive, with Trey Gunn and Pat Mastelotto providing both subtlety and thump in equal measure. A jolly if formidable presence, Mastelotto had Gunn to thank for setting up his gig with Sylvian and Fripp: "When they were auditioning in London, I called up Trey and said, 'Do you think they'd give me a chance to come over and play?' " the drummer recalled. "[The next thing] Richard [Chadwick, Sylvian's manager] calls, and said, 'Sure, come over', so I used my frequent flyer miles!"

As for David Sylvian, he appeared a changed man. Visibly more relaxed and considerably more energetic in comparison to previous live appearances, Sylvian's newly acquired command of the stage was as admirable as it was surprising. His live voice too, had improved markedly with age, projecting a deep and resonant quality on older material such as 'Riverman' and *Rain Tree Crow*'s 'Every Colour You Are'. "Over the last few years," reasoned Michael Brook, "to my mind, David has become an incredibly fantastic singer, and a very strong writer. I think he's going in a very good direction." Brook's comments were borne out by the new ballads David aired over the course of the Japanese shows. Both 'Damage' and 'The First Day' were vintage Sylvian fare, bitter-sweet, but never too emotionally cloying. Nonetheless, a new element had crept into his lyrics – the voice of experience. "So many things to say," he sang on 'Damage', "but these are only words, now I've only words . . . once there was a choice."

The Road To Graceland propelled itself across Japan throughout much of October, taking in dates at Sendai's Shimin Kaikan Theatre, Osaka's Festival Hall and Kyoto's Kaikan Dai-2 Hall before stopping at Tokyo's Nakono Sun Plaza for a two day stint on October 25&26 (the second of these concerts was filmed, and subsequently shown on Japanese/European TV). The USA and Canada beckoned next, with dates fulfilled in San Francisco (29), Chicago (31) and Toronto (November 1). On November 2, Sylvian found himself back in New York for a show at the intimate Beacon Theatre. By now, the band were really cooking, with the likes of 'Firepower' and Robert Fripp's distinctive and extremely funky 'Exposure' taking pride of place in the set. As live experiences go, *The Road To Graceland* was intense and atmospheric as well as extremely noisy. "We still have some of the atmosphere of the earlier shows," said Trey Gunn, "but also the other dimension of having a real band. We're a whole lot louder!"

The tour's next stop was Italy, where Sylvian as a solo artist commanded a surprisingly strong following. Ten dates were performed in all, with notable stop-offs at Naples' Tenda Partenope on November 7, Rome's Teatro Olimpico (8), Milan's Teatro Smeraldo (15) and Grappa's Teatro Astra (17). Suffice to say, attendances were high at all the concerts, and Robert Fripp ate particularly well. The next leg on *The Road To Graceland* took the group to Holland and Belgium for dates in Amsterdam, Eindhoven and Antwerp. A one day stopover in France saw Sylvian and Fripp bringing their wares to Paris' La Cigalle Theatre on November 28, before crossing the channel to the UK, and the final leg of the tour.

The English dates opened at Nottingham's Royal Centre on November 30, 1993, with the band heading off the following day for a particularly well-received show at Manchester's Apollo Theatre (Sylvian has always enjoyed playing the city, believing the crowds there to be greatly appreciative of his music). The group then ventured on to Glasgow's Royal Concert Hall, before flying back to London to end the tour with two concerts at the Royal Albert Hall on December 4&5. The final dates on *The Road To Graceland* were amongst the best of Sylvian's career. Aside from a jaunty take on 'Jean The Birdman' and a moving rendition of 'The First Day', the group performed an exquisite treatment of *Gone To Earth*'s least distinguished moment, the previously maudlin 'Wave'. New melodic life was also brought to 'Gone To Earth' itself, transforming the track from its former atonal origins into a gentle, but imperious ballad. The concert finished on a high note, with the suitably titled 'Blinding Light Of Heaven'.

A fine tour (with several bootleg videos doing the rounds to prove it), *The Road To Graceland* was more than ably captured on the album *Damage,* "a documentary CD" culled from the band's performances at the Royal Festival Hall, and subsequently released in September 1994. Bookended by Sylvian's haunting torch-songs 'Damage' and 'The First Day', the majority of the band's set (bar 'Exposure') was present, with Robert Fripp and David Bottrill's non-intrusive production allowing the energy of the shows to seep through in splendid fashion. Beautifully packaged (the CD box's design came courtesy of Russell Mills), *Damage* was jointly dedicated to the birth of David's daughter Ameera-Daya, and the memory of Robert's mother, Edie, who had recently passed away. The image of a heart-shaped rose in the CD's accompanying booklet added to the poignancy of their dedications.

Unlike previous excursions, Sylvian greatly enjoyed *The Road To Graceland* tour, believing that his friendship with Fripp, the skill of the musicians involved and the fact he was now a little older (35) all conspired to make him feel more relaxed in front of a live audience. He remained especially pleased with the sleek transition the songs had made from studio to stage. "You try and do your best by the composition," said the singer. "You want to service it the best way you can. So you bring in the best musicians possible to do that." Fripp was equally smitten with the results. "That is precisely what makes (the) music as powerful as it is, the fact that it physically effects the listener," he concluded. "Some music aims for the groin instead of the head, but the best music finds the middle way by aiming for your heart."

With *The First Day* and *The Road To Graceland* behind them, the duo turned their attentions to an intriguing audio/visual project entitled *Redemption (Approaching Silence)*. Described by Fripp as "an installation on the theme of redemption . . . it expresses some ideas on the buying back of humanity", the site of the exhibition was Tokyo's P-3 Gallery, a large space located beneath a religious temple in the busy shopping district of Shinjuki. The gallery itself was actually built on an old graveyard site, which according to David, gave out "a very potent energy". Opening to the public in September 1994, *Redemption* was more subdued in nature than Sylvian's previous installation *Ember Glance: The Permanence Of Memory.* Staged in two rooms (one large, one small), the exhibit used chairs, flickering candles, mirrors, skulls and a bathtub (above which hung a ghostly lantern) to invoke its central theme. One particularly striking piece was a semi-developed face lit in pastel shades of red and orange that looked on impassively at the skull/chair montage forming the centre of the main exhibit.

After struggling down a dark passageway to the smaller of the two rooms, observers were confronted with a video monitor displaying the text Robert Fripp had written for the project. While Fripp's words rolled by on the screen, his voice simultaneously seeped out of hidden speakers, reciting segments of the prose over a circular-sounding orchestral backdrop. As the music (entitled 'Approaching Silence') gently built, an eerie red glow enveloped the room. The whole effect was so unnerving that by the time one left the mausoleum-like chamber, Fripp's recitation had been largely forgotten. In short, *Redemption (Approaching Silence)* made for a somewhat intense afternoon's entertainment. "These offers often come my way," Sylvian later said of the installation. "It's not like I actually go looking for work. But when they do surface, it's too intriguing to turn down."

As was a request for a contribution towards the *War Child* project, a charitable organisation set up by musicians and artists to raise funds for children who lost their parents in the Bosnian civil war. Though Sylvian didn't appear on the high-profile album that accompanied the appeal (superstars only), he did donate a disturbing little item to an exhibition of paintings held in support of *War Child* at the Flowers Gallery in

Bethnal Green. Joining other artistic offerings from the likes of Iggy Pop, Russell Mills, The Rolling Stones' Charlie Watts and The Who's Pete Townshend, Sylvian's montage, titled *Intensive Care,* was a clever twist on the theme of suffering. Built to resemble a medicine cabinet, the piece housed a toy ambulance, Victorian-style pill jar and a hand-painted x-ray of a man's chest. It sold for approximately £700.

Following the *Redemption* project with Robert Fripp, Sylvian returned home to Minneapolis to spend time with his wife and child. However, the break was something of a busman's holiday, as he remained actively engaged in co-writing/producing songs with Ingrid Chavez for her second solo album. To quicken the pace, the pair decided to construct a recording studio in the basement of their home. As this would take time (and money), Sylvian announced tentative plans for a forthcoming CD compilation of his solo work, covering the years 1984–1994. The idea behind the release was to collect the better moments from *Brilliant Trees, Gone To Earth* and *Secrets Of The Beehive,* as well as provide a bonus disc containing various out-takes, B-sides and other obscurities.

Considering the quality of some of David's lesser known material, the prospect of such a compilation was greatly appealing. Forgotten little gems like 1984's 'Blue Of Noon', 1986's 'A Bird Of Prey Vanishes Into A Bright Blue Cloudless Sky' and the gloriously intoxicated *Rain Tree Crow* out-take 'I Drink To Forget' (featuring Mick Karn and Steve Jansen on 'wine glasses') all deserved a more lasting home than on the back of long forgotten singles. Nonetheless, Sylvian (or his record company) subsequently lost interest in the project, and the CD failed to see the light of day. Compensation came quickly though, when the singer offered a potentially thrilling alternative to the aborted album release. In the late summer of 1995, David confirmed he would be performing dates throughout Europe and Japan as part of "a personal retrospective". The tour, given the name *Slow Fire,* would employ no support band – or supporting musicians for that matter – as Sylvian intended to cover all instrumental duties himself.

Realistically, he was taking a serious gamble with a one-man show. After all, much of his music's appeal lay in the careful intertwining of instruments to create both mood and texture. Stripped of brass, percussion and secondary keyboard parts, Sylvian's songs might run the risk of sounding empty, or at least under-fed. Additionally, though he enjoyed *The Road To Graceland* tour, he had been part of a rich ensemble of musicians capable of making even the weakest of melodies sound grand and magisterial. While a creditable enough guitarist/synth player, he was also – by his own admission – no virtuoso. The subtleties of his material might suffer as a result. There was also the critical matter of establishing a rapport with his audience. Though Sylvian could partially trade on charisma, his long-time habit of staying silent between songs might lend the show an impersonal or even distant air. Faced with so many potential obstacles, one had to wonder whether he might be lining himself up for a fall . . .

In the end, *Slow Fire* proved to be a wonderfully judged show, with Sylvian at the top of his form as both a singer and surprisingly informal host. Kicking off in Yokahama, Japan on October 10, 1995, the tour slowly wound its way through Osaka (12), Nagoya (15) and Tokyo (17) before heading towards Italy, Belgium and the UK in early November. The prestige date on this leg of the tour was undoubtedly a one-off appearance at London's Royal Festival Hall on November 4, where British audiences could judge for themselves whether persevering with him through art, ambience, instrumentalism, botched reformations and audio-visual installations had ultimately been worth the effort.

Over the course of two hours, Sylvian answered the question with an august performance drawing on almost every aspect of his solo career, from the existential angst of 'Red Guitar' to the knowing classicism of 'Orpheus'. The show was made all the more notable by the fact that he relied little on backing tapes, preferring instead to tackle his songs on an acoustic guitar or lone piano. Thankfully, the material didn't suffer as a result of this pared down approach, with melody lines and tension both sustained throughout by the quality of his voice. Some new songs were aired, with the soulful balladry of 'Hallelujah' (a working title, by all accounts) particularly pleasing. However, if there was a highlight to be found, it had to be 'Boy With The Gun'. Chilling and evocative, the song was clear proof that Sylvian's compositions worked just as well on six-strings as they did with a full orchestral backing. As the lights went up after an abrasive rendition of 'Pulling Punches', the audience showed their affection by literally pulling him off the stage.

"He's become a guru, a god" wrote a suitably mortified Sylvie Simmons for *Mojo.* "People actually rush the stage and shake his hands, kiss them, rest their foreheads on his palms. From Candy to Gandhi – a long strange trip indeed." *The Independent*'s Ryan Gilbey also made much of the 'holy man' angle. "I swear I saw him turn somebody's mineral water into Chablis," said the writer, tongue firmly placed in cheek. While their reviews were mostly kind, both journalists were slyly alluding to the new look Sylvian premiered at the *Slow Fire* shows. Whereas before, he had chosen to greet his audience in distinctly unobtrusive apparel, this time the singer walked on stage wearing a long flowing silk shirt and traditional Indian suit.

The image was subtly reinforced by the merchandising for the shows, which featured blurred shots of David – arms outstretched, as if welcoming his followers – on T-shirts and tour programmes. Though Sylvian surely hadn't intended to promote himself as a 'fakir' (he actually dedicated the *Slow Fire* tour to Sri Sri Mata Amritanandamayi, a renowned Indian ascetic philosopher), both his choice of clothes and the iconographic aspects of the merchandising did create a certain 'messianic' aura. If one added the poetic, almost mystical aspect of his lyrics to the overall package, an uncomfortable religious undertone behind the marketing of *Slow Fire* began to emerge. In truth, such rampant mythologising of his image grated as much as it appealed.

Sylvian himself was wary of such charges. "The most universal [image of me] is the ivory tower thing, which is so far from the truth," he once said. "People get ideas from listening to the music or looking at the pictures – I don't know what they think!" Talented songwriter and singer, yes. God, certainly not.

Slow Fire marked the end of a highly productive four-year cycle in the life of David Sylvian. Through his marriage to Ingrid Chavez and friendship with Robert Fripp, he had escaped from the brink of torpor, and again found the confidence to confront his audience alone, and for that matter, relatively unbowed. However, as was so often the case with the singer, he chose not to capitalise on his good fortune, but instead withdraw from the marketplace to re-examine his wares.

20

Coda

Throughout the Nineties, David Sylvian had proved himself an able collaborator. His work with the likes of Robert Fripp, Russell Mills and Ryuichi Sakamoto, whilst never groundbreaking, was still worthy enough to merit serious examination and, as a consequence, Sylvian retained both his audience and the interest of the musical intelligentsia. Additionally, even when his collaborations bore bitter emotional fruit (as with 1991's *Rain Tree Crow*), the songs suffered relatively little: in fact, they may have even benefited from the emotional entanglements that gave birth to them.

Nonetheless, only the most devoted Sylvian acolyte would deny something was missing. The strident individualism, so important to the realisation of albums such as *Brilliant Trees* and *Secrets Of The Beehive*, seemed submerged, or at least partially diluted, in much of David's more recent work. Of course, his lyrical gifts and unswerving ear for a good melody were never completely absent, but one instinctively felt that, for the time being at least, the singer was content to hide behind the carbonised guitars of Robert Fripp.

In reality, the series of musical partnerships David Sylvian aligned himself to throughout the Nineties were critically important in maintaining his internal equilibrium. After a rocky late Eighties, his individual muse had largely deserted him: "Around 1988," Sylvian confirmed to *Mojo*'s Sylvie Simmons, "my private life took a turn for the worse – heavy emotional baggage – and I lost my focus. In fact, I had stopped writing on my own, completely. I found the only way I could work was to throw myself into collaborations. I don't think I would have done anything at all otherwise." In a matter of four sentences, Sylvian at last clarified why there had been no solo album from him since 1987.

The return to musical independence began slowly but surely in October, 1995 with the well-received *Slow Fire – A Personal Retrospective* tour, a series of dates which David undertook without benefit of other musicians. As we have noted, by freeing his songs from extraneous orchestration (he employed only acoustic guitar or spare keyboard sounds), Sylvian fashioned an intimate atmosphere between audience and performer – a far cry from the icy cliffs that surrounded his on-stage persona with Japan. Accorded considerable critical acclaim, *Slow Fire* not only had the effect of bolstering Sylvian's confidence in his own song-writing abilities, but as importantly, raised enough finance to underwrite some of the cost of his next solo album.

Atypically, David made the decision to dispense with the services of long-time musical partner, Steve Nye, and produce his comeback LP alone. The reasons were simple enough: new technology such as Pro-Tools (a form of computerised recording) allowed artists greater freedom in editing their own performances and, as a result, the need for an on-board producer to oversee the development of songs was lessened. In addition to the march of science, Sylvian's budget for his latest enterprise was limited. It made sound financial sense to keep studio personnel to a minimum. However, the burden of sole responsibility was partially eased by the presence of Dave Kent, an experienced engineer Sylvian brought in to aid him with the minutiae of the recording process.

Unfortunately, the project nearly fell at the first hurdle, due to a combination of odd circumstances and lack of inspiration. Eager to get his old friend Ryuichi Sakamoto involved in the album from the offset, David set up a three-week brainstorming session between the two. Yet the duo who had produced such inspired material as 'Bamboo Music', 'Forbidden Colours' and 'Heartbeat' found themselves unable to progress even the simplest of ideas beyond a few chords. The sessions were subsequently abandoned, with Sylvian returning to his then home in Minneapolis to continue the song-writing process alone. "It just wasn't gelling," he concluded at the time.

The next step of an increasingly tortuous process saw the singer flying to England, and setting up home at Peter Gabriel's Real World Studios near Bath. Here, Sylvian worked with various musicians in the hope their contributions might advance the ideas he had generated in the States. As before, these sessions proved largely unproductive, and he was soon on a plane home to his family. The only way forward, it seemed, was to take the approach of a musical hermit, and work solely on his own. In a series of fits and starts over the next twelve months, progress was finally made – enough, at least, to re-introduce other musicians to the project and record their offerings for posterity.

Sylvian's worries were far from over, however. While finding inspiration was now a past concern, both "technical and logistical difficulties" continued to plague the recording of the LP. Somewhat inevitably, these digital gremlins cut heavily into David's remaining budget, with the result that the vocalist ran out of money. In the end, final mixing of tracks took place in a humble barn/studio in rural California. Such financial anarchy (though not new for Sylvian) can hardly have eased the creative process.

"The pressures are very real," he later told *The Independent*'s John L. Walters. "I've never been in as much debt as I now find myself. We had to make major sacrifices, but I've had Ingrid supporting me all the way along. She's insulated me, to some degree, from the pressures so that I could continue working without thinking I've got to finish this week or else . . ." No doubt the financial settlement accorded Ingrid Chavez for her contribution to Madonna's multi-million selling single, 'Justify

My Love', proved a useful asset in combating her husband's ever-diminishing project funds.

And so it was that February, 1999, finally saw the release of a new David Sylvian single. Entitled 'I Surrender', the song was as much a calling card as 'Red Guitar' had been all those years ago – clear indication, in fact, that Sylvian's world-view had dramatically changed in accordance with his life experience. Over a lilting orchestra of strings, Fender Rhodes piano, bluesy guitar and leafy flutes, the singer outlined a new policy of emotional acquiescence, where free will bows before the selflessness of true love: "I've travelled all this way for your embrace", he sang, "enraptured by the recognition on your face, hold me now while my old life dies tonight and I surrender . . ."

For Sylvian, 'I Surrender' encapsulated the emotion of "desire, desiring the object of desire, and then finally surrendering to it until you disappear and become part of it . . . desiring the beloved to the point of total surrender . . . until you merge and your own self disappears within the greater whole". While David had made reference to notions of submission before in his work (the lyric to 'Darshan', for instance, had implied supplication to "a power greater than oneself"), 'I Surrender' somehow seemed more personal, perhaps more grounded in the message it sent to his audience. Only the most casual listener would doubt that this was a love song directed towards his wife.

Nonetheless, Sylvian still felt that the themes he invoked could easily be expanded to encompass broader, more spiritual horizons: "Some people have intimated to me that taking the path of surrender is an easy option," he told *The Wire*'s Rob Young, "I never felt that to be true. I've always felt that it's the hardest thing to surrender your will to a higher power or whatever. Or anyone. Or anything. It's not a one-time event, it's an ongoing process that you have to re-affirm in every second of your life."

As is now common practice in the singles market, 'I

Surrender' was released on two separate CDs, each containing different supplementary tracks. If such releases are an obvious ploy by record companies to increase potential sales, at least the Sylvian 'multi-pack' did not insult would-be buyers by offering uninspired re-mixes of the principal song. Instead, four new tunes (not available on the forthcoming LP) were aired: 'Les Fleurs Du Mal', 'Starred And Dreaming', 'Whose Trip Is This?' and 'Remembering Julia'. Of these, however, only 'Remembering Julia' really broke new ground, with Ingrid Chavez offering an enchanting spoken-word tale of a lost child-woman, seeking redemption from a distant God: "She's crying in the pulpit, waiting for a sign, she's pushed beneath the water . . . promise to be a good soldier . . ." The tale was made all the more touching due to the gentle keyboard/guitar swells Sylvian chose for musical accompaniment.

Reaching a semi-creditable No. 40 in the UK charts (the highest position Sylvian had attained for a single release since 1984), 'I Surrender' acted as an key primer for David's fourth solo LP, *Dead Bees On A Cake*, which arrived in record shops on March 26, 1999. According to the singer, *Dead Bees* . . . was a collection of "wholly auto-biographical (songs), the key elements being love, devotion and divine intoxication". It was as clear and concise an appreciation of the sentiments that made up the album as one could have hoped for.

Dead Bees On A Cake was, in truth, a fine distillation of both Sylvian's musical past and philosophical present. Sometimes flawed, sometimes heart-rending, it was nonetheless a work of real continuity, the themes raised encircling the listener in ever smaller spirals, until the inherent message becomes clear: one does not fail by surrendering to the gift of love. Instead, one might prevail.

Of the songs presented on the LP, there were several highlights. Aside from the aforementioned 'I Surrender', both the Asian-tinged 'Krishna Blue' and romantic jazz of 'Wanderlust' confirmed Sylvian's certain devotion to the love he had found: "She's prising the rope from my hands," he sang, "the fear and the hope I held onto . . . colour the river I swim back to you, Krishna Blue . . ." These sentiments were again echoed throughout 'Wanderlust': "Losing light, the selfish kind, and we're on the road again . . . it's given us this wonderful wanderlust".

The autobiographical nature of Sylvian's lyricism was hard to miss. 'Alphabet Angel', for instance, captured David recounting to his daughter the day he first met her mother in New Orleans, "the sun slipping into blue". 'Thaliem' was another poem of personal intoxication, its key line in direct opposition to the sense of regret voiced on 1994's 'Damage': "Take the shadow from the road I walk upon . . . you look and find someone, the damage is undone."

Yet, in amongst the optimism – the sense of inner completion that Sylvian hinted at – the dark themes that pervaded his earlier work still loomed in the background. Nowhere was this more apparent than on the desolate blues of 'Dobro #1' and 'Midnight Sun', where images of stolen lives, never-ending rain and orphaned stars gained lyrical dominion. Even the optimistically titled 'The Shining Of Things' flirted with haunting imagery as two lovers struggled to regain shared harmony following an argument: "She calls my name and I come running, I have lost the voice I listened to . . ." It was left to the concluding track on *Dead Bees . . .*, the ethereal 'Darkest Dreaming', to marry these images of light and shade into an aching, bittersweet whole: "I don't ever want to be alone," entreated Sylvian, "with all my darkest dreaming . . ."

As with all of David Sylvian's albums, there were occasional lapses of quality. Though 'Pollen Path' was a successful attempt at rock dynamism, its turbulent nature might have better suited Sylvian's collaborations with Robert Fripp. Similarly, the free-jazz experimentation of '. . . My Mother's Names', all wild guitars and uneven percussion, sat uncomfortably next to the more languid approach taken by tracks such as 'Wanderlust' and 'Thaliem'. And if one were looking to accuse Sylvian of pastiche, the lounge-lizard musings of 'Café

Europa' might easily be used as evidence. Essentially a personal travelogue, trading on images of planes, trains and automobiles, the song strongly recalled the 'life as tourism' manifesto that worked so well and so badly for David's previous group, Japan.

That said, *Dead Bees On A Cake* was a welcome return to form for Sylvian. While a far more gentile proposition than the likes of *Gone To Earth* and *Secrets Of The Beehive*, the LP still proved his effectiveness as a solo artist with much left to say. And if that old self-division or inner turmoil had been partially soothed by marriage to Ingrid Chavez, at least the singer had not fallen prey to the critical adage "inner peace is a synonym of mediocrity". After all, the clouded skies so effectively traced in 'Midnight Sun' and 'Darkest Dreaming' proved there was enough self-doubt left in him to keep the hounds of mediocrity at bay for a time to come.

Perhaps as intriguing as the album itself was the title David chose for it. Typically, the explanation offered was both as simple as it was arcane: "On most spiritual paths," he told Sylvie Simmons, "you'll hear people talk about the death of self – merging with the object of desire – so (that brought about) the image of the bees becoming one with the cake." A continuing motif throughout much of his work, Sylvian's bees seemed to represent a kind of kaleidoscopic beauty, their movement invoking an image of unparalleled splendour which simultaneously resided "before me, behind me, to the left of me, to the right of me, above and below . . ." The metaphysical and hermetic connotations contained within such imagery were all too apparent.

Of course, there were also many pragmatic aspects to the creation of *Dead Bees On A Cake* – not least the caucus of musicians employed by Sylvian to add necessary sheen to his rough song sketches. Among the familiar faces returning to active duty this time around were flugelhorn player Kenny Wheeler and David's brother Steve Jansen (the enmity born of the *Rain Tree Crow* sessions now firmly behind him). That said, the majority of instrumentalists responsible for the music of *Dead Bees* . . . were new recruits to David's cause, and included the likes of flautist Lawrence 'I Surrender' Feldman, bassist Chris Minh Doky and maverick jazz guitarist Bill Frisell, whose spare picking on 'Dobro #1' proved an unexpected pleasure.

Sylvian's approach to amassing the right musicians for his albums had not changed in years: if he enjoyed their work, he approached them directly, and asked if they might contribute. "I was amazed at how many people responded immediately to the invitation," Sylvian told the *Irish Times*' John Kelly. "That was an eye opener . . . people just don't get asked often enough! (Still), when musicians come in and respond to my work in a profound way . . . I'm always grateful."

The occasional surprise guest made for interesting listening. Mercury Prize-winning percussionist Talvin Singh brought the subtle sounds of the tabla drum to 'Krishna Blue', whilst Tom Waits' guitarist Marc Ribot (whose parts for the LP were recorded in a single afternoon) suffused songs such as 'I Surrender' and 'Midnight Sun' with an authentic blues feel. But the biggest contribution to the actual sound of *Dead Bees* . . . undoubtedly came from the keyboard of Ryuichi Sakamoto, whose welcome return to the project (following the aborted 1995 sessions) lent class and refinement to much of Sylvian's output. By creating various striations and patinas in David's songs, Sakamoto lifted the raw essence of the LP to new levels – sometimes far more than the actual tracks themselves deserved,

As usual, Sylvian retained the lion's share of his praise for his long-term collaborator: "Ryuichi has a wealth of knowledge of music of all genres," he confirmed. "He's one of the few people who can apply that knowledge (clicks fingers) like that. You can be sitting in a room with him, working on an arrangement, and say 'elements of Debussy would be nice', and suddenly there they are . . . that's very rare, and it all has his signature."

There were, of course, other influences at play on *Dead*

Bees On A Cake, not least David's wife Ingrid and his close friend/teacher Shree Ma. Though Chavez appeared relatively little on the LP itself (a lilting vocal on 'Krishna Blue', a few breaths and sighs on 'Café Europa'), her dual role as both muse and guiding influence cannot be underestimated. Simply put, Sylvian's abiding love for his wife is at the very heart of *Dead Bees . . .*, from the intoxicating atmospheres of 'I Surrender' and 'Krishna Blue' to the life-affirming sentiments expressed in 'Wanderlust' and 'Thaliem'. Additionally, Ingrid's record collection had a striking impact on her husband, with David incorporating new soul and blues ingredients into his own musical canon – the evidence writ large across tracks such as 'Midnight Sun' and 'Café Europa'.

The Hindu aesthete Shree Ma (a compatriot of David's main philosophical mentor Sri Sri Mata Amritanandamayi) also brought much to the making of *Dead Bees On A Cake* – the ideas central to her faith cross-pollinating with Sylvian's own internal ruminations to provide the album with a strong spiritual core. For instance, due to the interest David had taken of late in Hindu theology, 'the doctrine of introversion' he inadvertently preached throughout his time as a solo artist was altogether more subdued on *Dead Bees . . .* However, the importance of family, acquiescence of will to the greater good and fluidity of personal character were qualities positively championed within his new lyricism. It seemed that the fledgling existentialist, responsible for such separatist mantras as 'Ghosts' and 'Red Guitar', was now fully aware of his need to contribute – to those he loved, as well as the community they inhabited.

Interestingly, Shree Ma and some thirteen of her students came to stay with Sylvian and Chavez at their Minneapolis home in 1996, an experience the singer described as "tremendously transforming". According to David, "the house was kind of turned into an ashram for about a week", with Shree Ma leading her followers in devotional song each morning. The song in question, an ancient Sanskrit hymn entitled 'Praise

(Pratah Smarami)' so captivated Sylvian that he decided to record Shree Ma's rendition of it. The resulting session can be heard on *Dead Bees . . .*: "She used to sing the piece . . . every morning at the end of puja – worship," David told *The Wire*, "the voice, very fragile, echoing through the house. This yearning. We invited her to the studio . . . to perform the song . . . and (my) added guitar part just seemed to lift it."

Though Sylvian's admiration for Shree Ma and her teachings appeared boundless (he described her as a "truly devoted soul" whose work is "just pure light"), a final conversion to the ways of Hinduism remains an unlikely prospect: "Shree Ma (and her followers) come from a Hindu background, but that doesn't make me a Hindu. There's no need to belong to a particular religion to follow a spiritual path." As ever, the singer was content to remain on the outside, a perennial observer: "I've always been an outsider," he told *The Independent*. "I always will be. I'm not the sort of person that can belong, even to small groups. I'm not sure I've ever wanted to analyse why that is – I'm happy being on the outside. I'm comfortable there. I'm uncomfortable as soon as I feel like I should belong, or I'm thought to belong to a group. I rebel against it. More often than not, I'm kicked out!"

For Sylvian, the act of 'belonging' was still a step too far, a view no doubt entrenched by years of self-imposed exile from the artistic mainstream. Yet, his present circumstances confirmed that certain bridges had been built. He was now a man in his forties with a wife and children (Ingrid Chavez gave birth to the couple's second child, Isobel Ananda, in October, 1996). His relationship with his manager, Richard Chadwick, stemmed some two decades and remained as strong as ever. And though they had both gone their separate ways in the late Eighties, David still regarded former lover Yuka Fujii as one of his closest friends. This emotional stability, aligned with a new-found acceptance of "the shifting world", all pointed to the fact that David Sylvian's status as a 'outsider' was not as clear-cut as he may have believed.

Ultimately, it was left to the critics to apportion praise or blame to Sylvian's latest recorded work and the ideas it contained. In time honoured fashion, the songwriter managed to beguile and repel in equal measure: *Mojo*'s Phil Sutcliffe, for instance, found much to admire in *Dead Bees* . . . While raising an odd eyebrow or two in response to David's lapse into "vacuous . . . cabaret sauveness" ('Thalhiem' and 'Café Europa' were deemed prime offenders), Sutcliffe nevertheless responded favourably to the LP's charms, concluding that "This is a record to stir hopes that an artist who has fallen off the map of fashion and commerciality can at least do well enough to get his music out there once again."

Q's Stuart Maconie was less enthralled with *Dead Bees On A Cake.* In fact, he used his review to draw attention to a criticism that had haunted Sylvian for years: to wit, that the singer's vocal style often compromised the promise of his own songs: "It takes a few listens to realise what the nagging problem with the new David Sylvian record is," reasoned Maconie, "and when it comes, it's a shock. It's Sylvian himself. Musically, (*Dead Bees* . . .) is a rich and sensual hour's worth . . . terribly adult, stylishly redolent . . . but Sylvian's haughty, mannered vocal stylings are irksome when coupled with lyrics about mysterious women 'throwing books into the sea'. Put some of these vocal excesses to one side and (*Dead Bees* . . .) is almost enjoyable."

If the critics were divided about the validity of Sylvian's work, at least his supporters remained faithful to the cause. *Dead Bees On A Cake* debuted at No. 31 in the UK charts, an improvement of some six digits on David's last solo effort, 1987's *Secrets Of The Beehive.* He also managed a degree of international success, with the LP reaching the Top Ten in both Japan and Italy. Sales were undoubtedly helped by a whirlwind round of press interviews that saw the normally reclusive vocalist talking to anyone who might listen: "I'm happy in my solitude," he confirmed to *The Irish Times,* "and (courting publicity) has always been a problem for me . . . but less so now. I feel very rooted, very grounded in my life in a way I didn't before. (Consequently), I'm less vulnerable to this kind of attention. But the industry needs my support in promoting the record, so I do the best I can. I do want people to hear the record ... I mean, the whole point is to communicate."

The next step in Sylvian's return to the public domain was the release of another single/EP in the Autumn of 1999. The track chosen on this occasion was one of *Dead Bees ...'* stronger moments: the perplexing, yet occasionally brilliant 'God Man'. Underpinned by a wild confection of Prince-like drum loops, intrusive synthesiser sounds and detuned guitars, 'God Man's lyrical complexities left one both beguiled and bewildered: "From different maps, dead bees on a cake, you're sweeping the forest, man, it's getting late ..." With two dramatic, if inevitable re-mixes of the title track (courtesy of Luke 'Wagon Christ' Vibert and Guy Sigsworth) and a previously unreleased ballad, the rum-dark 'Shadowland', the 'God Man' EP represented some 23 minutes of intense listening.

Perhaps the most compelling reason to purchase the disc was for the CD-ROM element it contained – namely, a short 'press kit' film entitled *Time Spent*, which Sylvian and Chavez had shot themselves in the winter of 1998. Acting as an interior portrait of David, his family and the "philosophy behind (his) work", *Time Spent* was a welcome change from the more familiar promotional videos fans were usually served up by record companies. A stylised, yet still accessible piece, the film's technical shortcomings were easy to ignore, given that this was the first time Sylvian had genuinely attempted to cast aside his somewhat guarded public image, and present himself as an 'everyman' – albeit one with a highly developed worldview.

In stark contrast to the recorded drought of recent years, Sylvian-related product just kept on coming. In addition to a limited re-issue of *Weatherbox*, the five CD set collecting all of David's previous solo output, Virgin Records finally released

Approaching Silence, a three-track composite of the music recorded for the *Ember Glance* and *Redemption . . .* installation projects of 1991 and 1994 respectively.

Though these Russell Mills/Robert Fripp collaborations were familiar enough – the Mills/Sylvian pieces 'The Beekeeper's Apprentice' and 'Epiphany' were first made commercially available in 1991 – the serene, almost drowsy nature of *Approaching Silence* remained compelling, with sounds coming in waves, ripples and splashes – "a fine soundtrack", as one critic put it, "for an evening of inner contemplation". The year 1999 was rounded off by the publication of David's second book of poetry/songs, the aptly titled *Trophies II*, which aside from covering the lyrical waterfront from 1989's 'Pop Song' to '*Dead Bees . . .*', contained several new elegies, including 'I Do Nothing' and the charming 'When The Little One Came'.

As this book went to press (March 2000), more Sylvian-related merchandise would appear to be in the pipeline. For instance, the long-rumoured 'compilation CD', containing a mixture of David's better known songs and much sought after obscurities, may at last be on its way – though, as yet, no release date has been confirmed. Additionally, fans eager to hear Sylvian's 1992 collaboration with free-jazz pianist Keith Tippet could still have their wishes granted. The main problem with this project, however, is that it remains unfinished.

Finally, another tour seems inevitable, though what shape it might take (full band or solo performance) remains a matter for David alone to ponder. With two small children to tend to, a recent house move from Minneapolis to California's Napa Valley and an increasing association with the work of both Sri Sri Mata Amritanandamayi and Shree Ma, any decisions regarding time 'on the road' will have to be carefully planned. After all, intent and outcome are rarely co-incident.

What Sylvian can be sure of, however, is the body of work already behind him. Of course, he has often been quixotic in his analysis of that work, sometimes viewing his musical past with the eyes of a contented romantic, sometimes with a disdain that can compromise the importance of his achievements. Yet, in the same way that wolves make bad shepherds, seeking a definitive appraisal of David Sylvian's efforts from the man himself is a path fraught with difficulties. In fact, David has recently said that of the hundred or so songs he has written over the years, only a handful still remain satisfying in terms of content or execution. While he is perfectly entitled to make such a statement, it may be at odds with the evidence at hand.

In truth, Sylvian is one of the few performers to escape from the watery fields of pop music with his credibility more or less intact. By placing Japan in stasis at the height of their powers, he has ensured the group is remembered as a delightful curiosity of times past, their image and essential credo relatively unblemished by advancing years and bitter, if financially lucrative, re-unions. Even when the singer's resolve weakened in the early Nineties, and he sought the company of old friends to help him find his way, he at least had the good sense to cover his backtracking with a new name – Rain Tree Crow.

As a solo artist, there is also much to recommend him. At the start of his career, Sylvian was content to sublimate his desires, his essential longings, in a stream of beautifully executed, yet ultimately, dispassionate songs. Material such as 'Swing', 'Nightporter' and 'Gentlemen Take Polaroids' all hinted at a young man fascinated by the concepts of love and loss, but seemingly wary of engaging them in any real sense. Yes, he sometimes appeared interested, sometimes even touched, but never truly involved. Distance was all.

Over the course of 16 years and four albums, Sylvian has done much to counter this formative stance. By speaking of his own dissatisfactions, longings and expectations, he has not only allowed his audience to step closer to his work, but also given them an opportunity to examine themselves. In this respect, he serves as a fine example of 'the balladeer', a man whose tales of "loves lost and won" act as an emotional mirror to those gathered around him. "I know how music affects me," he once told *The Wire*, "and therefore I know it can work. People write and tell me that the work has moved them in many ways which helps them deal with the world. Enlightenment is a long way off but I think the work feeds back into life experience – the idea that it can be the catalyst in the process of self-awareness, focusing away from the external world and entering into the inner world: feeling comfortable there, and asking people to look a little closer, and in the process of questioning, develop."

Despite this gift for moving others, Sylvian still appears to cling to his status as an outsider – a position he remains reluctant to examine, but feels is intrinsic to his nature. Perhaps he instinctively knows that the person holding the mirror up to those seeking examination must remain perpetually "behind the looking glass". Nonetheless, such notions of perennial outsiderdom are difficult to maintain. As author/philosopher Colin Wilson, suggests in his book *The Misfits*, "even the most intelligent experience the desire to seek out – or create – a system of belief that can unite them with other people and rescue them from a sense of isolation. All reveal the craving to escape the burden of individualism and merge into some form of collective effort."

As previously stated, David Sylvian would seem to have escaped his particular burden through marriage to Ingrid Chavez, the children they have produced and the cultivation of some enduring friendships, collaborative, spiritual or otherwise. And if the rich lyricism present on *Dead Bees On A Cake* is anything to go by, the spiritual containment that ran deep in his earliest work has been replaced by a new emotional commitment – the desire to reach out superseding the urge to withdraw to the confines of self.

The quest for true peace has taken Sylvian down a long and arduous road, and one senses, the journey is not quite over yet. He readily acknowledges that the darkness that has snapped at his heels since childhood is still present – albeit now more a spectre than the all pervading force it sometimes threatened to be. Yet his current mind-set towards such adversity is strong, allowing him a new perspective that tolerates, even embraces, that which cannot be escaped: "There is a view that is not easily grasped on a moment-to-moment basis that whatever you are doing, whatever your predicament, however much your suffering, it is all entirely perfect – it is as it should be."

He continues: "Obviously this is hard to acknowledge, particularly at certain periods in life. I take this notion to mean that we are given the lessons most pertinent to our life. We are not given more than we can handle and that if we recognise this fact in the midst of the experiences, we can learn from the most difficult of circumstances and move on."

Over the years, David Sylvian has turned a mannered, insubstantial croon into an instrument of great emotional authority. He has also been responsible for writing some of the most touching ballads of the pop era – ballads that bring something out in the listener: at worst, sorrow, at best, joy. In this respect, he's up there with the finest of the bluesmen. "I think the goal is always the same," he once confessed, "to feel peace of mind and an enormous amount of love."

Blessed with all the thunder in the world.

Postscript

While the subject of this book has been the life and career of David Sylvian, his former Japan colleagues, Mick Karn, Richard Barbieri and Steve Jansen have been far from idle since the band split up in 1982.

Aside from 1982's *Titles* and 1987's *Dreams Of Reason Produce Monsters,* Mick Karn has released two fine jazz/fusion/ambient albums: 1993's *Bestial Clusters* and 1995's *The Tooth Mother.* Both LPs were critically well received by the rock press and represent some of the bassist's best work.

As a duo, Richard Barbieri and Steve Jansen have also produced several LPs worthy of mention. 1985's *Worlds In A Small Room,* 1991's *Stories Across Borders,* 1995's *Stone To Flesh* and 1996's *Other Worlds In A Small Room* are all eclectic releases, and should appeal to anyone who found Japan's music of worth. Karn, Jansen and Barbieri have also collaborated as a trio on the 1994 LPs *Beginning To Melt* and *Seed.*

Finally, mention should be made of Richard Barbieri's involvement with the progressive/ambient outfit, The Porcupine Tree, with whom the keyboard player continues to tour.

Discography

JAPAN

7″ & 12″ Singles:
(All UK releases unless otherwise stated)

Don't Rain On My Parade/Stateline
Ariola AHA 510 7″
March 1978

The Unconventional/Adolescent Sex
Ariola AHA 525 7″
August 1978

Sometimes I Feel So Low/Love Is Infectious
Ariola AHA 529 7″
October 1978

Sometimes I Feel So Low/Love Is Infectious
Ariola AHA 529 7″
(blue vinyl)
October 1978

Life In Tokyo (Part One)/Life In Tokyo (Part Two)
Ariola AHA 540 7″
May 1979

Life In Tokyo/Life In Tokyo
Ariola AHA 540 7″
(red vinyl)
May 1979

Life In Tokyo/Life In Tokyo (Short Version)
Ariola AHAD 540 12″
(red vinyl)
May 1979

I Second That Emotion/Quiet Life
Ariola AHA 559 7″
March 1980

I Second That Emotion/Quiet Life
Ariola AHA 559 7″
(red vinyl)
March 1980

Gentlemen Take Polaroids/The Experience Of Swimming/
The Width Of A Room/Burning Bridges
Virgin VS 379 7″
(special edition double pack single)
October 1980

Life In Tokyo/European Son
Ariola/Hansa HANSA 4 7″
April 1981

Life In Tokyo/European Son
Ariola /Hansa HANSA 124 12″
April 1981

The Art Of Parties/Life Without Buildings
Virgin VS 409 7″
May 1981

The Art Of Parties/Life Without Buildings
Virgin VS 409 7″
(special edition fold-out sleeve)
May 1981

The Art Of Parties/Life Without Buildings
Virgin VS 40912 12″
May 1981

The Art Of Parties/The Width Of A Room/
Life Without Buildings/The Experience Of Swimming
Virgin VEP 305 12″
(Canadian release only)
May 1981

Quiet Life/A Foreign Place/Fall In Love With Me
Ariola/Hansa HANSA 6 7″
August 1981

Quiet Life/A Foreign Place/Fall In Love With Me
Ariola/Hansa HANSA 126 12″
August 1981

Visions Of China/Taking Islands In Africa
Virgin VS 436 7″
October 1981

Visions Of China/Taking Islands In Africa
Virgin VS 43612 12″
October 1981

European Son/Alien
Ariola/Hansa HANSA 10 7″
January 1982

European Son/Alien
Ariola/Hansa HANSA 1210 12″
January 1982

Ghosts/The Art Of Parties (Version)
Virgin VS 472 7″
March 1982

Ghosts/The Art Of Parties (Version)
Virgin VS 472 7″
(special edition picture disc)
March 1982

Ghosts/The Art Of Parties (Version)
Virgin VS 47212 12″
March 1982

Cantonese Boy/Burning Bridges
Virgin VS 502 7″
May 1982

Cantonese Boy/Burning Bridges/Gentlemen Take Polaroids/The Experience Of Swimming
Virgin VS 502 7″
(special edition double single)
May 1982

Cantonese Boy/Burning Bridges/Gentlemen Take Polaroids/The Experience Of Swimming
Virgin VS 50212 12″
May 1982

I Second That Emotion (Remix)/Halloween
Ariola/Hansa HANSA 12 7″
July 1982

I Second That Emotion (Remix)/Halloween
Ariola Hansa HANSA 1212 12″
July 1982

Life In Tokyo (Remix)/Life In Tokyo (Theme)
Ariola/Hansa HANSA 17 7″
October 1982

Life In Tokyo (Remix)/Life In Tokyo (Theme)
Ariola/Hansa HANSA 1217 12″
October 1982

Nightporter (Edit)/Ain't That Peculiar (Version)
Virgin VS 554 7″
November 1982

Nightporter/Ain't That Peculiar (Version)/
Methods Of Dance
Virgin VS 55412 12″
November 1982

All Tomorrow's Parties/In Vogue (Live)
Ariola/Hansa HANSA 18 7″
March 1983

All Tomorrow's Parties/Deviation (Live)/
Obscure Alternatives (Live)
Ariola/Hansa HANSA 1218 12″
March 1983

Canton (Live)/Visions Of China (Live)
Virgin VS 581 7″
May 1983

Canton (Live)/Visions Of China (Live)
Virgin VS 581 7″ (special edition fold-out sleeve)
May 1983

Canton (Live)/Visions Of China (Live)
Virgin VS 58112 12″
May 1983

EPs/Special Editions:

The following EPs/Special Editions are all imports, originating from Germany, Canada and Japan. They were never officially issued by Ariola/Hansa Records or Virgin Records in the UK, and are therefore considered collectors items.

'Japan – Live In Japan'
Deviation/Obscure Alternatives/In Vogue/
Sometimes I Feel So Low
Ariola/Hansa HANSA 600 242 12″
1980

'Japan – Special Edition: Five Song Extended Play'
I Second That Emotion/European Son/Life In
Tokyo/Stateline/Adolescent Sex
Ariola/Hansa/Quality EPHA 001 12″
1980

'Nightporter – Mini Album'
Nightporter/Ghosts/The Art Of Parties/The Experience Of
Swimming/Life Without Buildings/The Width Of A Room
Victor VIP 4181 12″
1980

'Japan – The Singles'
Life In Tokyo/European Son/Stateline/
The Unconventional/Quiet Life/I Second That Emotion
Victor VIP 4106 12″
1981

Albums:
(All UK releases unless stated otherwise)

Adolescent Sex
Transmission/The Unconventional/Wish You Were Black/
Performance/Lovers On Main Street/Don't Rain On My
Parade/Suburban Love/Adolescent Sex/Communist China/
Television
Ariola AHAL 8004 LP
April 1978
CD re-issue only available on import

Obscure Alternatives
Automatic Gun/Rhodesia/Love Is Infectious/
Sometimes I Feel So Low/Obscure Alternatives/Deviation/
Suburban Berlin/The Tenant
Ariola AHAL 8007 LP
November 1978
CD re-issue only available on import

Quiet Life
Quiet Life/Fall In Love With Me/Despair/In-Vogue/
Halloween/All Tomorrow's Parties/Alien/
The Other Side Of Life
Ariola/Hansa AHAL 5011 LP
February 1980
CD re-issue only available on import

Gentlemen Take Polaroids
Gentlemen Take Polaroids/Swing/Burning Bridges/
My New Career/Methods Of Dance/Ain't That Peculiar/
Nightporter/Taking Islands In Africa
Virgin V 2180 LP
October 1980
Virgin CDV 2180 EMI CD re-issue June 1988

Tin Drum
The Art Of Parties/Talking Drum/Ghosts/Canton/
Still Life In Mobile Homes/Visions Of China/
Sons Of Pioneers/Cantonese Boy
Virgin V 2209 LP
November 1981
Virgin CDV 2209 EMI CD re-issue
June 1988
Virgin LP CENT 40 EMI LP re-issue (limited edition)
November 1997

Oil On Canvas
Oil On Canvas/Sons Of Pioneers/Gentlemen Take Polaroids/
Swing/Cantonese Boy/Visions Of China/Ghosts/
Voices Raised In Welcome, Hands Held In Prayer/
Nightporter/Still Life In Mobile Homes/Methods Of Dance/
Quiet Life/ The Art Of Parties/Canton/The Temple Of Dawn
Virgin VD 2513 LP
June 1983
Virgin CDVD 2513 EMI CD re-issue
April 1992

Compilations/Collections:
(All UK releases unless otherwise stated)

Assemblage
Adolescent Sex/Stateline/Communist China/Rhodesia/
Suburban Berlin/Life In Tokyo/European Son/
All Tomorrow's Parties/Quiet Life/I Second That Emotion
Ariola/Hansa HAN LP 1
September 1981
CD re-issue only available on import

Exorcising Ghosts
Methods Of Dance/Gentlemen Take Polaroids/Quiet Life/
Nightporter/My New Career/The Other Side Of Life/
Visions Of China/Ghosts/Life Without Buildings/
Talking Drum/The Art Of Parties
Virgin VGD 3510 LP
December 1984
Virgin VGDCD 3510 CD
January 1985

A Souvenir From Japan
I Second That Emotion/Life In Tokyo/Deviation/
Suburban Berlin/Adolescent Sex/European Son/
All Tomorrow's Parties/Communist China/Stateline/
Rhodesia/Obscure Alternatives/Quiet Life
Arista/BMG 260 360 CD
December 1989

Prophetique – 4 CD Box Set
Adolescent Sex/Obscure Alternatives/Quiet Life/
Bonus Disc – contains Stateline/Life In Tokyo/
I Second That Emotion/European Son
Hansa BVCP 644 646 CD Japanese import
(date not given)

Gentlemen Take Polaroids/Tin Drum/Oil On Canvas –
3 CD Box Set
Virgin CD TPAK 6 EMI CD re-issue
October 1990

In Vogue
The Unconventional/Lovers On Main Street/
Transmission/I Second That Emotion/
All Tomorrow's Parties/Alien/ Halloween/
Suburban Berlin/Quiet Life/Love Is Infectious/
Fall In Love With Me/Adolescent Sex/European Son/
In Vogue/Life In Tokyo
RCA/BMG 74321393382 CD
August 1996

Videos:
Two Japan videos were released commercially in the UK in 1983 and 1984 respectively. Unfortunately, they have both long been deleted by Virgin Music Video. However, copies are still in circulation, turning up occasionally on the net, at car boot sales or buried at the back of the music section in video stores.

Oil On Canvas
Overture (Burning Bridges)/Sons Of Pioneers/
Gentlemen Take Polaroids/Swing/Cantonese Boy/
Visions Of China/Canton/Ghosts/
Still Life In Mobile Homes/Methods Of Dance/
Art Of Parties
Live performance filmed at Hammersmith Odeon, November 1982
Virgin Music Video VIRV 055D (55 minutes)
1983

Instant Pictures
Gentlemen Take Polaroids/Cantonese Boy/Swing/Still Life In Mobile Homes/Nightporter/Canton/Visions Of China
Compilation of promotional videos circa 1980–1982
Virgin Music Video VVC 049 (30 minutes)
1984

RAIN TREE CROW

(All UK releases unless stated otherwise)

Singles:

Blackwater/I Drink To Forget
Virgin VS 1340 7″
March 1991

Blackwater/Red Earth (As Summertime Ends)/
I Drink To Forget
Virgin VST 1340 (cassette)
March 1991

Blackwater/Red Earth (As Summertime Ends)/
I Drink To Forget
Virgin VST 1340 12″
(includes album cover print)
March 1991

Blackwater/Red Earth (As Summertime Ends)/
I Drink To Forget
Virgin VSCDT 1340 CD
(includes album cover print)
March 1991

Blackwater/Red Earth (As Summertime Ends)/
I Drink To Forget
Virgin VSCDX 1340 CD
(special edition – includes album cover print)
March 1991

Album:

Rain Tree Crow
Big Wheels In Shanty Town/Every Colour You Are/
Rain Tree Crow/Red Earth (As Summertime Ends)/
Pocket Full Of Change/Boat's For Burning/
New Moon At Red Deer Wallow/Blackwater/
A Reassuringly Dull Sunday/Blackcrow Hits Shoe Shine City/
Scratchings On The Bible Belt/Cries And Whispers
Virgin CDV 2659 CD
April 1991

DAVID SYLVIAN

(All UK releases unless otherwise stated)

Singles/EPs/Cassettes:

Red Guitar/Forbidden Colours (Version)
Virgin VS 633 7″
June 1984

Red Guitar/Forbidden Colours (Version)
Virgin VSY 633 7″
(picture disc)
June 1984

Red Guitar (Full Length Version)/Forbidden Colours (Version)
Virgin VS 633 12 12″
June 1984

The Ink In The Well (Re-mix)/Weathered Wall (Instrumental)
Virgin VS 700 7″
(fold-out sleeve)
August 1984

The Ink In The Well/Weathered Wall (Instrumental)
Virgin VS 700 12 12″
(special edition fold-out sleeve)
August 1984

Pulling Punches (Re-mix)/Backwaters (Re-mix)
Virgin VS 717 7″
(3 postcard set included)
November 1984

Pulling Punches (Album Version)/Backwaters (Re-mix)
Virgin VS 717 12 12″
(3 postcard set included)
November 1984

Words With The Shaman – EP
Part One – Ancient Evening/Part Two – Incantation/
Part Three – Awakening (Songs From The Tree Tops)
Virgin 835 12 12″
December 1985

Alchemy – An Index Of Possibilities
1. Words With The Shaman:
Part One – Ancient Evening/Part Two – Incantation/
Part Three – Awakening (Songs From The Tree Tops)/
2. Preparations For A Journey/
3. Steel Cathedrals
Virgin SYL 1 Cassette
(limited edition)
December 1985

Taking The Veil/Answered Prayers
Virgin VS 815 7″
August 1986

Taking The Veil/Answered Prayers/
A Bird Of Prey Vanishes Into A Bright Blue Cloudless Sky
Virgin VS 815 12 12″
August 1986

Silver Moon/Gone To Earth
Virgin VSP 895 7″
October 1986

Silver Moon/Gone To Earth/
Silver Moon Over Sleeping Steeples
Virgin VSP 895 12 12″
October 1986

Let The Happiness In/Blue Of Noon
Virgin VS 1001 7″
October 1987

Let The Happiness In/Blue Of Noon/Buoy (Re-mix)
Virgin VST 1001 12 12″
October 1987

Orpheus/Mother And Child
Virgin VS 1043 7″
April 1988

Orpheus/Mother And Child/The Devil's Own
Virgin VS 1043 12 12″
April 1988

Pop Song/A Brief Conversation Ending In Divorce/
The Stigma Of Childhood (Kin)
Virgin VS 1221 12 12″
October 1989

Pop Song/A Brief Conversation Ending In Divorce/
The Stigma Of Childhood (Kin)
Virgin VSCD 1221 CD
October 1989

I Surrender/Les Fleurs Du Mal/Starred And Dreaming
Virgin VSCDT 1722 CD
February 1999

I Surrender (Single Edit)/Whose Trip Is This?/
Remembering Julia
Virgin VSCDX 1722 1C CD
February 1999

God Man (Album Version)/Shadowland/
God Man (Wagon Christ Mix)/Shadowland (Northfield)/
God Man (Guy Sigsworth Remix)
Virgin VEN D8 CD
September 1999

With Ryuichi Sakamoto:

Bamboo Houses/Bamboo Music
Virgin VS 510 7″
August 1982

Bamboo Houses/Bamboo Music
Virgin VS 510 7″
(special edition gatefold sleeve)
August 1992

Bamboo Houses/Bamboo Music
Virgin VS 510 12 A 12″
August 1982

Forbidden Colours/The Seed And The Sower
Virgin VS 601 7″
July 1983

Forbidden Colours/The Seed And The Sower/
Last Regrets
Virgin VS 601 12 12″
July 1983
N B: 'Forbidden Colours' also appears on the soundtrack CD to the film *Merry Christmas, Mr Lawrence,* released in 1983. Catalogue Number: Virgin CDV 2276.

Heartbeat (Tainai Kaiki II) Returning To The Womb/
Nuages
Virgin America VUS 57 7″
June 1992

Heartbeat (Tainai Kaiki II) Returning To The Womb/
Nuages/The Last Emperor (End Title Theme)
Virgin America VUS 57 12 12″
June 1992

Heartbeat (Tainai Kaiki II) Returning To The Womb/
Nuages/The Last Emperor (End Title Theme)
Virgin America VUS CD 57 CD
June 1992

With Mick Karn:

Buoy/Dreams Of Reason
Virgin VS 910 7″
January 1987

Buoy/Dreams Of Reason
Virgin VS 910 12 12″
January 1987

With Robert Fripp:

Jean The Birdman/Gone To Earth/Tallow Moon/Dark Water
Virgin VS CDT 1462 CD
August 1993

Jean The Birdman/Earthbound (Starlight)/Endgame
Virgin VS CDG 1462 CD
August 1993

Darshan (The Road To Graceland) – Re-mixes
Darshan (The Road To Graceland)
(Translucent re-mix by The Grid)/
Darshana (Re-constructed by The Future Sound Of London)/
Darshan (The Road To Graceland)
(Album version)
Virgin SYL CD1 CD
February 1994

Albums:

Brilliant Trees
Pulling Punches/The Ink In The Well/Nostalgia/
Red Guitar/Weathered Wall/Backwaters/Brilliant Trees
Virgin V2290 LP
June 1984
Virgin CDV 2290
June 1984

Gone To Earth
Taking The Veil/Laughter And Forgetting/Before The
Bullfight/Gone To Earth/Wave/River Man/Silver Moon/
The Healing Place/Answered Prayers/Where The Railroad
Meets The Sea/The Wooden Cross/ Home/Upon This Earth
Virgin VDL 1 LP
September 1986
Virgin CDVDL 1 CD
September 1986

Secrets Of The Beehive
September/The Boy With The Gun/Maria/Orpheus/ The Devil's Own/When Poets Dreamed Of Angels/ Mother And Child/Let The Happiness In/Waterfront
Virgin V 2471 LP
October 1987

Secrets Of The Beehive
September/The Boy With The Gun/Maria/Orpheus/ The Devil's Own/When Poets Dreamed Of Angels/ Mother And Child/Let The Happiness In/Waterfront/ Forbidden Colours (Version)
Virgin CDV 2471 CD
October 1987
(Note: The Japanese CD release of *Secrets Of The Beehive* substitutes 'Forbidden Colours (Version)' with a previously unreleased track – 'Promise (The Cult Of Eurydice)')

Weatherbox – 5 CD Box Set
Disc One: Brilliant Trees/Disc Two: Alchemy – An Index Of Possibilities, The Stigma Of Childhood (Kin), A Brief Conversation Ending In Divorce, Steel Cathedrals/Disc Three: Gone To Earth (Vocal)/ Disc Four: Gone To Earth (Instrumental)/Disc Five: Secrets Of The Beehive
Virgin DS CD 1 CD
December 1989
(Weatherbox is a limited edition box set, of which only 30,000 copies were produced by Virgin Records)

Dead Bees On A Cake
I Surrender/Dobro #1/Midnight Sun/Thalhiem/God Man/ Alphabet Angel/Krishna Blue/The Shining Of Things/ Café Europa/Pollen Path/All Of My Mother's Names (Summers With Amma)/Wanderlust/Praise (Pratah Smarami)/Darkest Dreaming
Virgin CDV 2876 CD
March 1999

Approaching Silence
The Beekeeper's Apprentice/Epiphany/Approaching Silence
Virgin CDVE 943 CD
November 1999

With Holger Czukay:

Plight And Premonition
Plight (The Spiralling Of Winter Ghosts)/
Premonition (Giant Empty Iron Vessel)
Virgin/Venture VE 11 LP
March 1988
Virgin Venture CDVE 11 CD
March 1988
Flux And Mutability
Flux (A Big, Bright, Colourful World)/
Mutability ("A New Beginning Is In The Offing")
Virgin/Venture VE 43 LP
September 1989
Virgin/Venture CDVE 43 CD
September 1989

With Russell Mills:

Ember Glance – The Permanence Of Memory
The Beekeeper's Apprentice/Epiphany
Venture/Virgin DSRM 1
1991

With Robert Fripp:

The First Day
God's Monkey/Jean The Birdman/Firepower/Brightness Falls/20th Century Dreaming (A Shaman's Song)/Darshan (The Road To Graceland)/Bringing Down The Light
Virgin CDVX 2712 CD July
1993
(Boxed CD containing postcard set also available)

Damage

Damage/God's Monkey/Brightness Falls/Every Colour You Are/Firepower/Gone To Earth/20th Century Dreaming (A Shaman's Song)/Wave/ Riverman/Darshan (The Road To Graceland)/Blinding Light Of Heaven/The First Day

Virgin DAMAGE 1 CD
September 1994
(Boxed CD containing booklet also available)

Other Appearances/Contributions:

Over the last 20 years, David Sylvian has made a number of guest appearances on various albums, singles and music/ poetry related projects. Unfortunately, many of these little gems have now been deleted. What follows are the details of those appearances I have been able to rescue from the vaults of friends and colleagues.

Virginia Astley –
Some Small Hope/A Summer Long Since Passed
WEA YZ 107 7″
1986

Sylvian makes a guest appearance on this single. He also contributes to Virginia Astley's 1987 album *Hope In A Darkened Heart.* Sadly, neither single nor album is currently available in UK shops.

Mick Karn –
Dreams Of Reason Produce Monsters

Sylvian appears on two tracks on this album – 'Buoy' (subsequently released as a single) and 'When Love Walks In'. Unlike many of the releases in this section, *Dreams Of Reason Produce Monsters* should be easy enough to find in record stores.

Virgin V. 2389 LP February
1987
Virgin VCD. 2389 February
1987

David Sylvian –
Interview 1987
Sylvian in conversation about his career, views on life and music
Discussion Records TIND 1 CD
1987
(Recorded in Canada)

Hector Zazou –
Sahara Blue
Sylvian makes a brief appearance on this album alongside Ryuichi Sakamoto
MTM Privacy MTM 32
1993

Russell Mills –
Undark
Sylvian makes a brief vocal appearance on Mill's début album
EM:T/Land Records
1997

Ryuichi Sakamoto –
Discord
Sylvian makes a spoken word appearance on the track 'Playing The Orchestra – f'. Again, this CD should be readily available in record stores.
Sony Classical (Catalogue Number unavailable)
1998

Russell Mills/Undark –
Pearl & Umbra
Sylvian contributes lead vocals to the track 'Rooms Of The Sixteen Shimmers'. Mills' second solo album also features guest appearances from such distinguished musical luminaries as Peter Gabriel, Brian Eno, Echo And The Bunnymen's Ian McCulloch and Sonic Youth's Thurston Moore.
Bella Union BELLA CD
13 November 1999

Aside from the above listing, David Sylvian has also made contributions to albums by Sandii And The Sunsetz (Sylvian appears on 1982's *Immigrants.* He also co-wrote the track 'Illusion' on said LP), Akiko Yano (Sylvian appears on her 1982 album *Ai Ga Nakucha Ne*), Propaganda (Sylvian contributes guitar to 1983's *A Secret Wish*), and more recently, Nicola Alesini/Pier Luigi Andreoni's 1998 CD-ROM project, *Marco Polo.* Sadly, catalogue numbers for these records were unavailable as this book went to press.

Videos:

Whilst there are several bootleg tapes of David's live performances as a solo artist doing the rounds, only one *official* Sylvian video release exists – 'Steel Cathedrals' – a short, experimental film David made with Yasuyuki Yamaguchi and Ryuichi Sakamoto in 1985. Sadly, it is no longer available in shops. Like the Japan videos 'Oil On Canvas' and 'Instant Pictures', copies of 'Steel Cathedrals' do occasionally surface for sale, but in nowhere near the same volume.

Steel Cathedrals
Virgin Music Video VRV SC1 (30 minutes)
1985